FIFO'd

KATE VENN

Kate Venn

*Dear Waits,
I have loved you
forever. I hope you
like this story
XX*

BLUECITY
Enterprises

FIFO'd

First published in Australia by BLUECITY ENTERPRISES PTY LTD 2018
PO BOX 7290
GERALDTON WA 7290

National Library of Australia Cataloguing-in-Publication entry:

Creator: Venn, Kate, author
Title: FIFO'd

ISBN: 9780648240105 (pbk)

Subjects: FICTION/General
             FICTION/Family Life/ General
             FICTION/Women

Also available as an ebook: 9780648240112 (ebk)

Cover concept by Kate Venn
Cover design by Ren
Airplane shape Icon made by GraphBerry from www.flaticon.com
Couple in love Icon made by Freepik from www.flaticon.com
Airplane Icon made by Freepik from www.flaticon.com
Reading Sign Icon made by Plainicon from www.flaticon.com

Typesetting and design by Publicious Book Publishing
Published in collaboration with Publicious Book Publishing
www.publicious.com.au

For Zyla, Bodhi Venn, Captain Steve

and

all the indefatigable

FIFO Mums

JODIE

Dastardly easterly. Evil twin to the southerly, who soothes and medicates. The easterly licks with hot breath. Punches faces with fists of heat and desert sand. The wicked scorcher, twisted burner. The scorned brother who whores and imposes, suffocates and burns with vengeance. When he is in his element, the people peel away, photos curl, animals pant, birds come closer to share my shade. The easterly snap-dries everything. He rages with trapped hungover heat. Always raising his fists westward, knowing that daily his cooler twin will find favour. Out here, it feels like I am slow roasting in the fan-forced fucker easterly wind.

Most of the time when it is dark and the children are asleep I hear the fridge. It quavers like tinnitus. My head rests in one hand and one eye waters. I struggle because I am not a true farmer's wife. I never dreamed of wearing pearl earrings, tucking a checkered collared shirt into my jeans and vowing to be buried in my Blundstone boots. I would not have put my hand up if anyone had asked me, even once, did I want to be a farmer's wife? I look ridiculous under a broad-brimmed hat and as my eyes sweep the hectares of land there are always flies trying to get in my mouth. Sometimes I bend over and try to cough the flies up, dry retching in disgust. Despite the flies, I definitely did fall for Pete as he swaggered towards me with his scruffy hair and sunburnt lips. As Pete asked about specific chemical compositions of fertilisers, I looked at him as if he was pretending not to know me when we had always known each other. It must not have been subtle as ten hours later, we kissed after dinner. Chapped lips on mine. Suddenly silos were in my future.

For two years we had an old-fashioned long-distance relationship. No apps to bridge the kilometres. Just two flogged telephones and – it seems so unlikely now – letters. The smoky seduction of love from afar is surely extinct these days. Back then I used to yearn, smoulder, call out across the Nullarbor. Not being able to see or show.

I visited the farm three times before I came to live on her. She seemed so full back then. Flying along gravel tracks in Pete's ute I stuck my head out the window and saw a smear of cockatoos following the river line as it moseyed so damn slowly around each rock. Not exactly rushing towards the sea. Big trees lined that river system and I remember leaves, although maybe there were never as many as I recall. Emus and roos in the paddocks, snakes on the road, outcrops of rocks looking ancient.

When I told the Melbourne night skyline I was going, there were no surprises. We let go hands like ambivalent lovers, knowing there was a fair chance that we'd be bedfellows again if there was no one else left at the end of the night. Ella saw me off at the airport. Mum was too unwell, as she had been since I could remember. Ella and I chatted excitedly about her coming to visit, the gig she was going to after dropping me off, about strange passers-by. The pink noise of sisters. Even ten steps away from the gate I had not fully comprehended the amputation: me from Melbourne, me from her. At the gate I gurgled in shock as if stabbed in the neck. After turning and entering the skinny tube to the plane I picked up all the bits that were spilling out behind, gave myself some pointed stern words, inhaled as if I was going to be held under water, and stepped on to the plane.

After six hot years and three umbilical cords cut on that farm I realised that we were stuffed. Pete had been saying 'It's just a bad year' for four years. The bank was unsympathetic, and pleased when Pete secured employment at Majestic Mines, just south-west of Karratha. I had to stay on the farm with the kids. There was lino on all the floors and only one tree out of the window to break the horizon. Five thousand hectares of space and I rarely leave the house. It just doesn't make sense without Pete there. I don't make sense there without Pete.

Tonight, an hour before Pete rang, I sang in the grey galvanised steel wheat silo, down near the sheds, and the sounds spiralled up and hovered above my head. A godless soul begging to be saved by something. Sascha's little arm reached up through the bottom manhole of the empty silo and grabbed my toes as they gripped the lip so I could hold myself inside. Gus and Bon watched and witnessed through the manhole opening. It was not something their dad would do. I could smell and feel the wheat dust from the past. It itched my skin and was another layer to rise above. Inside the silo my voice hula hooped, a warmth touching the metal sides around and around. Calling out for reassurance, serenity, my lover, a homecoming that I never sensed in these paddocks of ploughed dirt.

'Imagine a gospel choir in here; they'd be able to hear the hum in town.' The boys weren't interested.

'Can we go home now Mum? I want to watch my shows,' whinged Bon.

'I'm getting bitten by something Mum, can we go home?' A hopeful Gus.

'Mumma?' Sascha was watching the top of the silo where the sound hung. I closed my eyes and raised my face up to the circle of light where grain used to cascade down in thick streams.

'Ok then, let's get going.'

'Beat you to the car Gus!'

'Beat you!' Gus ran after his big brother with no chance of being faster or stronger for a decade.

My voice felt warm as I ducked out of silo, lifted Sascha up and headed back towards the ute, singing a sad song into her curls.

ELLA

The woman who raised Ella never took into consideration the time difference between the east coast and the west coast of Australia; two to three hours depending on whether the east coast was stretching out sunshine or not. Two or three hours in the middle of the day is neither here nor there. In Ella terms, two hours in the middle of the day is nothing; a Melbourne afternoon cuppa meeting a Geraldton midday swim. At either extreme of the day, it had more distressing effects. When Ella answered the phone to her mum at 9:00 p.m., it was to an incoherent lady, cork tainted, deep in the depths of her night. Ella could barely make words out of the sobbing and vino warble. Later, Ella's phone would ring at 4:00 a.m. Ella imagined the goon bag with vertical wrinkles from one tip to the tap. Her mother's left hand would have held the plastic valve to open lips and her right would have held the far silver tip of the bag in a clenched fist above, to maximise the flow.

'Mum?'

'Ahh, is that you Jodie?'

'No, you've rung my phone, Mum—'

'Ella?'

'Yes, Mum?'

'Where are you Ella?'

'In WA, same as last time you asked.'

'How could you fucking do that to me?'

'I'm going now Mum, it's late—'

'Don't, you fucking bitch...'

Ella liked that she could calmly press the little red receiver icon and feel the thick padding of central Australia between her mother's rage and her Abrolhos pearl-adorned ears. It never used to be like that. Before Ella married Max, her mother's words would ruin her for hours. When Max was home, he would tell Ella that her mother's cursing was the last thing she should worry her pretty little head about.

LYLA

Lyla perched behind a counter at the front of Salacious. She took money off blokes on the tear and tried to glean some insight into the bikie women who lusted after diamonds and white leather as they took lace off their skin in layers.

'How is front desk going, Lyla?' asked Barb, who had been the manager of Salacious since it opened its Northbridge legs. Barb was tough as kelp, tanned like leather, worn like a favourite pair of sandals. If Barb ever heard anyone had complained about the girls her response was invariably, 'I don't give a fuck, love. Those punters can get stuffed.'

'Yeah, I think I am getting the hang of it, Barb,' Lyla replied.

'I like your style Lyla. You greet the customers with a look like you'll give them a head job and then a home-cooked meal. You look so wholesome they would feel bad pushing their cocks in between your teeth, so they happily come into the club.'

'Thanks Barb, but you can be sure that I have been getting a few offers from punters who would happily do just that. They don't even get the message when I stick security onto them.'

'Is that true? Saint Lyla isn't getting as much respect from the punters as she deserves? I'm going to get you a halo. Stick your tits out even more but you need the halo.' Barb's finger lassoed a halo in the air.

'Thanks, Barb, you are all I have ever dreamed of in a manager.'

The blokes piled in. Suits, high-vis, t-shirts tucked into jeans. Lyla watched a hundred tattooed arms hand over money and walk past her. When the dinner rush was over, Cherry, one of the dancers, came to the front counter.

'Hiya Lyla.'

'Quiet in there now, Cherry?'

'Yeah I get jumpy when I sit around.'

'It's still early though.'

'Yeah, want to go for a smoke?'

'Yeah, I'll go for a quick one.'

Lyla and Cherry stepped out on the street, just to the side of the entrance so that Lyla could whip back in the door when another punter had crossed the threshold, dreaming of carrying one of the girls back out in his arms.

'Lyla, I can't stand being near when deep throat Lucy is hustling around. She is pissing me off. I'm going to smack her.'

'Oh yeah, why is that?'

'She is in there, her fat arse spanning a meter either side of her skanky G-string banging on and on about how she is going to sign up for one of those shows where desperate farmers go on TV to try and find a chick. What's it called? Farmer wants a root? She reckons she would love to go and live on a farm. What a load of shit! She has never even been half an hour out of Northbridge. She grew up on the game, that girl. She has shoved her fist up too many guys' arses and now she thinks it's a natural progression to go on TV and put her fist up a poor cow to try and snag a farmer.'

'Cherry, I'm sure I saw her last night in a cowgirl costume. Plaits either side of her head, tall pink cowgirl boots, crotchless chaps. It's probably every desperate farmer's wet dream to see a girl like Lucy in some crotchless chaps.'

'Yeah, well if she made it on that show you would need to have a really, really wide screen to show her fat arse in some chaps. We'd end up with her getting some contract with a fat chick clothing line and have to put up with her mug on the TV every night, just because she fisted a cow and got the man.'

'Oh, Cherry. I won't be able to look at her now without seeing that visual.'

'The farmer takes a cow, the farmer takes a cow, hi-ho the dairy-o, the farmer takes a cow.'

'Gross. Go back in?'

'Yeah.'

Two hours of sleazy music later and Cherry strutted back out to the reception cubicle.

'Smoke, Lyla?'

'Yeah, just wait a tick, we just had a rush. Buck's night boys. They are green. Hopefully you girls will get some money out of them.'

'Not usually my friend. When they come in packs there's more chance of it getting back to their missus that they slipped a chick fifty dollars just to stare where her g-string hides the flaps. They expect a show for nothing because it is a gimmick for the night. I like my regulars who come in and take a liking to me. They'll sit and talk and feel like they are my personal bodyguard for a drink and slip me fifty for nothing. No grubby talk of sitting on them or sucking their cock. No staring at my crotch or tits as if there is not a head attached a bit further up.'

'Ok, Cherry, let's go...'

Backs against the brick wall freshly painted charcoal grey, Lyla and Cherry looked every bit like working girls. Cherry lit two cigarettes. One for Lyla and one for herself. There was a hum from the adjoining latin bar.

'You got a man Lyla?'

'Nuh.'

'Why not? You've got the goods.'

'The timing's never been right I suppose.'

'What about Austin? Have you met Austin? He's loaded and not bad looking.'

'Who is he?' Lyla frowned as the bitterness of the blue smoke hit the back of her mouth.

'A friend of Barb's. I think he has some financial interest in the club. I know he wasn't one of the original backers but he might have bailed them out once. Barb is always charming when he comes in for a drink. He has some kind of bikie connection.'

'What about you Cherry? Who's popping yours?'

'I think I was born with a popped cherry, it seems so long ago. Yeah I guess I'm kind of taken. I don't wear my ring to work for obvious reasons but I went on *Biker wants a wife* a few years ago and the rest is history. You might have seen my man in here, York. He comes in all the time. Probably wouldn't have introduced himself as the Cherry Popper or Cherry Picker. He's alright. We're going through a good patch at the moment. I guess he made me an honest woman. He doesn't let me drink. Gives me a hiding if he sees me raise a glass. The drink is my poison. Better to be scared of him than become a born-again fundamentalist Christian to give up the booze.'

'I'm pretty sure AA don't use floggings to keep their members away from methylated spirits.'

'Maybe they should. The 12 steps of AA were always too steep for me to climb in these stilettos.'

'Ready to go back in to the bucks?'

'If they're wearing R.M. Williams I am coming straight back out again and leaving them for loose goose Lucy. Her fat arse will prepare the buck for what lies ahead in married life…'

JODIE

After working two weeks on, Pete usually blows the froth off a few beers at the Yuna Pub; a ritual that reminds him he is home. I think it allows him to switch from hard-working bloke to family man. He tells me he's had a gutful of other blokes by the time his ute reaches home and he's happy to sit on the couch and relax. Pity; all I want to do is go away. To the coast. To smell the sea. Riding shotgun with Pete, kids in the back, windows open towards the ocean, I feel all the sadness and loneliness drain away.

When Pete returned this swing, I had the trip all planned out. I had precooked meals in foil trays, ready to be warmed up in the camp oven: apricot chicken, beef stroganoff and spag bol. I told Pete that the trips would be harder when the kids were older so he happily packed half of our worldly belongings into the car, again.

Less than two hours north of Geraldton, I watched a soil turned terracotta. As the car sped north, it blurred the big gums and banksias outside my window. By 3:30 p.m. the bitumen on my side of the road was being fingered by the tall shadows of gum trees. Gus and Bon were watching a movie in the back seat and a fly buzzed around Sascha's sleeping face. Pete looked deep in thought as the kilometres gently passed away behind us. Brown beer bottles sparkled on the roadside. The shiny mosaic of the outback; a glittering legacy for future generations who will fail to fathom why drivers would fling empties to the edge of Highway One.

Leaving the Batavia Coast and entering the Shark Bay Shire, the soil cut from ochre orange to resource-boom red. By the roadside there were gravel skids, tufts of wildflowers, a murder of crows. Behind fifty metres of trees there were gates and fences. I squinted through the gumleaf glare.

'Pete, I wonder who owns all this barren, shrubbed-up land?'

'Mum, can we have another movie?' whinged Bon from the back seat.

'Ninjas?' called out Gus.

'Not ninjas, that's for babies. Mum, we want that dinosaur one where the dinosaurs come back and kill all the children.'

'What? That doesn't sound good, Bon.'

'I'm hungry Mum, can we have something to eat?' Bon begged from the back.

'Mum, I'm hungy, can we have sompting to eat?' echoed Gus.

'Mum, can we get out of our belts now? I need to go to the toilet...' Bon whined as he punched the window softly with his fist.

'Pete, they're saying Mum, but what they really mean is Dad, Dad, Dad,' I responded.

'Righto boys, we'll be at the roadhouse in five minutes so stop the whinging or you won't get anything.'

Overhead, the clouds were the same as city clouds. The westerly wind pushed those clouds above the roof of the car, towards the desert where anything could happen to them. One hundred metres before the next roadhouse there was a sandwich board advertising 'Big and Meaty Beef and Gravy Rolls and even Gluten Free Food.' The roadhouse was not letting anyone drive by. By the time we pulled into the driveway, the kids were squirming to go to the toilet. Pete and I undid our seatbelts and assumed our normal roles; I did the toilet runs, Pete took care of the fuel and the mashed-up insects on the windscreen. On route to the toilets at the roadhouse the kids and I passed a wall of cheap plastic toys, unlikely to last more than fifteen minutes. Fifteen minutes north or south of the roadhouse no one would ever backtrack, not for a cheap plastic toy.

'Come on boys, come on Sascha, straight through to the toilets. Look, but don't touch...'

As we waited to pay for our fuel, we stared in amazement at the roadhouse's wall of tattoo photos. Arms, wrists, shoulders, backs and rumps full of ink. Lots of dolphins, Ned Kellys, Celtic patterns and Chinese symbols for happiness and prosperity (or wok and dim sum, the tattooed being none the wiser).

'Which tattoo should I get, boys? Sascha? Which one should Daddy get, darling girl?' Pete asked. Sascha tried to pull a photo of the St Kilda football club emblem off the wall with slobbery little hands. 'No, Sascha, St Kilda? I don't think so.' Pete visibly winced. After a quick conference,

Bon, Gus and I agreed that Pete should copy a bloke called Steve who had a can of baked beans inked on his upper torso.

Back on the road, our car took one turn left towards Shark Bay.

'Kids, as soon as we turn this corner we are heritage listed. Are you ready?'

'What does heritage listed mean, Dad?'

'Well, that is a good question for your mother, Bon,' said Pete, skilfully handballing to his teammate. My mind was already thinking about the wallaroos, dugongs, sea snakes and stars and it didn't seem that I needed to answer.

The timing of the trip had us pulling up in glamorous Denham for the night. Well, Denham wasn't fabulous, but it had the potential to be if it had found itself broken off another continent, and not stuck in no man's land, ten hours north of the world's most remote city. Staring out at the coastline of Denham as a cheddar moon hung low, you could almost see the casinos, the dancing girls, the spangled shine of an exciting night life. Almost, but not quite. Instead, we shared the promenade with five hungry seagulls and strolled onto Denham's little jetty splattered with squid ink and bait juice. The boys peered into the empty bucket of one antisocial fisherman, who may also have been imagining smoking cigars with high-heeled ladies on yachts in Denham, not slouched in a camp chair on the jetty with an esky that was never full enough and a fishing line that never pulled.

The next morning we drove out of Denham and towards the little point where we set up camp. Three beautiful days camped on rocks right near turquoise water. Pete jumped to action setting up the tent and the portable toilet, and fixing up the firepit that others had left behind, all before the easterly wind dropped off. For three days we would be chasing that gap: the precious hours between the easterly dropping off and the southerly kicking in.

As soon as our camp was organised, Pete launched the dinghy in the water straight off the rocks and we were flying over the water. I fussed around applying zinc on noses, putting hats on heads and distributing snack after snack after snack. Pete took his role as captain of the vessel seriously, describing wind direction, tidal movements, points of navigational interest. He showed the boys how to scour ground, ensure that we were out of the marine reserves and set up four functional fishing rods. Forget physics and biochemistry, Pete was hothousing his children in something that might, he told us, be of some real use to them. Sascha gripped a plastic rod as she kicked her feet up and down.

'Dad, how long do fish live?' Bon asked, as he stared over the side of the dinghy into the spangled water below.

'Not very long at all in Western Australia, my son.'

'Why, Dad?' asked Gus as his dad juggled fishing rods, hooks and bait.

'OK, say your prayers to Huey, boys!'

'Is he your friend, Dad?'

'No son, Huey is the spirit of the ocean, the waves, the soul of the deep blue. He is the force that whooshes through the sandy bottom of the ocean and sends fish darting. Huey decides if we have grilled fish or two-minute noodles for dinner. We're in Huey's gilled hands. C'mon, Huey. C'mon.' It was clear the boys weren't quite sure what their dad was on about. Would this Huey rise out of the depths with seaweedy hair to hook a fish on to their dad's line? The boys' eyes squinted and blinked into the sun as they quizzically watched their dad, a grown man, groan and hold both hands heavenward. Within minutes Pete pulled up sharply with his rod.

'We're on boys! We're on! Get ready Mum, clear the children, I think it's a big one.' The line was bending Pete's rod down hard as the fish struggled to get free.

'Thank you Huey, thank you,' Pete said reverently as he pulled up the line and a blue vein grouper slapped onto the deck. 'He has been kind to us today, boys.' Pete nodded to the boys who were shrinking back towards me as the fish flapped loudly on the floor of the dinghy, pierced by a hook to the side of the mouth. Eyes rolling, I opened my arms to all three children. I had always made a place for Huey in my relationship with Pete.

When the fishing tour finished, we returned from our exploration of the shallow seas and alighted from the dinghy. We were approached by Ken and Glenise, an over-tanned couple from Mandurah, who were also at the camp. It appeared that Glenise and Ken no longer cared about dental work, or even teeth for that matter. Why would you, when you could kick back in camp chairs, suck down some beers and read some paperbacks in paradise? Ken and Glenise were keen to have a chat to us about life on the road; about gleefully shrugging off any grandparental duties and going wherever the road took them. They were about to shift their van to another camp within the station for another couple of nights before travelling further north.

After sharing a beer, Ken handed Pete a pink snapper. We had discussed earlier on the boat that catching pink snapper was prohibited in these waters, but Pete took it from Ken's outstretched hand.

'No use throwing a fish back in the water when it's dead,' Pete said, with hesitant gratitude.

'I've got some biscuits in here the kids might like lovey, want to come and get a few?' Glenise led me over to her van.

'Wanna cuppa or a wine lovey?'

'Yeah Glenise, I'll have a wine with you. I have one in our esky – want me to go and grab one of our bottles?'

'No, I have a cask here. Haven't drained it yet. Ken jokes that if the time comes and we need colostomy bags, we'll have a stash of silver ones ready to go. I'd love it if you'd help me empty it – it'll give me a reason to go back into town. Not sure that anyone is delivering booze out here,' Glenise handed me a tin mug. 'Hope you like Fruity Dyslexia?' I didn't but I couldn't be rude.

'Thanks – if there are no kale smoothies to be had, Fruity Elixir is the next best thing.'

'What's kale then, lovey? Never heard of it. Fruity Lexia is smooth enough for this gypsy.'

'It's a new...ah it doesn't matter. Who is this then?' I touched a scratched photo of a gentleman on Glenise's fridge door.

'That there is the love of my life.'

'Ken when he was younger?'

'Nah lovey, my first husband. He was Ken's best friend. He got cancer. Died before we could catch our breath. Had a sore back one day, went to get it checked out and never came home from the hospital.'

'No!'

'Yep, best years of my life with that man. Four kids. But Ken, he picked up all the pieces. Never really recovered himself. You just never know love, when your time is up. Got to live a life you love. Love long into the night. Say what you want to say. Don't get too caught up in all the details. Take care of your feet, all that kind of stuff.'

'So you and Ken never had kids together?'

'No love, too busy with the four I had around my ankles already. Ken was great with them. He really did Fred proud. He's a good man. Fred was my soulmate though.'

'Ken doesn't mind the photo on the fridge?'

'No love, things were different back then, that is forty-something years ago. Everyone seems so jealous these days – not so safe for a woman in the home if you listen to the news. Ken, he's happy enough. He lost his best friend. That's all he sees in that photo. Fred gave us a gift when he died; Ken and I never took one thing for granted ever again. We never got caught up in all the trappings; we are happy. Always have been happy enough, love. Did you say you live in Geraldton?'

'Yuna – have you heard of it? Pete works away, two and one. I make him take me away when he is home; being on the farm…it's hard when he is away.'

'Work widow hey? Fly in fly out? One of my daughters is FIFO; no children so she works away. Tells me about all the men out there missing their kids.'

'Yeah, the kids miss Pete.'

'What about you when he is away?'

'I survive I guess. Not sure what other options we have at the moment. I would love to have a van like this and hit the road, the five of us.'

'You gotta do more than survive lovey. I know it's hard when you miss your partner but there is something to be said for standing on your own two feet – not feeling like you can't have the good times without your partner there. Where's your mum? Is she around?'

'Oh, my mum, she's not very well…and in Melbourne. My sister is in Geraldton so I can call her, see her. Her husband works away too so we can have a wine and a whinge together.'

'Sounds like your boys are calling out for you love. Lucky to get one wine down I suppose with three little ones. Work out what it is love, the thing that makes you feel like life is not on hold because, sure as sure, our days are numbered. You remember that photo of Fred: life can be over in a flash.'

'Thanks Glenise. I will remember. Thank you for the wine. It was way better than a glass of kale.'

After grabbing Glenise's biscuits, Bon and Gus scattered off and Sascha played with stones as Pete and I prepared for the approaching evening. Pete walked down to the water's edge and started filleting the fish for our dinner. I started the fire and chopped up some salad. Ken and Glenise started packing up their sprawl.

I wandered down to where Pete was masterfully filleting the grouper; his right wrist zig zagging, the knife neatly separating the flesh from skin. Then he picked up Ken's pink snapper. He bounced it a few times in two outstretched hands and looked confused. He lay it down on an angular rock and cut through the scales. Pete shook his head as he opened the pinky's frame.

'Dodgy,' he whispered. 'What a dodgy operator...'

Ken had stashed an almighty sinker in the fish's guts so he could have ditched it. If he'd sighted any Fisheries officers, the pink snapper would have sunk like so many ships off this spiteful coastline.

I finished stirring some homemade mayonnaise in a cup and looked up when I heard a small skid on the stones. Ken and Glenise had their dinghy on the roof, van packed and Glenise was calling out, 'See you in the bush some time, love!'

With the neighbours gone, we had isolation. Not a dusty quarantine like at the farm, but isolation with an ocean view. A headspace away from spilt drinks, rosters and boarding passes.

After dinner, exhausted from salty living, the kids were asleep. Pete and I washed the dishes together, squatting next to the camp oven filled with warm soapy water. Two specks under a disco ball sky. All the constellations mashed together above our contentedness. Pete shook his soapy fingers and tucked a strand of hair behind my ear. I am sure I looked wild. A couple of days out of my normal habitat and I was a wench of the coast. I looked up at Pete, my hands still in the warm suds avoiding the late onset of evening chill.

'You want to go to bed Pete?'

'Yes, I'm shattered. I'm not used to all this parenting. How do you do it?' Pete asked this question with a shy smile. I knew that his question was FIFO foreplay. 'I have it easy working away, you are amazing, Jodie. I don't know how you do it. You just seem to handle the kids so effortlessly. I'm home for a few days and my blood's already bubbling.'

I narrowed my eyes to his open, excited face.

'Can't we just ask them to look after themselves from here on in? Surely they'd survive on cereal for breakfast, lunch and tea. How many boxes of that stuff did we bring? It's obviously like crack for the kids. They love it hey? Soon they'll need a box a day just to feel normal. They'll think that no one is noticing their downward spiral,' he said, drying the boys' bowls.

'Let's go to bed, Pete.' The foreplay had started to lose its potency.

'Like I was saying, I don't know how you do it babe, you are an incredible mother.'

All around us emus, big roos and small grey wallabies searched the darkened shrubs for food; none of which cared at all about our family, camp lantern swinging inside a swaying tent.

Months fell off us as we spent the three days fishing, walking, cooking, laughing, singing and crabbing. Then the days were over and the drive home was fast. The shrubs turned into gums again, taller gums, and dead gums on the ground. We sped through the grass tree protection zone, yellow cropping fields and then slam, back to reality, we were stopped at traffic lights in Geraldton reading an 'Eat beef you bastards' sticker on the car in front. A day later Pete was gone again and he took all the salt water, colour and excitement with him.

ELLA

Ella had spent a full day being plucked and pampered. She had some fresh lash extensions, a spray tan, and her hair cut, coloured and styled. She looked stunning; out of place, so far from any fashion capital. Skinny brown toned arms, skinny brown toned legs. The dark of her lash extensions contrasted with her green eyes. She had been working hard at the gym and her tummy felt tight under her singlet dress. Her nails were painted; duck egg blue on her fingers and Egyptian turquoise on her toes. She had splashed out on a stunning Abrolhos Island pearl that hung on a white gold chain above her chest. Jesus was meant to have said that the kingdom of heaven was comparable to a pearl of great price. Ella knew nothing about that but she definitely agreed that a pearl of great price was heaven.

Ella strode up her path with flair, hair fluttering and body bouncing. She turned the key and let herself in the front door, flicking her hair in the hallway mirror as she walked. She dropped her bags on the kitchen floor and stood in her empty kitchen. She stood in one place, her breath quickening. Time passed. Ella slowly sank down to the ground, her head resting on her bent knee, warm tears flowing down her cheeks, over her jawline and down her neck. Max was not swinging home for another ten days.

Ella knew that she'd been happy enough before she met Max. Back then she had the feeling of having a complete circuit, energy purring through her. There were always little dark days but no total circuit breakers. These days she felt like she was pouring energy down the sink. No one was there to witness her, celebrate her, guide her.

'C'mon, Ella,' she whispered. 'C'mon, Ella.'

She knew if Max was home alone he would be happily couched, beer in hand, in front of a movie, napping in and out of vital plot scenes. No way would he be wrought, catching eye slop in his hands.

Ella and Max had bought the shell of a two-storey kit home on a block in Geraldton with ocean glimpses. It made Ella breathe easier to see that sliver of bluey green. Her mind would go to kelp forests, the remaining whale sharks, her honeymoon in Coral Bay where big fish had slapped her ankles in the shallows and turtles had pushed rubbery eggs out under a fluorescent moon. A chandelier hung down from a steel rafter. It looked gorgeous spraying light on the walls, now that they had been able to afford some. Initially Max and Ella had joked about having enough cash to build one wall in their bedroom; a feature wall. The money had started fluttering down when Max began at the mines.

After making a small dinner of boiled eggs and steamed greens, Ella made her way up the stairs and sat on the balcony of their colourbond palace. Cyclone proof, though she had never heard of a cyclone in Geraldton. The sun had just set and Ella considered the block of time between now and bed. It always seemed so full of promise during the day. That time to complete projects, sort out her superannuation, and touch up her nails. When the horizon was backlit it seemed more difficult to be productive. For the first couple of hours she usually fuzzed the silence with the news, soapies and whatever was on after that. She ate, washed dishes and put a little load of laundry on. Thought about, then decided against, mopping the floor. At eight-thirty Max usually rang.

'Hi babe.'

'Hi babe.'

'How was your day?' Ella always wanted to know.

'Yeah ok. How was yours?'

'Ok, busy. What about you?'

'Pretty fucked. Long. I'm exhausted. Looking forward to coming home.'

'Ten days?'

'Ten sleeps babe.' Sometimes Max walked away from the wet hall, phone to his ear and talked softly about licking Ella. She would unzip her jeans and close her eyes.

Nine o'clock was Ella's danger hour. After a couple of wines, ringing a few friends and picking up things around the house, she would find herself holding the plastic bottle, taking the pill. Half an hour later she was happy to lie on the couch listening to music with the TV on, sound turned down. Ten sleeps to go. Sometimes she would write love letters to

Max in this state, more out of guilt to water down how angry she was with him. Ella wished she had never given up cigarettes. Her nights could be crammed full of cigarette smoke. Maybe there's some patch or pill you can get to gradually build up your taste for cigarettes again. Maybe the pill she had popped was doing just that. But that tiny pill had the power to relax her mind and stop it focussing on the rattling of the southerly along the corrugations of the roof. It stopped her mind wondering about the wet hall Max was in. Without the pills, it became like a bar at a resort with half-dressed admin girls, skinnier than her, everywhere. With the pills, it was full of ruddy workmen, showered and boozy.

Ella thought she could hack the separation from Max for the money it would bring them. A pocket of diamonds. Loosen the mortgage noose. Pay for expensive clothes for the kids that they would one day bring into the world. Pay for the massages that Ella was convinced she needed on a weekly basis to ward off the loneliness caused by lack of physical touch for three-quarters of her life. Ella's masseuse, Carmen, understood loneliness, so she put an extra layer of sensuality into the massages. Carmen and Ella had an unspoken understanding. There was a feeling that if one of them had been male, or both had not been so inflexibly hetero, they would have fucked for hours, hard against the padded massage table. The way Carmen touched Ella set her sex life off kilter as she looked wistfully for this softness from the rough hands of a mine worker.

LYLA

When Max walked through the automatic doors of Perth Airport, bag over shoulder, sunglasses on, looking for her from left to right, Lyla felt the urge to pounce on him. To jump up on his chest, climb up his torso, sit on his shoulders and wrap her body around his head. The chemistry always took her a bit by surprise; the hard to describe but irrefutable attraction she felt for him. Like chocolate on a dashboard, she held her form but melted soft. She never ran out to him, nor waved, but just waited by her car. He knew where to find her. She always parked in the far right of the car park, the less in demand spots, a bit out of view. When Max approached her, he dropped his bag, held her face and kissed her with the tenderness reserved for people you think you are going to lose.

Each time Max returned, Lyla chose a new place for them to eat. It was never sparkly or frequented by Perth's spray-tanned socialites. It was usually small, a family business, in the suburbs; businesses that did not benefit from many walk-ins. They ate at the kind of place that Lyla used to go to with her mum on Friday nights, when they were too tired to cook. Dimmed lighting in any ethnic style; Vietnamese multicoloured silk lanterns, Indian red chilli lights on a table centrepiece, Chinese pink and blue cherry blossom tree lights. Lyla felt warmth for the restaurant owners, like they were vintage, precious and something endangered as the world sped towards franchises and the enforcement of health standards. Those same health regulations would probably shut down every restaurant that Lyla and Max had been cocooned within as he drank beer and she, red wine, as they celebrated their borrowed time.

Tonight Lyla had chosen Sudanese. It was close to home, not too off course on their return from the airport. They never indulged themselves with love making in the car in the space of time between the airport car park and the restaurant. Lyla enjoyed the smouldering. Every time the hairs on her arms would stand on end and the car door would give her electric static. Every time she was puberty blues nervous. They played a coy courtship in the restaurant, watching each other's lips as they spoke. The love was thick and mystic as they ate and readjusted to having each other there.

'So how have you been, babe?' Max asked.

'Yeah good, I got a call from my friend Matt, who is doing a job for a production company who are putting together a play called "Love and a Violence Restraining Order", about screwed-up love. Glamcrime. An inside story into biker girlfriends. For Perth residents looking to glamorise their own underbelly. Sanitise it. Lots of good sunglasses, tits and arse. Riding on the wave of underbelly telly I suppose. People love it. Showcasing how murderous and immoral we can be. He asked me to just give him a hand doing some research – paid research – you know, meeting some women...'

'So a nice safe 9–5 job for you?'

'I've done a few shifts at a club in Northbridge. Salacious it's called. I can't wait to get my gear off in the name of research—'

'Lyla, I'll line you up a job at the mines.'

'Don't be silly, I am joking; I'm on reception, keeping myself nice. It will be much more exciting than the last job I did for Matt, researching the life of a rouseabout. Remember? That was way dirtier and my fine research wasn't even used for anything in the end. No, I am really looking forward to it. Matt sent me a big package of court transcripts, biker assaults on their partners, affidavits from violence restraining order applications. We can read some together tonight when we get back to my place...'

'That wasn't exactly what I had in mind...'

'How was your swing?'

'Long. It felt like I was just doing time. Punishment in advance for my obsession with you. Even now when you hold your red wine glass, I imagine those fingers pulling down hard on my cock. Every time your mouth opens for a mouthful of Ajali, I imagine my tongue entering it to explore...'

'Max, you are...just eat up.'

'I have so many memories of meals with you in my memory bank. Sometimes there is a short circuit in the wiring and these memories are directed to my wank bank, where you're suddenly parting the material of your shirt to rub Khoodra Mafrooka into your chest and then motioning for me to climb across the table and feast on you...'

'Ok, here comes the waitress.'

The waitress placed the black vinyl folder that enclosed the bill in front of them and retreated back to the kitchen.

'Forty-eight dollars...that can't be right, can it Lyla? Two mains and two drinks?'

'This isn't Cottesloe. What were you expecting?'

'The bills are always much less than I think the food was worth. I'm going to have to tip.'

'Rightio, big spender. You can come and tip me at Salacious one night...'

When Max went down on Lyla later that night she instructed him, 'Softer, softer, so I can barely feel it.'

So Max licked her with feather weight, petal weight, the weight of a gentle breeze. A warm feeling spread across her whole groin. The feeling of firelight flickering, a heat pack soothing a sore back. The touch of his tongue was like water trickling.

Max anchored Lyla. He secured her to safe ground. When the coastal winds were howling she was nestled in calm waters. He stopped her from drifting and running off course during the night hours. Only very rarely did it feel like he was chaining her down with heavy cold metal.

JODIE

In the Midwest, the sea breeze corrodes steel like a cancer. It makes rust-coloured lace out of edges of metal, eats away manmade structures. I longed to be affected by the sea breeze. In Yuna, I was not in its path. It was an hour's drive from farm dirt to sand. Saturday is our town day when Pete is away. The supermarket is sometimes an excuse to drive towards the ocean. Two hours return to buy a bag of bananas and a take-away coffee. Just don't tell Pete.

The kids and I arrived in Geraldton a couple of hours before the Fremantle Doctor. My three ran at different speeds from the pavement, across the Council reticulated grass to the water park at the foreshore. I sat under the last remaining rectangular shade cloth; strangely left untouched by the teenagers who often scaled the poles and bounced on the shade sails until they broke in the dark of a boring small town night. I thought fondly of those teenagers, unlike other residents who encouraged the Council to cover the foreshore in CCTV cameras to catch their hooded heads. Aerial shade cloth antics were an inevitable consequence of safety proofing all other play equipment so that barely anything moved any more. Lest the young folk hurt themselves.

I texted Ella to see if she wanted to join us at the foreshore, knowing that she was working and my chances were slimmer than the teenagers in denim shorts and trucker caps who weaved through the little kids under the fountains. All the other mums seemed to be in little huddles with banquets of chopped up fruit spilling around. For an hour I sat in a strange quiet with shrieks and calls all around. I rang Pete, who I knew wouldn't answer. I looked at my mum's number on my phone and scrolled on. I pulled out my own pre-prepared banquet of chopped fruit so that my kids had a reason to run back over to me. The water park was a soft, lycra-filled isolation; not hardcore like on the farm. I took some deep breaths, feeling a little bit panicky. Maybe I shouldn't have had that coffee. It is all ok. Loneliness feels stranger on hot days. I packed up the fruit.

'Anyone want an ice cream?' I called out to my kids. Suddenly, like a sharp change in the weather, I was smothered by the love of three grassy wet human beings.

After eating ice creams I took my happy children to the foreshore playground so that they could throw themselves down slides and bounce off unknown kids. Pete seemed so far away. I picked up a local newspaper that was lying on the seat next to me. After taking out the Mingenew Expo Official Program from the middle, the paper was lightweight; an article about local shearing entitled 'Quick go the shears', a feature on the ignored business of agriculture and a warning about quad bike fatalities. I flicked to the latter pages and an ad for an ocean-side shack caught my eye: 'Owner relocated overseas no longer needs property. Seller wants it gone. 3.58 acres 300m to ocean.' I watched Sascha hovering near the slides as the boys got air in their descent. What would it take to lure Pete from Yuna and replant him 300 metres away from the ocean? Surely he would adapt to the coastal climate? Would the farm sell? Who would want it? The farmers were reporting better seasons; maybe someone would be interested? Was there any chance Pete could be convinced to see a different future for Gus and Bon? Was it something I was prepared to push? Would it then lock us into a chopped-up life, where Pete would always have to fly away? Could I work in town? Would it be possible with three young lives to guard? Did I have the right to stand up and say that I needed to leave the place that would be forever under Pete's fingernails? Would he forgive me? Was it another impulsive whim of mine? To move from Melbourne to Yuna? To leave Yuna for 3.58 acres 300 metres from the ocean? To not want roots to travel too deep?

As Bon rushed up speckled with sand, I folded the newspaper and put it guiltily in my bag.

'Can we have another ice cream Mum, please? Dad would let us.'

'You are hilarious! No! Grandpa Jack is expecting us, anyway.'

Arriving at my father-in-law's place, I heaved Sascha out of the car and squeezed her hand between my knees to hold her captive as I used both hands to help Gus down. Bon leapt down by himself, and pushed Gus over onto the bitumen.

'Mum, I just jumped down, Gus was in my way.'

'Up you get Gussy, we will see if Grandpa has an ice pack. You'll be ok. Come on, sweetheart. Say sorry Bon…quickly, sorry…I'll count to three.'

'Sorry Gus.' A totally unconvincing big brother.

We walked up the driveway of the Batavia Wrecks Retirement Complex. 'Nothing too complex about it,' Pete's dad had said to me when his hip betrayed him in a fall and he was transplanted there, 'You bloody get old and they put you somewhere to die.' There was a rude explosion of dark pink bougainvillea to the left of his doorway covering over a window that led into his living room. 'Ironic,' he had mused on that first day, 'bloody bougainvillea, impossible to kill.' Jack's first day at the Wrecks Complex was over four years ago, before Gus was born. Was I pregnant? It is hard to remember. Yuna women still weight-bear when pregnant. Heavy loads. No allowances, no excuses; hardy. 'Taking me to the wreckers, Jodes?' he had asked as I had hauled his easy chair, embroidered with 'I Love Jack' in a love heart at the mid back height of the chair, up the pathway past the bougainvillea. Pete's mum, May, had loved embroidering in an 'I Love Lucy', 1950s mid-century font. Flowing lettering, like it was on a Hollywood director's chair.

Bon and Gus rang the doorbell and ran around the side of the brick doorway out of sight. I backed up to the bougainvillea and felt its thorns grab the threads of my light silvery cardigan. Jack always played along, gruffly cussing at the empty doorway; shed-talk that made me cringe and the boys giggle with pure delight.

'Who is there? Fark me, I must be going mad. Is there anyone there? John ya sneaky old bastard, is that you?'

'Gampa, it's us,' called out Gus, losing it and choking on laughs.

'Shh Gus, he can't see us. Now you've told him!' Gus was pushed to the ground again as Bon jumped out, 'It's me, Grandpa Jack, it's me.'

Jack and the boys grappled at the doorway and Sascha squealed and bounced up and down in my arms to be released. 'Boys, come on, you'll knock Grandpa Jack over. Watch his walking stick, don't trip over. Gus, listen to me, stand up please, Grandpa will trip over you.'

'Stop fussin Jodie, they are fine. C'mon boys, come inside, help your mum and sister. Don't let the neighbours hear you, they'll want to come over and kiss you and they have no bloomin teeth. Come in quickly, cricket's on!'

Jack led us in to his perfectly organised unit.

'Small plot this is Jodie, not hard to organise after running a farm. They are just preparing us for the smaller plot, Jodie; that one will be hard to keep clean after a few days. Know what I mean, boys? You ever seen a rotting carcass on the farm? Of course you have – that will be me, flyblown. Just dig a hole on that farm and chuck me in when I die, boys. Will you help your dad dig a hole? I don't want to be in the cemetery here. It's full of smelly old people – talcum powder and piss. Take me out to the farm again – promise, Bon? It'll probably be your job. Your dad will be too busy earning the big bucks; you'll have to take care of business.'

'Yuck, Grandpa Jack. Mum can do it. Mum, can you bury Grandpa Jack at the farm when he dies?' Bon, tummy down, in front of the telly.

'Any day now I reckon.' Jack said closing the fridge door, milk in hand.

'Mum!' Bon shrieked, 'Grandpa Jack says he is gonna die any day.'

'Shh Bon, you don't need to shout, I'm right here. The neighbours will start knocking on the walls.'

'Grandpa Jack, Mum always says she wants to move to the beach, what will we do then? Can you dig a hole in town? Will that be ok?'

'Over my dead body will that farm be sold, Jodie.'

'Well, Jack, you said that was any day now, so I can contact the real estate agents.'

'You think you can leave but you never can – like me. My old broken body is here but in my mind I am always on that farm, still checking fence lines…checking for pig tracks…'

'Cool, that's two less jobs for me; I hate doing the fences when Pete is away.' I sat down at the poor excuse for a breakfast table in Jack's kitchenette.

'Ahh, Miss Jodes, you are a sort. Pete is lucky to have you. My May would be proud of how you run that place with the kids when Pete is away. Not all women could do that.'

'Not many men, either.'

'May would still want to clean out your fridge though, clean your windows, cut the boys' hair…'

'You reckon they need a haircut, Jack?'

'Unless you are happy with their schoolmates mistaking them for girls…'

'It's fashionable for young boys to have wavy rock 'n' roll hair these days.'

'Not in Yuna it's not.'

'You're right – maybe tomorrow.'

'Nails too love, May would cut their nails.'

'Jack, are you going to make me a cuppa or keep nagging at me like an old farm wife?

'You won't leave the farm, will you Jodes? These boys, they will want to run that farm one day. Keep it in the family, love. May would be proud if you did that. I'd be bloody proud if you did that.'

'Pete wants to stay on the farm, Jack. What do you think my chances are of getting him to move to town?'

'Hmm, next to farkin zero love. Sugar?' Jack loaded us up with the abandon of someone who has no regard for health risks. We dipped our sweet biscuits in our milky tea and Sascha pulled at my skirt.

"Mumma, more? More?' The biscuits were distributed in rounds until the plastic crumpled empty on the table and Bon, Gus and Sascha had all grabbed at it just to check.

LYLA

Lyla swerved so a butterfly crossed her path as she walked from her apartment to the car. She watched its wings flutter, musing on its haphazard path. So inefficient, the flapping so constant. No soaring, no making use of the Fremantle Doctor that takes junk mail and distributes it vertically a metre off the ground to random houses down the street. The butterfly jumped up, flopped down, shot sideways. Lyla could not understand the design, the intention, the eons of evolution that kept the butterfly jiggling in the blue skies. Lyla had a large pink flower on her t-shirt and the butterfly soared, dived, and bumped into her chest.

From the outside, Lyla's path also seemed inefficient, comical, a butterfly following any shift in the breeze. From the inside, Lyla had always been led by a very powerful compass, to Perth, to London, and back to Perth. Lyla knew that Max was married to Ella; in fact she had flown back from London for the wedding. At the time she thought that it was important, like seeing an open casket. To stop thinking that Max was going to be there when she decided to return. She had masturbated about him that night, thinking of him in that black suit. As the orgasm racked her body one tear had fallen to the pillow. She had rejected Max and suffocated the flames of the future he had conjured up for them. She had refused to concede that her future lay in Australia where no one believed your brilliance. She wanted to live a fantasy for a while; give herself to the world wrapped in tinsel. So she returned to London, with the sound of country Oz hillbilly rock bouncing inside her head.

Back on Shaftsbury Ave, strides before Dean Street heading towards Chinatown, Lyla had swayed out of the path of the Number 19 bus. She gasped with grief as the bus swerved out of control and pinned an elderly lady to a shopfront. Lyla heard bones crushing like white cuttlefish underfoot on reef back home. When the bus reversed, a brown wig with tight curls fell to the pavement in a pool of red blood. Lyla watched with disturbed eyes as an ambulance with paramedics arrived, the police, and the vaguely interested lunch-eating public.

Lyla was invited to parties by men in pointy shoes and fabulous hairstyles. She attended and sometimes gave away her love to one of them for an hour or so when it seemed the most interesting thing to do. The auditions Lyla endured were for non-speaking roles in advertisements and there was always some excitement and confusion about her accent. London seemed polluted with people. When she got a phone call from her mother saying that her GP had detected a lump in her breast, she got online and booked a ticket on her credit card. One way back to Perth. She would save money once she was there to return to London.

Initially Lyla was ashamed to tell Max that she was returning. She explained her return as being all about her mum, the illness. Max was devastated. Not that she was returning and not that he happened to be married to Ella; just the timing, he cursed the timing. He had believed Lyla when she said she would never return. The time she rang him from Perth he knew that she was in the country from the moment she said 'Hi.' The distance was no longer there. Within months, Max told Ella that he was being pressured into a different roster, three weeks on, one week off, for the same pay as a concession so that the mine did not shut down. Ella had believed with beautiful big eyes. Max had carved one week out of every month for Lyla. A bonus mystery week. A week in one wormhole of the universe. Undetected, that is how they lived.

Spending time with Lyla in Perth worked beautifully for Max. He didn't believe she would stick around for long so he savoured seeing her in the airport car park waiting for him once a month. Lyla would always wait nervously around her car until he arrived and pulled her towards his mouth. After the week, Lyla would drop him back off in the airport car park at 5:00 a.m. to fly out. One week with Ella, two weeks at the mines, and he was Lyla's again. The three weeks in between his stays were getting longer and longer.

ELLA

When Max's car churned up the driveway, Ella was already wet. She had buffered and painted every edge of her body. Sometimes she would strike a pose as Max entered the door. She had done 'draped on the staircase, high-heeled pins spread wide on different stairs'. She had done 'naked in the bath with fairy lights and patchouli oil burning', 'spread eagled on the bed, ankles tied high to the bed head', and 'naked on the kitchen floor, spreading raw cake mix on her breasts'. Just like Max was walking straight onto a porn shoot.

Max loved Ella when she craved his attention, and encouraged it. This night, Ella had pre-steamed the bathroom for effect and ran in when she heard Max's steps on the path. Naked, she pushed her breasts up against the glass of the shower wall and strategically placed her fingers so that they were revealing just a glimpse of her. Max always called out and she never answered. That was part of the act, for him to walk in and catch her with her hand in the cookie jar.

'Ella, are you home?' Max crooned, 'Ella, baby, where are you? Ella, I can't find you, where are you?'

Of course, Max had heard the running water from when he opened the door. Massive smile as he trod the stairs, Max put his bags in the bedroom and quietly opened the bathroom door. There she was, nipples hard on the cold glass, caught in the act, again.

Max and Ella crashed straight into love making. Porno as it was, it felt like love as Max gobbled at Ella's neatly manicured crotch and she fluttered like a pinned butterfly. Endorphined up, they ordered pizza and sat up watching movies, drinking beers in pink and blue stubby holders made to commemorate their wedding day: 'To have and to hold and keep your beer cold.'

JODIE

After another two weeks on swing, Pete arrived home. Sometimes when he returns, he drives around the farm taking stock. Takes his rifle and shoots kangaroos. Shoots emus. Tries to shoot pigs. I understand that farm people feel this is necessary so I hide my tears behind sunglasses as baby emus scatter away from their dead dad. I love my kids but they are different to me after growing up out here. Even at a young age they have the same self-righteous brutality. Animals were always pre-packaged where I grew up so I struggle to know how to handle death. It's better not to see the perfectly white bone of a snapped leg poking out of muscle. However, the busyness of being a mother on a farm has spared me from a fragile mind. There is never any time for fuss. The CWA mothers that meet once a month at the community hall are teaching me to be as tough as Patterson's Curse.

This time when Pete returned home I was singing about old MacDonald and his pigs to Sascha as he entered the door. He walked up behind me, leant into my body and rested his head on the back of my shoulder blade. He listened as the song hummed out of my chest cavity. He began sniffing my back, my hair as it rested on his face, my skin. It felt like Pete let himself slowly melt there on my shoulder, on the floor, as Sascha shook her hands shouting out sounds and I oinked along.

After dinner, when Bon, Gus and Sascha were stabled, Pete and I had a drink together sitting on the deep freezer outside the back door. He drank whisky from a plastic thermos cup and I sipped red wine from a latte glass. Deep breaths looking at the orgy of stars above.

'How are you Jodes?' he asked

'Ok. This trip was tougher than the last one – I think I got used to having you around.'

'How did the kids go?'

'We talked about you all the time.'

Sips.

'I missed you so much, babe.'

'I know.'

'What should we do this week? Is there anything special you want to do?' I asked.

'Kiss you.'

'You know what I mean. Do you want to drive out to Lucky Bay? Take the kids camping?'

'I know which Lucky Bay I want to be in right now.'

I smiled, eyes rolling.

'Ok, I'll ask you tomorrow.'

Sips. I still felt withdrawn, detached. I had not yet melted back into him. It was a soft resentment, a distant longing to breach the divide to being back in love, as one half of a whole, two bodies touching, not just one body, alone, in a dry, never-ending paddock of dust. Pete looked at me.

'Babe, I was thinking about you last night knowing that I was going to see you today and it made me so happy.' Pete often took the lead.

'It's just so weird when you are suddenly back. I miss you so much and then you are suddenly back.'

'Kiss me?'

I shut my eyes and felt Pete's big lips kiss my cheek gently.

'Kiss me?'

I hunched over and let the tears fall, feeling Pete's hand on my back. It was always a sad relief when he was back. To share the load. To remember that I was in love with this man, for whom I shared a life with hectares of grain. When I found Pete's lips it was with a frenzy of emotion that I don't think he entirely understood. I kissed his lips as if they were a latte after a two-week withdrawal. I kissed them over and over again. Pete put his hands up my top as if he was a fifteen-year-old boy. Two weeks away and he acted as if he was naughty. No longer entitled to touch me. He felt my tummy and hugged my back. With one hand he tried to unlatch my bra. Unfortunately the time away always seemed to most affect his ability to de-bra. With a big belly laugh I helped him. Perched on that deep freezer under the stars we tasted each other again. Clung to one another. Slapped at mosquitoes and laughed.

The next morning we headed to Horrocks Beach, as many farmers from the Midwest do to temporarily distance themselves from the dry land that is their livelihood. When Pete drove us away from the farm the kids and I sang and bounced up and down in our seats. Oceanbound, as always, I sang the loudest. Halfway to Horrocks Beach I noticed that Pete was uncharacteristically quiet.

'What's on your mind, Pete?'

'Yeah, nah, nothing babe.'

'Pete?'

'Oh, just more rumours at the mine. People have heard that the company is going to get rid of about seventy workers.'

'Really?'

'Yes, really, and I haven't been there that long compared to other blokes. LIFO, they say: last in, first out. Two guys got stung the other day. They were given notice and sent packing on the same day for "violation of the internet usage policy".'

'What happened?'

Pete lowered his voice, 'Apparently one guy saved a whole lot of porn on the company's shared drive, only temporarily as he was copying it for someone, and they jumped on it.'

'What kind of porn?'

'Poo porn.'

'Dad, why are you talking about poo?' asked Bon.

'I just like to say the word, Mate. Poo! Poo! Poo! Now just watch that movie while I talk to your mum.'

I lowered my voice to a whisper. 'Poo porn? If you said poo porn, then that is totally fair enough.'

'No, I'm kidding, it was just your standard, open leg, chicks with dicks porn.'

'What? Are you serious? Saved on the shared drive?'

'No, it wasn't even anything unusual, just stock-standard porn.'

'Is that the porn where you want to squint your eyes in case your mother's best friend is suddenly on the page in front of you spreading the pink? Who likes that stuff, Pete?

'Just a big dirty mother load of porn. Some man on man. Nothing crazy. Probably quite explicit, and I think it was a chick from Human Resources who stumbled across the files. They obviously inflamed her anger rather than any erogenous zone. Anyway, instant dismissal. The dude is going to the Commission; trying to run it as an anti- gay discrimination case. I would love to be in front of the Commissioner when the evidence is exhibited. Not sure he'll get too far though because another guy got instant dismissal in the same week for another violation of the internet usage policy for downloading porn onto a work laptop and that was for meat and potatoes "Wham, bam thank you Ma'am" hetero porn. They could probably cull most of the workforce if they wanted to for porn-related offences.'

'Really, Pete? I see…'

'You know me babe, I only watch my secretly filmed sessions of love making with you.'

'Shhh! Bullshit. You have not taped us without me knowing!' I hissed at him.

'Jodie, Jodie; maybe Paris Hilton was "taped", but I don't think you call it "taping" any more when it is straight on to your phone from behind when you are giving it doggy style.'

'You are full of shit, Pete. Anyway, I am sure you are right that all those miners with two-terabyte hard drives do not have them full of pictures of their family.'

'Sure we do, scrapbytes we call them. I love the shots when you and the kids are wearing matching outfits.'

'So anyway, is it really possible that you could lose your job?'

'Well, not for porn but yes, definitely. I haven't been paying my union fees for long, so I could be one of the first to go.'

'Do you think you could get a job on another mine?'

'Maybe, if they are not culling too. I don't get it. You hear CEOs of mining companies banging on about bringing half of China and India to Western Australia yet all my big tough workmates are trembling.'

'Is there anyone you think could get the axe before you?'

'There are two guys on our team that I would love to see axed. Real roughnuts. Units. Bullies. They have it in for this cleanskin named Mark.'

'Cleanskin?'

'You know, like I was, someone who has never had any underground mining experience.'

'Oh ok.'

'These two thugs just harass him every day. I'm not sure what is going on but they are targeting this guy. Fucked-up shit like drawing dicks on his hard hat, flashing their cocks at him, walking up to him in the mess hall and farting over his dinner. Classy stuff.'

'Pete, you should report them.'

'I know, I probably will. They are union backed so I just have to be a bit careful who I talk to.'

'Did you say the cleanskin's name is Mark? What does he say?'

'Not much. He's just a young dude and looks uncomfortable. He never really responds.'

'Want me to fly out with you next time and sort them out?'

'Yes please, Jodes. No, I am monitoring the situation. There is such a fine line between robust banter and merciless bullying. We all know they are bullies. Maybe there isn't really a fine line. Maybe there is a very clear thick white line with reflective squares that all of us can see apart from those two dickheads.'

When we arrived at Horrocks Beach, Pete pulled up into a car park just near the public toilets close to where there was a track straight onto the beach. I watched him dismount our two quad bikes from the trailer. I helped Bon and Gus out of the car and to fasten their helmets. I took the baby sling from the front seat and wrapped Sascha on to the front of my torso as if we were being mummified; until I was convinced that she would not fall out. The sling had come with an instructive DVD but my milky mind when Sascha was born had never retained the crucial sequence of knots and turns. I looked down at my dodgy job and was not sure if I was ever going to be able to remove her. I then climbed up onto our red quad bike and helped Bon to swing his leg over and onto the back of the quad bike seat. When Gus had his little arms wrapped around his dad's back we took off to ride the sand dunes.

The dunes looked Arabian, perfect white peaks with sand levitating upwards. Before Pete started working away I was wary of the quad bikes. Now I ride like I am in a Mad Max audition. It soothes the internal frustration, the mild irritation that I can't shake with caffeine. Pressing my right thumb on the accelerator button, I feel like the wind can't blow hard enough in my hair. Pete and I raced each other down sharp razorbacks and up pyramids of sand, egged on by two small boys who would race the sand dunes every day if they could.

Later, when we had secured the quad bikes back on to the trailer, we travelled further and arrived at our special spot. Pete and I set up camp under one big ficus tree on the beach. Gus and Bon crouched near the tent digging trenches and building skyscrapers out of bleached white sand.

Sascha hovered behind her brothers, eating the odd handful of skyscraper when the boys were distracted.

'Jodie, come swim with me, the kids will be fine.'

Pete took my hand and led me down to the white foam. A gentle shore break slapped our shins as we waded out through sparkle-painted water. I felt the old heaven and earth pass and a new one come into existence as the sun bore down hungry on my shiny brown shoulders. Birds flew low overhead and small white fish darted around a circuit board of sand. Pete dived ahead of me and turned back with a smile on his face and a hand poised ready to splash. Before he could have the satisfaction, I dived down underneath the salt and water, through the scattering fish, surrendering myself on this tidal altar, not quite a virgin but certainly no lamb. Within fifteen minutes, the past was forgotten and I felt a precious future had been delivered into my waterlogged, outstretched hands.

As the day faded, Pete washed the sand off the kids under a camp shower strung up to the functional ficus overhead. A quick rub of talcum powder to remove any stray grains of sand, and Pete looked like he felt fairly happy with his parenting.

'Did you see that Jodie? The talcum powder trick?'

'Yes babe, I told you that one, remember?'

'Yeah, I remember.'

Pete and I enjoyed meltdown hour more than ever before. Bon and Gus happily put their pyjamas and fluffy slippers on and ate their dinner in a bowl on a camp chair. Sascha sat in her camp high chair and slammed her happy fists down into mashed avocado. Carefully holding their dinner bowls with two hands, Bon and Gus had their torches lying next to their thighs, looking forward to the dark.

'I know, Dad...'

'What, Bon?'

'You could work away one week and stay home for twenty weeks.'

'I wish you were my boss Bon; that sounds like a great swing.'

'Ok Dad, you could do that.'

'Well, it is a bit tricky Bon. Because I have to take the plane to work, it takes a long time, so when I am there, they want me to stay a while.'

'Why do you work on the plane, Dad?' asked Gus.

'No, I don't work on the plane, I just go up, up, up, in the sky and then come down again to a place called Majestic Mines. When I get there I put on funny goggles and a hard white hat and some crazy overalls and go down under the ground to work. It would be much more fun working on a plane.' Pete grabbed the boys' torches and motioned some flight safety instructions showing the exit points to the front, sides and rear of the plane.

After dinner, we put head-torches on and wandered down to the shoreline. With soggy slippers and sleepy bodies, Gus and Bon asked us tricky questions, trying hard to comprehend the stars.

LYLA

Lyla knew she was in a relationship of sorts. She did not consider herself single but was still living alone three weeks on, one week off. She wondered if she didn't have a fly in lover whether she would go out and mix with other people more. Throw herself into more activities. Would she be more open to life? Less likely to stay at home if she wasn't anticipating that moment at Perth airport when Max returned? Salacious was almost made to measure for filling in the gaps. Lyla justified it as work; the research, the cash and the tips. It stopped her getting lonely. Salacious gave her human interaction, even if it was of an upfront, XXX, open-leg nature. Lyla thought, without Salacious, her fly-in fly-out relationship might fail. She wasn't sure when the need for human company would override love.

Lyla's chances to ponder the meaning of her existence or the calibre of her relationship were limited when she was sitting on reception at Salacious. There were lulls and rushes and Cherry reliably wandered out to the front desk when the club had gone quiet.

'Hey Lyla, you want to come outside with me?'

Lyla nodded, closed the till, pulled the straps of her shoes up over her heels and wandered outside behind Cherry.

'How is it going in there, Cherry? Many tips?'

'Enough to feed the kids, I suppose.'

'I didn't know you had kids, Cherry.'

'Two beautiful big Great Danes, Shorty and Snoop.'

'I love Danes.'

'Yeah, I love Danes too, I had two blonde ones give me a hundred bucks tonight just to have their photo taken with my tits.'

'You'll be on the internet, lady.'

'I'm pretty sure my face didn't make it into the shot. Unfortunately I haven't had any backpackers pay a hundred dollars for a shot of my face.

Maybe if my face had their love juice splattered all over it they'd pay the cash to send the images to their mates.'

'You never wanted kids, Cherry?'

'Well...I did have one early on when I was drinking, before I met York. He was taken off me. My heart didn't break until I sobered up. I don't want to fuck with him now by turning up and saying, "Hi son, I was so pissed when you were a baby that I couldn't look after you. What do you think about that? Yeah son, would you like to get to know me now? I am great at what I do. One of the best. I just happen to take my clothes off and slide up and down a pole a lot." Nuh, the little man is much better off without me.' Cherry inhaled deep, eyes glazed. 'I think I'll meet him one day. I'll be walking along the beach in Scarborough. I'll just know him; I'll know his walk, his eyes, his hair. My son, all grown up. Probably hanging out at one of those backpacker bars in Scarborough, smashed, if he really is anything like me.'

'What about York, he never wanted kids?'

'Not from me love. He's probably got a baker's dozen around Perth. I don't care, don't want to know about it. He's old school in some ways and I'm sure one day he'll impregnate a hooker and have a son that he wants to pass all his wisdom onto. He won't ever change a nappy though. When it comes to shit and vomit he is hopeless.'

'You don't ever think about having a kid with York?'

'Ha! You are lovely! I owe my looks to my surgeon and my ovaries didn't put up the same fight against the natural aging process.'

'You could still have kids! What are you talking about?'

'Shorty and Snoop are too much responsibility for me! I'm a sucker for their guilt trips too. I get home with stiletto sores and one look from the pair of them and I'm treading the bitumen down to Scarborough. York just shakes his head. He takes them pig hunting and that is it. It would probably be the same if we had a son. Anyway, I better go and do some hustling. Ciggie later?'

'Yes, later.'

Three young tradies looking drunk and sheepish had walked in the doorway of the club. Lyla squeezed past them, opened the little door to the reception area and sweetly requested their entry fee.

JODIE

It was a wild west decision for us to start fly-in fly-out work. It was a big deal for Pete to look around at the plot that had been the livelihood of his family for generations, bid farewell and start again. To pioneer something new, regardless of how long it would take to line bare bones with blood, muscle, skin. Before we made the decision our brains were drenched in cortisol. Stress reactions to power bills, the price of bananas, each decision handed down by the Reserve Bank of Australia. Sometimes my right eye would twitch involuntarily as I made strong coffee on the morning of the first Tuesday of the month. Now time had become the depleted resource. I want a pile of time. A box of assorted time, wrapped individually in foil. Long-stemmed time. Expensive cognac-tinted time. Cheap time made in China. A cache of pirated time from Bali. A maximum sentence of time. I rummage through my wardrobe, through disorganised drawers searching for spare moments. I look out to the horizon, take deep breaths, drink camomile tea but nothing gives me a craved sense of time.

Another week had passed with Pete home and it was time for him to pack up and leave again.

'It's no fun when I am the only one packing,' he implored, looking over at the kids and me watching him.

When his bag was packed, he walked out and threw it in the back of the car. Usually Pete takes his own car and leaves it at the airport for the two weeks he is away. No one seemed to care that it was parked behind a small eucalypt beyond the official airport car park. Not committing to short-term or long-term parking; just flying in and out at the side. I wanted to take Pete to the airport this time. The boys always asked to see the planes and Sascha was old enough now to wave at her dad walking the tarmac.

We helped the kids with their seatbelts and when everyone was settled, Pete started the hour drive to town. We drove mostly in silence as the sunlight showcased bugs on the windscreen.

'How are you feeling, Pete? Homesick for the mess hall?'

'Never.'

'Not even for the pork spare ribs?'

'No.'

'Oh.'

'Sorry, my head just starts to race when I am about to go back to work. I keep thinking about all the jobs I wanted to do this swing home. I'm worried there might be a water blockage; the bath water emptied out so slowy. I was going to check the drain.'

'I can handle it.'

'Are you sure?'

'Well, maybe I can't handle it but I can ask someone. Keith next door?'

'Ok.'

'I never got around to fixing the back station of the retic.'

'It's ok Pete, I can have a look at it. I can water by hand if I can't work it out.'

'And I think there might be a pig in the trap up near the east boundary. Sorry babe. I put some wet grain in there and just forgot about it.'

'Geez Pete. What do you want me to do about it? I'm not killing it.'

'Killing what, Mum?'

'Nothing Bon, Mum is not killing anything.'

'I don't know, just leave it?'

'What, just let it die in the pen?'

'If you have to.'

'No, I can't do that. I'll just give it some more feed.'

'For two weeks? You don't have time.'

'I'll deal with it, Pete.'

Arriving at the Geraldton Domestic Airport, Gus and Bon both wanted to help their dad with his navy-blue bag. The bag had roller wheels on the bottom but the boys made it seem tricky to achieve a forward motion, diverting to the left then overcorrecting to the right. Gus, with his shorter arms, was on the left and Bon on the right with eldest brother authority. Sascha's chubby legs carried her slowly towards the check-in counter.

When Pete kissed Bon, Gus, Sascha and me goodbye and walked through the security gate, I felt the promise of a little bit more time. I would have a reprieve from tending to Pete and his appetite for me. An appetite where only half an hour out of twenty-four was sexual. It was an appetite for attention. Pete wanted to hold me all night;have an arm or a leg over me. He wanted me to sit next to him on the couch. It never used to be that way. Before he worked away I would have to go and find him, tempt him to come in from the fields.

When I watched Pete turn around and wave a last goodbye as he placed his left foot on the steps to walk on to the plane, I knew it would be good for us to have the days apart. To reassess, to remember the parts that make up the union. To slowly unpick. When the plane started down the runway I felt some gratitude for Pete and my life on the farm. When the plane took off at 15 degrees to the horizon I lost that whisper of gratitude. I felt hope and panic enter the ring and put their mouthguards in. When the plane was at 45 degrees, my skirt had six fists grabbing a handful tight. It was at that moment I remembered when Pete left, there was always a rude spike in the price of time.

The sun had bailed by the time I had the kids in the car, cardboard boxes of chicken and chips on their laps; a greasy consolation for them losing their Dad to work for another fourteen days.

'Mum, it's so much more fun when Dad is home. When will he be home again?' Bon asked.

'Your dad has to work so that we can have chicken and chips, boys, so don't be sad about him going to work again.'

'Mum, I miss Dad already.'

'I do too, Gus. But we will be fine. It will just be really busy for two weeks and then he'll be home. Who is going to be on my team while he is away?'

'Not me, I want to be on Dad's team,' Bon answered.

'Oh well, what about you Gus?'

'Dad's team!' Gus called out without hesitation.

'Sascha, you want to be on Mumma's team?'

'Mumma!' Sascha piped with a fat chip in one fist.

When our family, minus Pete, arrived back at the farm I slogged through the night time routine: baths, pjs, teeth, stories, sleep. The first couple of days were always the hardest, adjusting to one less parent. My instructions to the boys became a little less Gandhi and a little more Kim Jong-Il. The kids were exhausted and gave in fairly easily to my dictatorship.

Five minutes after I sat down at the kitchen table to have a cup of tea before organising the house, the phone rang.

'Pete?' I asked, not paying attention to the screen of my phone.

'No Jodes, it's me, Ella.'

'Hey Ella, how are you?'

'I'm ok. Having a quiet night at home.'

'That sounds lovely.'

'Not really.'

'I dream of quiet nights. I've just put three tired children down after dropping Pete off at the airport. They've only just fallen asleep and it is nearly 9 00 p.m.'

'I know; it's different for you. I am jealous some nights thinking of you craving quiet time, when I'm sitting on the couch watching the walls.'

'I would love to spend a night watching walls, or even TV. I dream of watching TV from 5:30 p.m. Game shows, the news...heaven.'

'Trust me, all TV is shit. And the news – it's scary. Don't watch it...at least don't ever let the kids watch it.'

'No, don't worry, I turn down the volume in the car when the news comes on the radio.'

'Hey Jodes, are there ever nights when you get spooked? You know, a woman alone in the house? I know you have kids but they are not going to protect you if something happens.'

'Usually I am too exhausted to be scared, I just collapse onto my bed and sleep. Are you getting scared?'

'Depends how many Xanax or drinks I've had.'

'Oh...zero Xanax?

'Zero Xanax and I am hearing supernatural phenomena – not as in voices, or "They took me to their planet and I came back with an anal probe they forgot to take out." I mean, I do hear things that my mind turns into crazy shit – like mice in the walls sounding like someone digging outside the window.'

'Yes, the mice freak me out. All that scratching, how can tiny little teeth make such loud sounds?'

'And the wind makes my bedroom sound like a dungeon of domination; curtains whipping the window sills, colourbond moaning, curtain rings rubbing on metal curtain rods...'

'Have you tried closing the window? No, sorry, I totally understand, Ella, sometimes the crows walk on our roof here and it sounds like barefooted children stomping overhead. So, one Xanax in?'

'Xannys soften the sounds and let me appreciate the sound of the waves breaking. What about you out in that godforsaken place? You don't need to worry about getting attacked out there. Any psycho heading for you would get bored, turn on some sweet country and western tunes in the car and forget about savaging your remote agricultural arse, Jodie.'

'What are you talking about – haven't you watched any horror movies lately? They are generally not set in cute kit homes in inner suburbia.'

'So you get spooked when Pete is away?'

'Yeah, especially when there are guys out shooting. They can be trampling tracks twenty kilometres away and it sounds like they are coming up the front drive.'

'It is hard to feel safe.'

'Some nights I hear footsteps on the gravel. Some nights a dog is barking its head off at silence. Sometimes I hear the children calling, but when I go to check them, they are asleep. I like to think I am a tough woman who can march across continents but really I like Pete's protection on the mattress.'

'Well, you know me, Jodes, I have never been the cross-continent pioneering kind. I am only here because I followed you. High heels not mountain boots for these lickable feet. I'm easily scared – maybe I'll buy a pitbull? Chances are it would become too attached to me and maul Max when he returns. Maybe I'll look online and buy some pepper spray.'

'We'll be ok, little sister.'

'Let's call each other every morning or something so that if my blood is spilt it doesn't spoil for weeks like those poor old people that sit there for months before anyone notices them...yuck...their liquefied organs stinking out the suburbs before anyone notices they've gone to the comfy sofa in the sky.'

'Ok Ella, we can check on each other. We'll be fine.'

'Yeah...sleep well.'

'Goodnight Ella.'

'Goodnight Jodes.'

I joked and acted tough as big sisters are born to do but Ella and I had talked many times together about the blood spilt at different locations close to our homes. I am sure my reassurances were minimal comfort, barely bravado. Both of our partners made us feel protected, and with them away we were watching for the wolves from the window.

LYLA

Grabbing his bag and moving through Perth Airport, Max did not even notice all the tucked-in blue and yellow shirts, the laptops and hard drives. His mind was already with Lyla in the carpark. He just had to manoeuvre through clumps of travellers, lines of taxis, cars anxious to leave the airport.

Soon Max and Lyla were sitting across from each other at the Hot Corner Indian and Thai Restaurant in Forrestfield. Lyla was fascinated that they served Thai and Indian food together. Not literally together, but two menus. If you can't decide if you would like to have Thai or Indian, the Hot Corner is the perfect choice. Online reviews called it 'sadly disappointing' but Max and Lyla rated restaurants differently.

The waitress put down a plate of glossy teriyaki chicken and steamed rice, which Lyla had felt compelled to order as it was neither authentic Indian nor Thai food. Max had ordered a Penang pork curry, which arrived a good ten minutes later, piled high with shredded kaffir lime leaves and fresh basil.

'So how is the research coming along, Lyla? How is the investigation going? What's the dirt?'

'Well, you know how I was telling you about my favourite biker wife, Cherry?'

'Yeah, but I didn't actually know you were married, it makes me feel a bit uncomfortable sitting here with you.'

'Yeah, as I was saying, the favourite of all my wives, Cherry, is a rough nut but I like her. I haven't worked her out yet. I have got no idea about her world. I think she likes me but I couldn't really be sure, it could just be a "keep your enemies even closer than your friends" type thing. Her husband is one of the big players. His name is in and out of the papers, he's brazen. Quite the outlaw. I imagine even going to the supermarket with York Stanz would be like Ned Kelly's last stand.'

'But you never ever ever ever exaggerate, do you, Lyla?'

'Never, ever. As I was saying, Cherry is fascinating in herself but there is this other side to her that she's married to one of the dodgiest, most violent bikers in Australia but they have two great Danes called Shorty and Snoop. They take them out in sidecars.'

'And how do you think this York "psycho guns blazing canine lover" Stanz is going to react if he finds out that Miss Lyla Evans has been snooping around his missus and taking notes?'

'York will only find out if you tell him, Mr Max Bennett, and I am guessing that you would become York's bitch in the clubhouse before I even notice you're missing.'

'I can't believe that they wouldn't pick up that you are sussing them out, watching…'

'That's not what I'm doing, Max, I have a legitimate curiosity about Cherry, the life she's lived, the clothes she wears, what she and York do on weekends to wind back down from a frantic week of dodging and dancing. How they fuck and fuck each other up. It is social history. What is the use of documenting these characters when they are dead or worn out from the good life? I feel like Cherry is the quintessential bikie wife. She's the one I'm interested in.'

'I know babe – you said, your favourite wife…'

'Yeah, well here I am investigating the stereotypical bikie wife but she is so complicated. Delicate and fucked up. I have only skimmed the surface. I haven't caught sight of York yet but I can't imagine why she's married to him.'

'Seriously Lyla, what do you think will happen to you and Mr Bang Bang if they find out about your research? Mr Bang Bang is not exactly a guard dog. He's not going to be able to keep you safe. Meanwhile, I'm down a hole in the middle of hell's inferno where I can't hear your calls for help.'

'Max, this is who I am. Cherry and York will never know that I am conducting research because I have not really lied to Cherry. She knows my name is Lyla. That I live by myself in a nondescript yet climatically reliable outer suburb of Perth and I am interested in what she does. I will work at the club for a while, submit my research to Matt, and then look for something else to keep me occupied. Who knows, maybe I'll do a few auditions? Apply to the Western Australian Academy of Performing Arts? In any event, Mr Bang Bang and I will be happily wandering the streets waiting for the one week in four when we get to pretend that what is real is that there is a man in our lives who loves to go for walks with us, watch bad porn on the couch, and for the week he is with us, will not even think about his other realities. Ok?'

'Ok. I'm satisfied with your explanation, or sorry, was that a justification? I guess one week in four you get a personal bodyguard who couldn't be more closely watching your arse. And the rest of you. By the way, I would not feel comfortable watching porn on the couch with Mr Bang Bang. How is my little buddy?'

'He's ok. Last night there was a fat full moon and we drove all the way in for a stomp in Kings Park. His little stumpy legs are worn out.'

After dinner and the short drive back to Lyla's apartment, Max and Lyla settled in for their week ahead. Max held Lyla's thighs open and tinkered with her insides like a gentle mechanic. He never came brashly, splashing her with his seed. He rocked and restrained until she was a shuddering pile of orgasm and then quietly pumped into her. He nibbled on her, holding her buttocks up. Max would pull one side of her shirt away and sit back to see her brown hair fall on her sunbaked boobs. Boobs that were browner and browner the more she worked nights. There was scheduled time in her courtyard almost every day now.

Max thought Lyla was a long shot, a high-risk investment, totally unlikely to stay with him for more than a phase. Lyla thought they were heading towards happiness, the building of all sorts of better things. Lyla saw the dawning mists of their joint future; the promise of children, meals shared, dancefloors waiting for them. Max did not know that Lyla had changed and covered his heart like couch grass. She had taken hold.

JODIE

Days passed in rapid succession, staccato, in a daze after Pete travelled back to the Pilbara. It was 8:00 p.m. in Yuna; another evening in paradise. I could be anywhere, I told myself as I hauled laundry out of the machine, one arm in front of the other. Canada or Palau, I would be eyes weary, arms full. I lugged the laundry basket outside under the line, pegging little clothes out as insects flew smitten towards the spotlight Pete had rigged up for me just for these little moonlight sonatas. Floating in the shadows where the spotlight couldn't quite reach there was improvised fantasia, pegs flying, snapping on my fingers, the odd sock slipping and landing in the orange gravel.

From outside, I heard the phone ring. I rushed to answer it before the sleeping children were woken. I jumped over scattered toys and three wet towels before I found my phone on the couch next to two remote controls.

'Hi babe.'

'Hi Jodes.'

'What's happening out there?'

'Not much. Just a normal day underground. How are the kids?'

'They've been good today. Not too much trouble. I still needed a glass of port before story time.'

'Oh well, as long as you aren't giving them port before story time, I think it's all ok.'

'Surely a little bit wouldn't hurt? What's happening out there tonight?'

'There is a bit of a buzz in the wet hall. Heaps of blokes downing beers discussing the latest rumours of redundancies.'

'Are they just rumours?'

'I'm not sure. No one I know has got the cut yet. Everyone is still panicking about being in the firing line. Actually, the single men don't care. They gloat. "If you haven't had at least three redundancies you are just an apprentice." Years of experience and a tally of redundancies make the worker, they say. But babe, I'm shit scared.'

'Really, Pete? Oh my darling.'

'What would we do, Jodie? I could commute but what could I do in town? We are only just getting back on our feet. I can't bear the thought of being broke again. I don't want to feel like we are slipping backwards. Everyone is nervous. Not a good vibe at all. It must affect people on the tools. I am casting my mind back trying to think if I have given them anything to use against me. I'm not the only paranoid one. Gecko is sure he will be in trouble for constantly swiping protective gear. He thinks he has taken home hundreds of Majestic Mines safety goggles. In up times, Majestic wouldn't care, but when they are looking to cull, they could use any excuse. Everyone is on their best behaviour. Even so, they could double the amount of random drug tests and shake off a few guys on our site who I'd say were lucky to get the job in the first place.'

'You can't worry about it, Pete. If it happens, it happens. You could come home. We could go on the dole. Watch movies all day. Cask wine breakfasts? I guess that isn't such a good look with three kids watching.'

'The Department of Child Protection would take them off us pretty quick so we wouldn't have their beady eyes watching us descend into hopelessness.'

'Should we just wait and see? They'd be crazy to get rid of you, Pete.'

'Thanks, babe.'

'We could move into town, live near the ocean; I could get a job doing something.'

'And leave the farm?'

'Yeah, we could leave the farm. We could just pack up and buy a little house in town. A little shack near the beach – start again?'

'I couldn't leave the farm. Jodes, we couldn't do that – my family have been on that farm forever.'

'Not technically forever – just thinking back to Captain Cook. Pretty short kind of "forever".'

'You know what I mean. Anyway, we're locked in. The bank won't let us walk away. We would never be able to sell it to cover the money we owe and buy another place. We just have to focus on getting through the dry. The farm will flourish again in a couple of years…Jodes? Then we'll have options. Are you still there, Jodes?'

'Yeah, I'm still here. I just didn't quite realise you felt we were so locked in.'

'Wouldn't you love for the boys to take over the farm one day?'

'Yes, yes, I know you'd love it. Sascha too if she wants.'

'We just have to put in the hard yards now, keep it all turning over, wait for fatter days. Jodes, I promise you, things won't always be this hard.'

'Speaking of fat, what did you have for dinner anyway?' I wasn't really prepared for my opening argument, my submissions; I had to do my homework first before explaining to Pete that in my heart I was already 300 metres from the ocean in a little shack with sea anemone shells hanging from the veranda roof and footworn paths from our door to the wet lap of the coral coast.

'Barramundi again. It was beautiful.'

'We had baked beans on toast, the boys thought it was the best thing ever except Gus stuck one up his nose and it took me about ten minutes to teach him to exhale out of the nostrils to clear it out.'

'I miss my kids. How were they today?'

'Monkeys. Sublime. Excruciating. Cute little terrors. Hard work. Sorry, I had to put them to bed tonight early, I needed Mummy time. I tried to ring.'

'I know, I didn't hear my phone.'

'That's ok. They cried and carried on a bit: "Daddy, Daddy, I want my Daddy." I just told them that I really missed you too. How many sleeps to go?'

'Four days down.'

'It will be lovely to have you home. I've got so many jobs for you already.'

'Oh great! You'll forget about those jobs when I walk in and wrap your legs around my waist.'

'Possibly.'

Living on the farm, I had started a compilation of all the jobs I had to do while Pete was away that I would usually delegate to him. Top of the list was dealing with half-dead baited mice and rabbits with myxomatosis in need of palliative care. I cannot stand inflicting harm on animals, nor seeing them writhe in pain, so I dreaded the days when a cute little bush mouse was panting in front of the fridge or when one of the dogs would bring in a sick, disfigured rabbit, barely alive. Closely following in second place was having to remove festering baited mice or dead myxomatosis rabbits after their last breaths. Next on the list was mechanical breakdowns of any kind; the car, the automatic garage door; things randomly malfunctioning or beeping rudely at me. The next subgroup were the heavy lifting tasks; for example, carrying Pete's metal ladder from the crowded shed to the bathroom where I've scaled the steps to wipe the bubbling remnants of a mouse out of the clear panel of the sun roof. Tool usage was also on the list; I have conquered the hand drill for little jobs, and the high-pressure hose for industrial cleaning. Well, that was actually all the tools I have conquered and Germaine Greer might well object to a high-pressure hose being on the "too hard for a chick" list. Setting up reticulation systems, checking for blockages in reticulation systems and clearing dead mice out of the hose, those jobs were definitely on the list. I am sure little sacks of testosterone are building up somewhere inside me.

LYLA

Some days when Lyla dropped Max back at Perth airport she wondered how much weight a relationship could bear. Some times the fly-in fly-out lifestyle seemed to weigh heavily on her. With so many relationships failing, Lyla wondered whether she and Max were fooling themselves as they went through the motions.

Lyla had not yet been tempted to be with anyone else. She watched porn but it was rarely anything more than a shallow excursion. Fleeting. Not of any real nutritional value. Lyla wanted romance: romance that crept through the night; in and out of dreams. Romance that was not forced. She wanted Max to be unable to stop kissing her. For him to want to kiss her face whenever he was talking to her. For Max to actually feel sad at goodbyes; to not want to leave. Lyla wanted Max to buy her presents, not for her material gain, but to show that he walked through the world when she was not there and thought of her. She wanted him to want to make her happy, not bring her down. She wanted him to want to stay well clear of pressing the buttons he had found upset her.

Generally, after two weeks at the mines Max was not exactly as clear on what was romantic and what was not. He knew that when he flew back into Perth airport, the farting and burping had to stop. Contrary to what other blokes told him about how they seduced women, Max understood that constantly asking for head jobs was out. He was learning that there had to be real excitement in your voice, even if you were exhausted from a gruelling twelve-hour shift, or two weeks of gruelling twelve-hour shifts. Kisses should not just be used to lure your lover into sex. Emotionless kisses were not acceptable. He would never just get a drink for himself. He would never leave and not look back.

Working at Salacious, Lyla wondered about the intersection between partnership and freedom. She gauged that most of the dancers were in relationships. The girls often came to the front desk and gushed to Lyla about the rings on their fingers. Their boyfriends often came to the club, checking that no one was hassling them; that there was no reason for them to be jealous. Lyla wondered how much freedom there really was in the relationships the girls described. It sounded like sometimes the intersection between partnership and freedom was lubricated and smooth, other times the girls were grazed by gravel, pinned to the wall.

Driving into Northbridge from Forrestfield, Lyla beat the traffic but was twenty minutes early for her shift. She spent ten minutes in her car reapplying her makeup, a task she found easy with her theatre background. Makeup Northbridge-style was heavy, let alone makeup for a skin club in Northbridge. Lyla drew on dark plum lip liner, filled in her lips with blood plum-coloured lipstick and then painted a layer of thick clear gloss on top. Lyla sprinkled some fine silver glitter on her face, picked up her handbag, locked her car and walked down from the car park to Salacious.

'Lyla, want to come for a quick ciggie before you clock on? There's still fifteen minutes before the after-work rush.' Cherry was just walking out the front door as Lyla was walking in.

'Sure, Cherry.'

Lyla and Cherry walked out and lit cigarettes in the balmy late afternoon air.

'Why are you here, Lyla?'

'I'm rostered on at five – why, what do you mean?' asked Lyla, slightly confused.

'No, I mean working here. Haven't you got anything better to do with your life? At least I get paid shitloads.'

'I get tips from some of the punters.'

'C'mon Lyla, you could work in a pharmacy and earn the same money. What is the attraction? You think you are going to meet a man here? Because I can tell you right now, sister, you are invisible to any genuine guy who might come in here.'

'Who knows, maybe one day I'll try dancing. I always wanted to grow up and be an actress; pole dancing in Northbridge is close, isn't it?' Cherry smiled and inhaled, eyes following cars as they travelled up James Street.

'Hey, can you let me know if you see Honey tonight?' Cherry asked.

'Ok, I don't think she's rostered on until seven or something. Why?' asked Lyla.

'Well the rumour is that she won't be in until she can line up some major prosthetic dental work.'

'What?'

'The other girls are saying that her man Jez went crazy on her last night at close.'

'What? But I was here until close last night.'

'Bambi said that she saw them in the car park and Jez was dragging Honey by the hair. Bambi said that she called her this morning and she couldn't talk as he smashed her teeth in so badly.'

'Fuck. Did Bambi call the police when she saw them last night?'

'No darl. Otherwise it would have been her spitting her incisors out into her wild turkey when she got home.'

'So has anyone seen Honey yet?'

'From what Bambi could make out, Jez finally called an ambulance last night. Not sure what he told them. "Yep I just didn't like her teeth Dr, they had to go." Fat disgusting prick of a man. I don't know why Honey was ever with him. Well, I can imagine. Fucked up childhood. Thinking that money can make a shit life look more glamorous. Jez is a real mongrel. York has told me stories before. Apparently he reversed his car into his ex- girlfriend on the night he found out she was pregnant. Of course she lost the baby.'

'Shit Cherry, Honey told me the other night that she was living at home with her parents and she was just dancing to pay her way through studying town planning.'

'Gee, was she asking you to pay her to sit on your lap too? Fuck Lyla, you are green. Honey's hopes of studying anything were dashed when her stepdad smashed two Besser blocks together with her head in between when she was about seven years old. All the scars are thick, she's shown me. No, the only thing Honey ever studied was the Nimbin gutter through hazy heroin eyes.'

'Shit.'

'She wound up here a couple of years ago and I think things were fairly stable for her until Jez spotted her in here about eight months ago and started feeding her party drugs. Silly bitch. Ignored everything she had heard about him for a bit of glitz. It was always going to end in tears. Barb should start doing random drug tests like they do at the mines.'

'If everyone had to blow clean before starting work here there would be an empty stage and lots of punters asking for their money back.'

'Empty stage? Excuse me? But, yes, you would be looking right now at Salacious' only dancing girl. Hmm, I would clean up. I'm going to have a talk to Barb...'

'So Cherry, before we go back in, what should we do about Honey?'

'Do? What do you mean?'

'Is there anything we should do for her?'

'What, like send a bunch of flowers?'

'Um, yes?'

'Ha! You are a classic, Lyla! Flowers! Would you like me to hand around a hat for contributions to her dental fund? You know that's a dead giveaway that someone is a biker's girlfriend: private health insurance, massive dental plan, the maximum dental coverage available...'

'Cherry, you are a harsh woman.'

Still laughing and shaking her head, Cherry butted out her cigarette and walked towards the doorway.

JODIE

Relationships mutate and scramble to adapt when love goes long distance. There is something monastic and bitter about people who suddenly lose their partner to work. I try not to be one of those people. Sometimes Pete and I lurch for the bedroom when he flies back in. As long as the kids are out of earshot, it is the most direct method of reminding us that we are two halves of a partnership, intimate with another human being, in love. Two weeks away often seemed to weaken the memory of those facts. Each time we reconnect I realise that I am getting softer around the middle and harder in my attitude. Pete's tongue and hands are getting rougher and rougher. There is a space under the cotton sheets where the coals of our past work to spark up our relationship. My anxiety always lifts as soon as the coals have done their job.

I am more attracted to Pete than ever. He is always exhausted when he comes home. I have lots of couch time to consider his torso passed out on the floor in front of the television, next to me on the couch or on our inflatable camping mattress if I convince him to take me away from the farm. Sometimes I am so choked up with love that it doesn't come out right. Reluctant to scare him off with my tsunami of pent-up emotion, I am always measured and a little bit false; a bit too pornographic for the massive heart that beats my insides. Pete is oblivious, and stoked that the mother of his children seemed conflict-free. His radar wasn't detecting the tsunami that was heading for the coast.

LYLA

Lyla was irritable as she sat in her booth at Salacious. Something was taking its toll: the music, the sexism, an intensifying craving for nicotine. Max was still five days away from returning and she felt a growing intolerance of him being a one-week special. Lyla felt herself snarl a greeting at two young men and asked for their identification as they held out a fifty-dollar note to pay their way. Cherry came and blocked the door so that the boys had to beg her to let them inside.

'Lyla, you look premenstrual, love, why is such a pretty young thing like you looking so sour? Come and talk to Auntie Cherry...let's go out the front. Is it all that sexual frustration of being single and seeing Perth's most eligible men passing you to come inside and look at me?' Lyla already had a cigarette in hand and was squeezing out of the narrow doorway of the booth she worked inside.

'Cherry, you can have every single one of them. I have not seen anyone eligible since I started work here.'

'You sound jaded, Lyla. Are you disillusioned from Salacious' unique strain of tainted love?'

The women laughed together, as if working at a place like Salacious was perfectly normal, like it was the workplace they had prayed for since childhood.

'I am sexually repressed, you have that right. Looking for love, I suppose. Maybe I should find myself a bikie man like you?'

Cherry raised an eyebrow as she sucked hard on her cigarette.

'Why didn't you ask earlier? I am not quite sure about you though, Miss Lyla. I am guessing that bikie men may not actually be your flavour.'

'What is it with the biker men, what is the attraction?'

'Well, one day York and I were at the clubhouse, everyone relaxing, drinking, and I saw two guys in the kitchen standing together looking into a cupboard, talking quietly to each other. I instantly knew that major shit was going down so I calmly walked outside, lining up my escape, when the first sounds of violence erupted. Shots fired, heads taking fatal blows, front teeth smashing. You don't get that kind of excitement with suburban love.'

'Thank goodness.'

'No, that was scary and you do get paranoid walking around. I love him because when he is around, things are larger than life. The big money exaggerates everything. York has a little old man down south near Dunsborough who cultivates rare breeds of lavender and rose. York organised for him to send a harvest to a perfumery in Paris. A scent was produced, named after me, arriving on my doorstep one day out of the blue in a massive designer-made glass bottle containing about two litres of a subtle, beautiful fragrance.'

'Uh huh...that does sound good.'

'One day he hired a team of students to write me a love letter. Three handwritten words, "I love you", written over and over. York had heard that in 1875 a citizen of Paris called Marcel de Leclure had written the longest love letter ever to his lover, Magdalene de Villalore: "I love you" written 1 875 000 times. York made sure that the students completed 1 875 001. Beautiful; obsessive and competitive perhaps; still gorgeous.'

Lyla coughed out her smoke. 'I'd be happy to compromise; "I love you" written a couple of times would be fine. Would you say York is your typical biker though? I can't imagine some of the men I've seen on the road ordering perfume. I know that heaps of bikers these days look more like fly-in fly-out workers than bearded Harley riders, but some still look like they would rather knife you than romance you.'

'Lyla, you have to come off reception and into the club. None of the bikers look at me as if they want to knife me. When I say me, I probably mean my tits; when they look at my tits they don't look like they want to knife me.'

'But what happens if one of those bikers has to choose between loyalty and their women; like if York was given an order that you didn't agree with?'

'I don't get too involved, Lyla but I know that York gives orders rather than takes them.'

'So York is high up then?'

'Like I said, Lyla, I don't get too involved.' Cherry wrapped up the conversation and gestured to Lyla that it was time to return inside.

ELLA

It was with a beautiful skin full of alcohol that Ella achieved some sort of survival. Her steps along the footpath were deliberate. Don't step on the cracks and everything will be all right. She traced her finger along picket fences; some old, some newly painted, some newly painted to look old. Two wines was all it had taken to make her optimistic that she could survive this swing, that her life was fashionable and not a lonely joke. Ella's heels were too high so she took them off and held them in her phoneless hand. She couldn't ring Max during the day as he would be working underground, so her phone was only really useful for safety and duckfaces. Francis Street provided opportunities for selfies that other streets didn't. That wasn't the reason why Max and Ella had purchased their house back from the beach; but it was panacea and distraction as Ella walked towards the beach, towards town and back again in a fairly useless loop.

Sundays were hard to bear when Max was away. Ella always made plans; with others who surfed or jogged along the foreshore; with couples who took their dogs to jump over shore breaks at Page's Beach; with single girls who worked in the shop. She tried to avoid anyone with kids or meeting couples at a café for Sunday brunch. No way. If she wanted to hang out with kids her niece and nephews were an hour away and did not annoy her in the way that other people's kids did. Too hard to keep still for a photo, and couples seemed to insist on continually trying to take photos of their children. As if they would ever really look back at them. No one wants their Facebook feeds choked with pictures of other people's kids or pets and those people themselves just have them bloat their phone until someone steals it or they accidentally drop it down the toilet as it falls out the back pocket of their not-so-skinny-now jeans. Why bother? Images of her complexion against the pale limestone blocks of old stony houses, on the other hand – Ella could not get enough of those. Ella sent one to Max, as if he hadn't seen enough rock in the background of his day already.

Ella walked booze-happy across the grassed area near the Port. The low-tea sun felt fit to inflict skin cancer and the grass only semi- scratchy under her pumiced feet. Ella liked seeing action; action around her that made the world seem like it was moving forward, not still with two vertical lines over everything; paused. When Max was away time seemed to drag lethargic. When he was home the days disappeared: bang, bang, bang. Ella walked quickly with light steps across the bike track, through the line of sand-grass and down onto the beach. So close to the Port, yet so sparkly, Ella never once thought of lead and its inevitable invisible touch. She was wondering whether she should leave her shoes on the beach and swim. They'd cost her one-fifth of Max's daily wage or twice her daily wage, so she wasn't sure she wanted them snatched while she was wading around oblivious. She didn't have bathers on but her bra and undies would pass and probably excite someone along the way. But it was only two hours since she'd straightened her hair so she decided to keep walking.

Ella was near the public toilet block south side of the foreshore playground when she realised she needed to go to the toilet, but her steps did not veer one degree closer to them. She had shuddered on the one occasion she had found herself perched high above the seatless stainless steel toilets, utkatasana. She guessed that toilet seats were dispensable for some good reason in the Council's eyes but at the moment the bottom of her soft thigh accidentally came into contact with the cold metal bowl she could not think of one godforsaken ratepaying justification. Ella could never quite remember if it was the GFC or GCF but she definitely wanted toilet seats, even in hard times. So she turned right up Fitzgerald Street and paused for a second to contemplate entering the Sandy Beach Hotel to use their toilets.

The grand entrance to the pub was not grand. It was circa old days and had never had the cash injection it needed to hold its own among other restored old Geraldton buildings. As she slipped on her shoes she balanced with one hand on a sign to the right of the door. Under her fingers the fluorescent sign advertised that between 4:00 p.m. and 8:00 p.m. the Sandy Beach Hotel had a free sausage sizzle, a meat raffle and Western Australia's best raunchies. Ella could hear a rumble from inside as she stepped a sandy heel over the threshold. She walked in hesitantly. She hadn't been in the Sandy Beach before and it felt like she was entering a secret gentlemen's club. A bogan version. With each step the music got louder; indistinguishable rock at a distance.

When Ella peered around into the front bar she saw a girl in a red g-string standing in front of three blokes. Ella couldn't hear what they were saying and all she could think was that she wanted the girl's red heels; she had seen some online that had similar lines: rounded at the front and extremely high heels; not quite fetish.

'Excuse me darl, mind if I come past?' A man in board shorts placed one hand on Ella's left shoulder as he passed her at the doorway.

'Yes, is it…is there…' Ella coughed her discomfort into the doorway and flicked her hair out behind her right shoulder. One wine, she thought. Just one. It would be rude to use the toilet and not have one drink.

Ella self-consciously walked to the bar and stood behind a bar stool waiting to order a drink from a raunchy wearing navy and white horizontally striped bikini bottoms and a sheer navy bra with anchors embroidered over the nipple area. Ella looked ahead, not to her right, not to her left. The back of the bar had four big beams lined with alcohol and an odd collection of stuff: a cone shell, old glass Morse Indian Root Pill bottles, shale from the Abrolhos Islands, compasses, nautical paraphernalia. Some of it looked dusty and old but almost perfectly in line with the coastal theme designs Ella had seen recently on Instagram: shells and string and other forgotten things. How lucky for the Sandy Beach Hotel to come unwittingly back into fashion.

Coming out from the top of the shelves above the bar and spanning the room was an old-style string fishing net: knotted squares 10 cm by 10 cm. Some red Japanese glass fishing floats hung from rope amidst hundreds of fishing lures: antique, soft plastic, sprocket, hard body, spinners and poppers. Lures hooked up by men who would never put a padlock on a Parisian bridge for their wife, but took great pride in having a lure hanging from the fishing net above the front bar at the Sandy Beach Hotel.

'Just a house white thanks,' Ella requested from the skimpy behind the bar.

'No worries lovely, come in for a drink? Nice in here on a Sunday ain't it?' the skimpy asked, English as breakfast muffins.

'Oh…I…yeah…I guess I thought one drink would be nice.'

'Of course. There you go – I think that's a Margaret River blend. Have you been down there?'

'I—' Ella turned around as the skimpy had moved down the other end of the bar without waiting to collect her answer.

Ella held her glass in front of her face for longer than usual before she took a sip. The music pulsed and she moved her glance around, not wanting to linger on the three topless women circulating in the room, collecting glasses, chatting, wiping tables.

'A beautiful sight, isn't it?' Ella turned her head to look into the face of the man sitting to her left who had made the observation. She stared down quickly at the floor of the front bar. Ella's brow and lips scrunched closer to each other. She turned back to look at him. The man's face was a shit fight: a glass eye, enlarged pores on his nose, extremely long eyebrow hairs on one side. A scar marked the site of a prior slicing from the right cheek to where the top of his ear was missing. Ella had never seen such a face. His glass eye looked illfitted, secondhand. Ella's chest rose as she quickly looked back to the open room.

'Yes, I haven't been in here before, I like the pressed tin roof.'

'Oh, I thought you might have been here for the girls.'

'Oh no...no...I mean...I don't know...I definitely like their shoes...' Ella cringed as her eyes dodged tits.

'Don't worry, lots of girls come in for the skimpies, by themselves or with their fellas.'

'My husband hasn't brought me here.' Ella's eyes were starting to twinkle. 'What a dud, I knew I shouldn't have married him,' Ella smiled at the face next to hers.

'Oh well, no reason why you can't bring him in here. Most blokes seem to rate the Sandy Beach Hotel.'

'Higher than they rate being with their families or anywhere else on a Sunday afternoon, by the look of the number here.'

'They probably tell their families they need to buy something at the hardware warehouse – a light globe, a new joiner for the hose, something essential...then whoops, they remember they've forgotten to have any lunch and it's sausage sizzle time at the Sandy Beach Hotel.'

'I hate sausages but they smell good...'

'Hey, Kaylee is coming over – you want to give her a goldie? Tell her you like her shoes?'

'No, no, I'm good thanks.'

'It would probably be rude if you didn't.'

'Ok, ok. I don't have change, though. I have a five-dollar note.'

'Kaylee will take that for sure.'

'Hiya, I'm Ella, just really came to use the toilet. I like your shoes.'

Kaylee laughed with a head flick that brought all her brown hair to the left side of her chest. Ella noticed Kaylee's mineral foundation and bronzer that sparkled under the unrigged scented soft plastic lures overhead. She scanned Kaylee from head to foot and would say that she was probably on par to Kaylee in looks and fitness but guessed that she probably looked after herself a bit better than Kaylee. Kaylee's heels would have to be blistered, her little toes corned.

'Hey Kaylee, this is Ella. Hasn't been in here before – I'm trying to teach her what the go is.'

'Hi Jimmy, how are you? How was your week? Thanks love. Hi Ella, I'm Kaylee, don't worry love, I've only been here a couple of weeks, came up from Perth, doing a tour of the Midwest: Mount Magnet, Meekatharra, a bucks party on a property in Wiluna and then home.'

'Wow. I haven't been out to those towns – I grew up in Melbourne.' Ella was going to say something sarcastic about Meekatharra not being exactly Las Vegas and just caught the words before they slipped out.

'Wanna come? It's not bad money – lots of mining men in Meeka and Magnet happy to splash a bit of cash at the pub.'

'Yeah, probably my husband. He's up that way. Sounds like fun. I'd love to catch Max by surprise. If he saw me topless in a bar in Magnet holding out a glass to him asking for some cash he'd probably have a coronary from the shock – and all the deep-fried sweet and sour pork he eats out there.'

'Yes, they work hard but make up for it with desserts from what I've seen. Thanks Ella, thanks Jimmy.'

Ella and Jimmy sat on bar stools as Kaylee picked up a tray with three beers on it and walked towards a table at the back of the room; relaxed shoulders down, red knickers swaying.

'From Melbourne are you, Ella?' asked Jimmy, one eye on her, one vaguely on Kaylee.

'Originally. Came here about three years ago now.'

'I'm telling you, Geraldton is a lot different these days. You can barely recognise it from when I grew up. The Norfolk Pines stand their ground but a frenzy of development has happened around them.

'So you've never left?' Ella asked, not expecting that he had migrated far. 'Why would you? Leave Geraldton and the Sandy Beach Hotel? I've crayfished out of the Abrolhos Islands for eighteen seasons now…'

'Wow, you must have seen some changes,' said Ella, not particularly sure she wanted to hear a whole catalogue of them but at least it saved her from feeling ridiculous sipping wine and looking at Kaylee by herself.

'Ella, changes – for a town where nothing fucking ever happens, I have seen some changes.' Ella thought Jimmy wasn't going to elaborate and was trying to think of another question to make the conversation last the duration of her one standard drink, when he continued.

'The crayfish industry has changed – the number of boats for sale at the wharf would bring tears to the eyes of anyone who remembers the glory days, when crayfish paid for houses along ridges with town's best ocean views. Geraldton was one of the last bastions of cheap housing before the boom. Even after the bust, properties for sale ten years ago have more than quadrupled in price. Top prices for fibro cottages that once were state housing stock. Sometimes past residents still pissed or lost knock on the doors of pimped-up cottages and ask to see the insides of the homes they once knew. Of course the new residents have more money and distrust and don't let them in to view the contents of their home.'

'Did you grow up in—' Ella started.

'Now every bastard is scampering around a bit disoriented because we are subject to the bust; a breakdown of the spoils we thought were ours from the boom. Every second house is for sale in a bid to stake ground won in the boom but the bust is upon us and encroaching, like a monstrously big pair of tits bearing down on us and squashing our dreams...'

'Wow.' Ella was wincing at having taken Jimmy somewhere deep with just one question.

'Ella, you see families going to the beach more and watching the tide, hoping they can rely on life's ebbs and flows.'

'Beautiful. Are you, like, the hotel's resident poet?' Ella watched as two blokes in dirty high-vis work shirts entered the bar.

'You're too kind! So your hubby works out of Mount Magnet?'

'Somewhere up there. I haven't really got my head around the geography yet. Near Newman? I probably should look at a map. Anyway, he does three and one.'

'How's that then?'

'Not great. FIFO widow three weeks out of four.'

'Not now you have your new family at the Sandy Beach Hotel – Kaylee, me, Axl here.'

Ella followed Jimmy's thumb pointing to a punter to his left, reading a newspaper at the bar.

'What have you dobbed me in for now, Jimmy?' Axl turned around and nodded at Ella.

Ella had never seen anyone look so clean and shiny, hair still wet as if he had just stepped out of a shower at the Sandy Beach Hotel. Brown eyes. Ella felt shy.

'Hi, I'm Ella, I haven't been in here before – had no idea what I was missing out on.'

'Well, you've struck gold meeting my man Jimmy and myself on your first visit. We are more or less Sandy Beach royalty. The probability of meeting us was pretty high, though, as we try to cover opening hours between us.'

'Oh, don't worry, I understand, my mum was an alcoholic…'

'Hey, hold up, I am not an alcoholic, this is mineral water.' Axl held up his glass of amber liquid with a centimetre of white froth on the top.

Ella sipped her glass, smiling, making the cold wine disappear into her.

'Axl here is planning to put in a land rights claim on the Sandy Beach Hotel so he can't change his beliefs or customs, not a millimetre or he has no chance. Has to remain stuck in his old patterns, can't evolve…'

'Are you really making a native title claim on this land?' Ella cocked her head in confusion. Axl burst out laughing.

'Jimmy, shut your mouth. Ella, don't ever believe anything that comes out of Jimmy's mouth – don't be deceived by his charm and beauty, he is a mongrel. Came out in a litter in the car park behind the Sandy Beach.'

'Ok, nice to meet you.' Ella put down her sweating glass on the bar towel.

'Had enough of us already? Stay and have another wine – I'll shout you one.' Jimmy dug his hand into the pocket of his shorts and pulled out his wallet.

'How come you never offer to shout me one?' Axl folded his newspaper over and stood up to the left of Jimmy.

'Just this once, I'll buy both you bastards a drink.'

'Bastard? Ok, you definitely owe me a white wine after calling me a bastard.' Ella's eyebrows raised a long way up from her mouth.

'Sorry love, you're not a bastard, I just meant this bastard.' Jimmy's right fingers started fiddling with his incomplete ear. He turned around to face the bar and buy a round.

'Classy, hey?' Axl was loving seeing his bar mate squirm under the canopy of lures. As one beer anthem switched to another Axl looked at Ella's side profile longer than he ever cared to look at the raunchies. Ella didn't notice, as she was looking at a long hair on the back of Jimmy's neck and wishing she had her Italian nail scissors in her bag to have a little snip.

JODIE

The morning after Pete flew back out to the Pilbara, I invited Jenna, one of the mums from school, over for morning tea. An hour before she arrived I looked around the house and felt shame. There were kids' clothes everywhere: a school uniform from the day before at the foot of the toilet bowl where it had been taken off before a much-protested shower, scattered boys' pyjamas lining the lino hallway, and a light peppering of dirty clothes in all other areas of the house. Housework is an overwhelming, relentless and unrewarding experience. A sacrilege against life. That doesn't stop the shame, though. I wish I had some obsessive side to my personality; some preference for organisation. Instead, I'm used to a frantic skidding around before someone is due to arrive. Pete often joked that if shame was the only thing that motivated us to clean, it was damn lucky we felt pain at the thought of losing the respect of others. The dreaded reflection on one's soul of a dirty and out-of-control house. I placed Sascha in front of two episodes of *Play School*, spot cleaned and closed some doors to minimise exposure.

At ten o'clock I heard Jenna's car blustering up the gravel. I turned off the television and Sascha made a high-pitched, wordless complaint.

'C'mon Sascha,' I said as I picked her up and used my spit to wipe stuck food off her cheek, a manoeuvre that was instinctual and disgusting. Queen Victoria died in 1901 and here, in Yuna, surrounded by snakey agricultural land, I was spitting on my daughter's cheeks to increase the level of Victorian propriety in my world.

'Jenna, hi. Come in. How are you going today?'

'Hi Jodie, yeah, I'm good, how are you?'

'I'm good. Pete's just gone back so it's always a bit hectic. Excuse the mess. Come in. I'll make us a cuppa.' I led Jenna into the kitchen, picked up one of Bon's books from a seat and gestured for Jenna to sit down. I lowered Sascha down; she waddled over to the fridge and put a dried bit of banana stalk that she found on the floor into her mouth. 'Sascha, no, don't put that in your mouth, yucky.'

'Morning tea time, Sascha!' Jenna said with a generous smile.

'Yes, if we ever run out of food we can live off what's on the floors for at least a week,' I joked tentatively. I knew Jenna's partner also worked away so I had banked on a bit of camaraderie in the trenches.

'Yes, I know, my floors were like that until I bought one of those swivel mops. Have you seen one? I can show you mine one day if you like. Yes, tea will be fine. White. One sugar. I love it. Don't know what I did before that mop. The other mums at school have them too. Changed my life!'

I took a deep breath with my back turned to Jenna as I plunged her tea bag into scalding water. At least the trenches would be spotless. 'When does Dan get home? What swings does he do?' I asked, placing Jenna's tea and some shop-bought banana cake in front of her.

'He does eight days on and and six days off. Pretty crazy. The six includes his two days of travel. He gets paid for one day of travel so it's okay. Not ideal I guess. He gets home in a couple of days,' said Jenna, both hands cupping her hot tea, the diamond-ringed finger softly tapping the ceramic.

'How do you go when Dan is away? With the kids and everything?' I asked, hoping for some fraying around Jenna's neat country edges.

'Yeah, it's fine.'

Damn.

'When he goes I just focus on keeping things in order: the house, the farm, the kids.'

'Ha! Me too! "Chaos is a friend of mine",' I said, quoting Bob Dylan. My shoulders relaxed.

'Do you struggle a bit when Pete's away?' Jenna asked.

'Yeah, I do. It's hard. I miss him. The kids miss him. The wheels fall off a bit when he's away.'

'I can give you some tips if you like. Some of the girls said that I should start a blog or Instagram site or something with all my household tips.'

'Oh, okay...' Oh, God help me. Jenna proceeded to enlighten me with her top ideas for how I could get more organised: the best paper towels to use, multiple options for toy storage, weekly linen washing techniques, tips for toothbrush and toothpaste storage. I smiled politely thinking about the senseless, reckless manner in which I had stored the kids' toothbrushes up until now.

Before she passed away, Pete's mum had regularly visited and tried to teach me the golden rules of housekeeping: at a very minimum, make the beds and do the dishes every day. It never seemed easy for me.

'The key to organisation is that everything must have a place,' she would gently teach, hoping I would change.

The housework lapsing and catching up was my new pulse. The dishes spawned all over the kitchen, and were put back in their place. The clothes flew out of the cupboards, and were contained. The rubbish rose then fell. When Pete was away, this was my pace, my blinking of time. I approached housework like a bulimic approaches food. I messed everything up as if someone else was going to clean up after me, then it dawned on me that it was actually me that would have to roll up my sleeves, my fingers that were going to have to do the work.

When Jenna finally left, I put Sascha down for her middle-of-the-day sleep and wandered into the bathroom. I looked at the toothpaste-splattered mirror, the gunk around the plug hole, the greeny-blue scale around the taps. I grabbed a microfibre cloth and started wiping the toothpaste off the mirror in wide strokes, like waving for help in a riptide. The farmhouse we lived in was old. It had always been used for workers. There was another house on the property, the main house, which we preserved in case Pete's dad ever recovered from old age. I have to check it now and again to make sure no pythons have moved in and ensure the mouse bait is keeping the mice from taking over.

Pete has said we will move into the main house one day. I have never told Pete that moving from our farm house to the main house would dry out my soul. I would wither, packing boxes to move deeper into the farm. To take up the main house would be to resign myself to a humming sadness; a life at odds with my rhythms. I brought my suitcase here in the first place and made vows that some might think bind me to this grainy life but all I think about now is moving to the sand dunes. I must talk to Pete, give him the inkling. Say careful words. Do the thinking to devise a plan for evacuating to other ground. Pete will not understand. I know he'll resist, say I made choices. He will talk of his ancestors and make me feel uncertain about why mine are calling me closer to the coast, away from the inland curl.

LYLA

It was twilight when Max walked through the automatic doors of Perth Domestic Airport with a rush of workers, all single-minded in taking the leap from work to home. Some were imagining throwing off their high-vis work wear, showering and heading down to a happy bar in Fremantle. Some were imagining gently re-entering family life. Others were heading to a nearby hotel, suspended for the night in between what they do for money and what they do the rest of their lives. Some of those blue and yellow workers were dreading going home, for home had become a place much more difficult than work, where accusations flew and they were never able to make up for the time they'd been away.

Max felt only relief as he moved with the crowd across the road to the short-term car park. He veered right and saw Lyla, neck strained, waiting by her car, looking for him. The last fifteen steps towards her were the worst when he had a stupid grin on his face, but he was still too far away for her to hear his words. When his bag dropped and he reached for her, both of their words departed temporarily. Eyes closed, they guiltily realised that despite all the other complications of meeting here in the car park, as the light was dripping out of the sky, they had both allowed themselves ridiculous happiness.

'Hi babe,'

'Hi Max.'

'How are you going?'

'Good,' Lyla said, looking at him, slightly thrown again at how handsome he looked to her. 'I've found us another restaurant.'

'Let's do it, my lady.'

The Phuket Elephant Restaurant was a gem Lyla had found while walking around one day with Mr Bang Bang. It ticked all the boxes for the next instalment of Max: cheap plastic chairs, deep pink carpet with plastic pink and red floral arrangements that were in no way minimalist. She had been impressed by the signwriting on the front window, 'Food to Thai for'. As they entered the premises, Max and Lyla were greeted by a smiley young girl who led them to a table by the back wall and brought them some menus and a jug of water.

'Mum would have loved this place,' Lyla said, still gazing at Max. 'How was work this time?'

'Yeah, it was okay, the hardest part is the paperwork – Job Hazard Assessments.'

'Well, I did see online this week that there was another workplace death in the Pilbara.'

'I know. I know there's no escape from the paperwork and I know that it is preventative and butt covering, but it's torturous. I hope whoever made the pyramids didn't have to have every brick moved covered by a Job Hazard Assessment. It would have blown the project out by a thousand years. We had an alert the other day that explored the risks of placing toothpicks in the normal garbage. Lyla, promise me you will always break the toothpick in half and never be so reckless as to throw it, totally intact, into a rubbish bag.' Max threw his hand up in the air and flicked his fingers downward.

'Any highlights in the food hall this swing?'

'I can't complain about the food. Do I look chunkier? I can't resist the salt and pepper squid and racks of lamb. I don't want to think of how depleted the animal kingdom is as a result of my dinner plates over the last two weeks.'

'Do some guys go crazy at the bain marie?'

'I saw one guy have two whole plates of those battered sweet and sour pork balls. Piled up high. Dangerous. If it wasn't for the Job Hazard Assessments you would probably be able to work it off, but there is no chance of burning many calories these days.'

'Did you think of me, in your donga?'

'I thought of you being in my donga, spread-eagled, little strips of high-vis material just covering your bits.'

'Max, the waitress is coming.' Lyla kicked him under the table.

'Would you like to order now, please?' The waitress must have been a family member; she looked about fourteen.

'Yes, could I please have chicken satay skewers for entree and gai med ma moung for main.'

'And could I please have tom yam goong for entree and a green curry chicken for main.'

'And drinks for you, Miss?'

'Yes please, just a house red will be great thank you.'

'And I will have one of those Thai beers, thank you.'

'Max, that is very exotic and adventurous of you, a Thai beer? There is hope, then.'

'Come on...'

'Do you think this is what happy couples do, Max? Find something they love and keep replaying it?'

'I would replay this; the last forty-five minutes from the automatic doors of the airport until now. I'd be happily stuck in those forty-five minutes for a couple of years.' Max looked at Lyla. Lyla looked back at Max, forgetting the shame she focused on when he was away.

'So how's the job going, Lyla?'

'I met York this week.'

'Who was York again?'

'Cherry's husband, the dodgy one.'

'Oh yeah, I remember.'

'He's a very smooth character. Not my type, of course. Although he too is married.'

'Carry on.'

'Cherry introduced me on Sunday night. He was just in for a few quiet drinks so I was able to observe the vibe between them.'

'And?'

'I'm not sure. He seemed lovely. Charming. Quiet. Informed. And all the time I am thinking of the tally of jaws he has smashed.'

'Great. Please, I do not want you to have your jaw smashed, it's important to me.

'Max, if I can get your mind away from head jobs until entree arrives, there is more to the story. York is a fitness nut. Vegetarian, Buddhist, into yoga and jigong. Will not let Cherry look at a drink. Yet he goes pig hunting and has this flipside criminal mind. No one has told me exactly what his trade is in. No prosecution against him has ever stuck. He is clean. Bleached clean. Crisp white Thai fisherman's pants in the morning sun clean. Squeaky. A man version of Miranda Kerr. I am sure, like her, he buries his biodegradable toothbrushes in the garden every three months. But I am sure, unlike her, he is cracking skulls behind the scenes.'

'Cherry hasn't let slip what sort of business he is running?'

'No, and she is a smart woman; I imagine she's too clever to ask many questions.'

'It has to be drugs, hasn't it?'

'Probably. I am not totally up with black market commodities but I guess it is drugs or guns. Some kind of illegal gambling? Prostitution? Something slightly predatory or...immoral? Yeah, it has to be drugs, Cherry kept on referring to York's "big money".'

'Well, a guy at work the other day was saying that the Government is testing our waste water and guess what? Per capita, Western Australia has the highest number of ice addicts in the country. The resources boom heralded good days for the drug trade. Even after the bust there must be cashed-up workers paying way more for crystal meth here than in the east. Apparently the police are expecting turf wars to stake a claim on the profits. I don't know how the blokes get away with it at work. I'm obviously not imaginative enough, as daily drug testing turns me off taking any detectable substances.'

'I can't really imagine you on crystal meth.'

'I've heard guys get up to all sorts of shenanigans to evade detection, getting their kids to piss in containers and then having some rig up so that when it is time to leak, they siphon out the clean gear. I definitely don't have the nerves.'

'Lucky you get high off me.'

'I do. My one-week Lyla binge.' As Pete spoke those words Lyla looked down at the butcher paper covering the table below her face. She suddenly felt sick and anxious. A swarm of bees massing in her stomach.

'Do you think Ella detects me in your system?'

'Shit, Lyla, I don't want to talk about it.'

'Well, every month you go from me to her. You don't think she picks up on anything?'

'She is in love with me and trusts me.'

'Fuck. Max, what are we doing?'

'I don't know, Lyla. When I'm flying from Perth to Geraldton I convince myself that I am coming back from three weeks' work. My limbs start to ache, I feel exhausted and then I am there, coming home after a strenuous swing, needing to collapse on the couch and recuperate. So what are we doing, Lyla? Where do you see this leading?'

'I don't know. Some days I look up at that eternally blue sky and think I would be crazy to leave this town.'

'So your life decisions hinge on the weather?'

'Among other things.' Lyla was confused whether to recklessly abandon her instinct for self-preservation or ensure that she never asked a question that would garner the reply, 'I'm sorry Lyla, I'm married to Ella, and I will never leave her.' Awake at 2:00 a.m. she often realised that if he was going to leave Ella, he would have done so by now.

'It's easy for you, your work is here.'

'So now it's about job opportunities? You think you might leave here for a job elsewhere?'

Lyla looked back at him with wide eyes. Neither of them had the balls to ask each other for what they wanted.

'Who knows what the weather will bring.'

'You still think your ambition is too big for this one-horse town?'

'Damn right it is, Max Bennett. You know it is.'

So, with Lyla's lead, the conversation drifted gently to Thai-style wontons and sweet rice layer cakes and safely away from adulterous husbands and impotent dreamers.

The next morning Lyla lay completely cocooned in Max's arms and legs.

'Tell me about your pussy,' Max whispered into Lyla's hair.

'I don't understand it myself, Max. It is such a weird thing. A strange little Buddha. Sometimes it wants its belly rubbed hard and then other times it just wants a little tickle. I honestly don't know most of the time what is going on with it. Sometimes it is so alert that even the gentle rub of my knickers makes me horny and I go to a toilet or somewhere else quiet and pull down those knickers and I could rub myself raw and I can't come. A mystery.'

'I know,' answered Max, 'Sometimes I have found a technique and for a few days it makes you scream, in a good way, and then just when I get cocky and think I am on a winner you will squirm, in a bad way, and I know it's time to find something new.'

'See what I mean? I have no control. It is unpredictable. One thing I can tell you is that that you are far better talking to me up here than down there.'

'What?'

'Well, if you lowered yourself down to my crotch and started slowly saying, "Your pussy is so gorgeous, you have the best-looking pussy in the world, I love your pussy so much", it would fall on deaf ears but if you stay up above for that same amount of time and say, "You are so gorgeous, you are the most beautiful woman in the world, I love you so much," you will reap far better returns down below.'

'Really?'

'You can have me panting by looking me in the eyes and telling me those things. Do you need me to write them down?' Lyla laughed and grabbed a pen from the bedside table and started scrawling on Max's forearm, 'Lyla, I have so much respect for you, you are an amazing woman.' That was all Lyla got to before the pen malfunctioned; Max's coarse blond hairs choking it up.

'So all those times I've talked I wasn't actually getting anywhere?'

'Sorry Max, I probably started thinking about all the things I had to do the next day.'

'Oh really, is that right?'

Lyla knew that Max took every scrap of advice she gave and from that point on he made sure that for every secret communication he had below her belly, he came upside and whispered all the love he could into Lyla's heart and mind.

JODIE

Ever since Pete started to work away I've had dreams that he is being unfaithful. Last night in my dream Pete had called one of my friends 'sexy' and pulled her on to his lap. Boutique night terrors tailor made for me.

Tonight inside the dream, Pete was being a party boy. He was being charismatic in front of two young women and was ignoring me. He had invited all these people over and they were lounging around in our bedroom, joking, flirting. Pete pulled out a bag of mull and started rolling a fat joint. When he put it to his lips and picked a lighter up from the floor I said, 'Pete, not in the bedroom.' He looked up with an expression of disregard. 'Yeah right,' he said and flicked the lighter. The young women looked at me and giggled. I stood my ground. 'Pete, the kids are in here all the time, I don't want it stinking of dope.' 'They'll love it,' Pete said, his nostrils flaring as he inhaled deeply. As he exhaled he looked me in the eye quickly as if to say, 'I don't care what you want.' The dream went on. There is a young woman with flawless skin, no freckles, no sun damage, no blemishes, no body hair in need of harvesting. She is in bikinis. Pete can't take his eyes off her as she talks to me.

'You can understand why Pete wants to be with me. He wants to lick me and rub his fingers all over my soft skin. I mean look at you, there are so many flecks of stuff all over your skin, so many marks and folds of skin. I am hot, so hot even you probably want to touch me. Have a look.' The young woman took off her bikini top and came closer to me. She shook her breasts in my face, turned around and bent over in front of me.

'Now,' the young woman said as she stood back up, cocky, 'Now, I am going to take your husband and he is going to have the best night of his life with me, and you are going to deal with it.'

I looked at Pete, bewildered. His eyes were transfixed on the woman as she turned to him, placed her bikini top over her breasts and asked him to help her tie the bikini at the back.

'No, way, I'm not covering them up,' Pete said, as if I was kilometres away, and not looking on in disbelief. Looking back at me, the woman smiled and wet her lips with her tongue as, one by one, she placed her boobs back behind the bikini material. I knew if I stormed out Pete would not follow; if I slammed the door, he would barely hear. I didn't know which strategy would work to break him out of the trance. I tried to think of something to say to Pete, to make him realise that a night with that woman wasn't worth throwing away the years we had shared. Wasn't worth the kids growing up wondering why their dad wasn't living with them and why Mum could be heard sometimes screaming and crying into her pillow.

'I'm going now,' I said, with summonsed-up pride.

'Ok,' Pete said with no emotion. As I walked out of that room and past a swimming pool that we don't really have, I could see two other women licking each other, with their bikini bottoms pulled aside. Then I woke up, my eyes filled with black. I could not see any light though the blinds. My stomach was turning. Only 4:30 a.m. on the bedside clock.

Splintered parts of the dream stayed with me for the rest of the day and gave my voice an edge of resentment when Pete rang that night, exhausted from a day of tending to machines, some that had malfunctioned down a black hole deep in the ground. Some days my subconscious could not accept that Pete could be physically away from me and not be a cheating bastard. I always have a searing dream like that in the week after Pete flies out and one in the second week before he returns. When I sit in our quiet kitchen at 8:30 p.m. alone night after night I start wondering what he is doing, who he's talking to in those camps. I start wondering how many women work on the mines, whether Pete actually likes working away. However, I know that suspicion is not a remedy for distrust, and to keep living on the farm and keeping the show rolling, I tell myself to take a leap of faith that Pete was worthy of my trust. Sometimes when that didn't work, I took one of the pills Ella had left on a high shelf in my bathroom.

LYLA

On the front desk of Salacious, Lyla began to unwrap the grief of losing her mum. Like a striptease, her sadness was being revealed to the muffled pulse of commercial house music. Cancer ran like a mad woman down her line of ancestors. Descendants who had milk then finally blood run from breast to belly. Lyla was now the last one in line. Without siblings, she felt a duty to pass on her genes, to keep clasping hands from one generation to the next. She did not want her hand to be the first one left reaching, unmet. She smiled sweetly at the punters as her mind traversed her mother's last weeks. She remembered her mother's severe discomfort as she tried to help her to the toilet, her swollen arm and hand. The breast cancer had spread to the lymph nodes behind her breast bone and washed into her liver.

Having returned from London, Lyla could lie on the bed next to her mother, not wanting to look away, for fear of regret. She collected all those seconds and read her mum poetry: Shakespeare, Les Murray, Dorothy Hewett, and her own words from their own shared life of sandy feet and days that were so sweltering the redback spiders crawled out from the roof space. Lyla recounted her mum's life for her: the journey from Gin Gin to Geraldton for the love of Lyla's dad, growing Lyla up in the old part of Beachlands, the trek to Perth after Lyla's dad broke lightbulbs, dinner plates, and the family unit. Lyla reminded her mum of the happiness she had found in a little South Fremantle house just before gentrification. Lyla's mum had learned to laugh and grow jasmine on her crimped wire front fence before Lyla decided that Geraldton and Fremantle did not fit her ambition. When Lyla left the country, her conversations every few days with her mum warmed the bleak London winter. Lyla's mum had never questioned her about Max or her choice to leave and fly, economy class, so far away. She just talked of the characters in South Fremantle: her long walks up to the site of the old Fremantle deadhouse, the young Aboriginal kids doing cartwheels along the shore line, the buskers playing late at night on the cappuccino strip.

'You right love?' Barb asked, standing in the doorway, flashing lights behind her head.

'Um...yes...of course. Just a bit of a headache today.'

'Want me to put some Mozart on for the group dance? It would really fuck with the girls. And the punters.'

'You don't have a headache pill, do you, Barb?'

'Yes, sure, I'll get you one. I'll be five minutes. You want a Scotch too?'

'No, thanks Barb, just a couple of pills will be fine.'

Lyla took a big long sip from her water bottle and pushed her tits up higher in her bra. Employee of the Month. Five deep breaths, her counsellor had said, to reboot the brain. The beats descended from disco reverberated on the skin of her skull. Lyla tried to remember why she was there at Salacious: for the research, for the money, not to mourn her mother.

Honey popped her head around to the entrance to the reception cubicle with two little white pills in her French manicured fingers. 'Here, Lyla, Barb said you needed these. I could get you something a lot more effective – makes the evening fly...' she said with a cheeky smile.

'Honey, you're back. Are you ok?'

'I'm fine, I just had a chemical peel and didn't want to scare the boys.' Honey deflected like an expert.

'Oh,' Lyla said, a little stunned. 'I was just a little worried when you hadn't come to work for so many days.'

'Barb knew I wasn't in for a while, didn't she let you know?' Honey said lightly, looking over and cocking her head to one side, 'I think you're uneven, love.' Lyla looked down at her chest and noticed that one boob was bolstered up, nipple almost exposed, and one lay flat down, deflated.

'Ok then, thanks, have a good night back there.' Lyla repositioned her cleavage as Honey's unbroken stiletto soul walked deeper into the club, tongue licking the back of her two new prosthetic teeth. Lyla grabbed a pen and scribbled down on a blank piece of paper, 'Why? Why cover? Why not admit that you have been hurt?' It was a question Lyla resolved to explore. She had seen hints of it in newspaper articles where girlfriends petition to have charges against their partners dropped, despite a hand of harm, dealt to them most grievously. Jealousy that takes love to a harrowing realm where tenderness and violence merge in car parks, bathrooms, against living room walls. Lyla winced as her head ached and swallowed the two white pills down.

JODIE

Closing over the boys' door after checking them, I heard the quiet buzz of my phone, which had been silenced lest anyone call in the crucial half hour when the boys could wake up from where they were shallowly drifting.

'Hi babe.'

'Hiya Pete.'

'How was your day?'

'Fine. You know...the same.'

'How were the kids today?'

'Yeah, they were good. Grumpy and tired and crying for you again but they were fairly well behaved. How was life underground?'

'Ok except things have got pretty bad with those two blokes I told you about – the bullies.'

'Why, what happened?'

'Things escalated today.'

'In what way?'

'Well, one of them, John, apparently pulled his dick out and masturbated in front of Mark on the bus this morning.'

'What, are you joking?'

'No – I know, it does not do much for the integrity of our team, I can tell you.'

'Why would he do that?'

'They are bullies. Apparently John was calling Mark a "poof" at the same time. Probably something was not quite right in his upbringing, I would guess.'

'Imagine if I pulled one of the mothers aside at mothers' group and started rubbing myself at her?'

'Jodie, don't make me horny.'

'Pete, that is totally crazy behaviour.'

'I know. As a result, Mark finally complained to the health and safety rep about everything that's been going on and unfortunately, the rep was dismissive of the whole thing.'

'Even dismissive of the wanking on the bus?'

'The rep asked if he had any evidence. Mark said he asked the rep if he wanted to take a look at his scarred retinas.'

'It probably would have defused the situation if Mark had grabbed out his phone and started recording.'

'Except we're not allowed to take our phones on site for occupational health and safety reasons. Then when Mark came back from seeing the rep into the crib to have lunch, all the blokes knew where he'd been so heaps of them were being arseholes, calling out "Boo hoo, do you want a hanky?", shouting "soft" at him when he walked past. One guy snarled at him that he should stop whingeing and go and push a pen in Perth if the job is too dirty for him.'

'What is Mark going to do?'

'Well, I worry he is not going to do anything because now that the health and safety rep pretty much told him to harden up, it's almost like it's now three against one. The Rep told him he would soon adjust to the "robust" work environment.'

'Are you going to do anything, Pete?'

'I'm going to talk to Mark again tomorrow. I'll try and stick close to him anyway. I don't think those guys would pull any of those stunts on me. I tried to stick up for Mark today. I told Chris, the other mongrel, to fuck off when he was providing a running commentary on Mark's work, calling him Princess Mark and Sook, just trying to unnerve him.'

'What did Chris say?'

'He hissed at me that he couldn't hear me halfway out the door, as I was going to be made redundant anyway.'

'Ouch, they sound like thugs.'

'That's nothing. They're always talking up their connections with management, threatening to have us all blacklisted. I don't think they have any influence, but there is a little part of me that is a bit worried if I speak up, I'll be shown the door.'

'It sounds like you had a rough day. I was feeling sorry for myself just toilet training and nagging the boys to clean up their mess. I would be a whimpering cot case if someone was wanking at me and telling me to harden up at the same time.'

'Yes, I will not have anyone wanking at you. That's for sure.'

'I miss you.'

'Just over a week until you all arrive here for the family site visit. At least we get to spend Christmas together – well, some of it.'

'I can't wait. Good night babe.'

'Good night.'

'Good luck for tomorrow.'

'Yes, thanks. Good night.'

LYLA

After four nights in a row on reception at Salacious, Lyla had a night at home. At 6:00 p.m. she had a bath with a glass of red, Mr Bang Bang snoring on the bathmat. As she submerged herself in the water and gazed at the square of last light pushing through a translucent window, her mind started to fire; circuits spanning both hemispheres, trying to find patterns. Watching from the safety of the bath, Lyla thought about Max, Cherry, Honey, Barb, her mum, Matt and what research he was seeking. Salacious was sleazy, no doubt. Lyla felt uncomfortable as her hand rested on her pubic mound and she felt her nipples harden. She would fight arousal as she did when she nipped into the bar to grab a soft drink and saw a man, sleeves rolled up, sitting on his chair, eyes penetrating the girl in front of him, lying on a table, legs spread, the thinnest strip of lycra and cotton keeping her barely inside the regulations policed by the Western Australian Department of Racing, Gaming and Liquor Compliance Inspectors, or the 'flap police', as the girls referred to them.

How many layers of observing does one minute of reality hold? Bambi, spread-eagled, watched by a man, watched by Lyla, to be relayed to Matt for his show to be watched by audiences in Perth, re-enacted for festivals in other countries. A game within a game. And what if one of the layers was corrupt; if the man watching Bambi was secretly recording her pelvic movements or Lyla was secretly recording his entranced expression as she walked to the bar and ordered her lemon, lime and bitters? Would Bambi's fiancé recognise her belly button jewellery online? Would he be unable to contain his rage? Would he appear in one of the transcripts that Lyla rested precariously on the edge of the bath? Would the man slipping club dollars into Bambi's g-string have anyone in his life who would care if they saw the image of his hand gently lifting the elastic? Did Ella know what was going on? Was there any justification in the over-violated name of love for her affair with Max? Where was her mum now? Lyla suddenly felt overheated and turned the cold tap on until the water level threatened to overflow over the ceramic lip of the bath. Mr Bang Bang stood up with a look of disgust as a line of cold water seeped down and waterlogged the apple-green bathmat. He walked out slowly, leaving Lyla alone.

ELLA

Five days into his week home, Ella climbed down the stairs to find Max, eyes closed, beer in one hand, Hawks and the Dockers chasing the football on a lonely television.

'Hey Max, are you awake? Want to go out tonight? Have a dance?'

'Nah.'

'C'mon, when do I ever get to go out if you are away three weeks out of four and you won't leave the house on the week you are home? You had your boys' night out but what about me? I'm losing it. There's a band tonight at the pub. It's Saturday. I want to go. I think it's Latino.'

'Great – dancing to Latino music, my favourite.'

'Well, you won't go to the eighties or nineties nights. You say you don't like cover bands or when emerging bands try to do originals; I don't care if you don't want to – let's just go for a couple of hours.'

'Really? Can't we just hang at home? The footy is on. It was crap when I went out with Jono – smashed units everywhere. I'll make you dinner…'

'Chilli con carne again? I love your cooking but I want to get out of here. One night out of twenty-eight? Do I have to beg?'

'I prefer it when you beg…'

'C'mon babe, just get changed and fucking buy me a couple of wines. How hard is it? I'll take you to the Sandy Beach Hotel for a couple, you'll love it. Best raunchies in WA, they claim.'

Ella felt Max owed her for her loneliness and sometimes punished him by being lavish with their money. She called it penalty spending. Ella justified this to Max when he was in town by making it seem as if she was spoiling him. Life had to be condensed then reconstituted to be lived one week out of four. So she bought triple cream brie, a king sized bed, and saturated every minute they spent together with intensity. Max could never really be bothered. He would have been happy to watch season after season of his favourite series, spend hours gaming or trawling the internet. Any activity that let his body rest. So even when he was home, Ella didn't get the attention she was seeking.

JODIE

I wearily ran a bath when the children gave up their gallant fight to stay awake. I poured lavender and baby oil in the water and turned the light off so that I could lie, eyes closed, in darkness. The nights were short and the days were full of flies and heat. There must have been pollen in flight as my skin had been itching all day. This night, I was only just coping. I had lost all momentum, my body felt heavy, my vision hazy. As I laid in the bath I saw myself from above, as if there was a satellite, hovering among the space junk, scanning earthward for the exhausted and deflated. I saw the image of my pink body in the dark, so isolated in the night's terrain. I inhaled the lavender and wondered about the buzz of New York City, the swing clubs, seeing human sweat from close proximity. I pictured the Jemaa el-Fnaa Square night markets in Marrakech; colourful images I had seen from other people's travels; magnificent spices and grisly stacks of sheep heads, a vibrancy I hungered for. Within half an hour my mind was as empty as the hectares surrounding me. I sank deeper into the hot water and melted into sleep.

Rattled awake by the call of my phone, I clutched a towel and ran wet from the bathroom to the kitchen.

'Hi babe,' said Pete's calm voice.

'Hey Pete, sorry, I think I was asleep.'

'Kiddies wear you out today?'

'Yeah. So many questions, so much craft. The boys had their last day at school, so taking them and picking them up with all the excitement seemed to take half the day and Sascha and I just stayed at home for the rest, trying to organise the chaos. How did it go at work? I was wondering all day how the situation with Mark was going. Did you get the chance to talk to him?'

Silence. 'Pete? Are you there?'

'Sorry Jodes, there is really bad reception here tonight; it's been a horrible day. Tell me more about my family?'

'We're fine. I think the daily tally was five drinks spilt and about four injuries that required the ice pack, which had not frozen again after the first injury. What happened today, Pete?'

'I can't wait to come home.'

'Pete, what happened?'

'Well, I tried to talk to Mark this morning but he didn't respond. I asked him if it would help if I went to talk to the health and safety rep as well and he said that he didn't think so. He just shrugged me off really. He seemed a bit aloof. Not angry or sad or anything. So we caught the bus to the site and John and Chris were relentless as usual, saying that they had some drinks last night with Darren, the rep, and that they had all laughed together, calling Mark a "snivelling grub" and a "piece of shit". Mark didn't really react when they were hassling him. I told them they were maggots and bullies and that they were making the job unsafe for all of us. They just turned around and asked me if I was a "poof" too and whether Mark and I were "bleeding from the bum" after spending the night together.'

'Oh my god, Pete.'

'So then all morning I was fuming, which is crap because my mind wasn't on the job. I couldn't concentrate. All I could think of was the poor young lad. I don't care what they say to me as I can see straight through the bullying. But the young dudes, like Mark, they feel like they have to put up with it.'

'So what happened next?'

'So before lunch I went myself to see Darren, the rep—'

'Go Pete!'

'Well, unfortunately it didn't achieve anything.'

'What?'

'Darren, the prick, told me I should access the counselling service if I wasn't coping in the job.'

'No way!'

'Darren told me that because he was looking out for me, in the climate of job insecurity, he would not report how I was not coping any higher up the management chain.'

'What did you say?'

'Well, the whole thing threw me. He wasn't hearing what I was saying. He just latched on to the fact that I said the whole situation was affecting my concentration and ran with it.'

'Oh Pete, that's terrible.'

'Anyway, I don't want to waste one more thought on those guys. Tell me more about my kids – only six sleeps before you guys arrive.'

'I know, and seven sleeps before Christmas Day. I have so much to organise before we drive out of here.' I looked around at the kitchen: piles of papers everywhere, artwork done at school, dirty dishes, dry stores that had not been put away in the cupboard since last weekend's shop.

ELLA

Ella preferred to surf. Swimming was way too boring for her. She hated that her hair was affected, that the chlorine overpowered any fragrance in her stockpile. But on late-night television she had seen a girl with an apron of skin, thick skin girdled around her body as a legacy of fat lost in the ultimate of doomed battles; a war temporarily won except for the apron. The memory of the apron got Ella out of bed, allowed her to stand awkwardly in the swimming pool change rooms on tippy toes to minimise contact with other people's hair, which lined the ground on the way to the pool and hung in the water itself. The thought of the apron pushed Ella do ten, twenty, thirty laps, forty on a morning full of frustration where it took that many strokes of anger before the peace set in.

The Juggler was a handsome man but Ella didn't pay him much attention in the beginning. For about a week they swam separated by two or three lane ropes. The Juggler was just a smudge on the other side of Ella's goggles. She left the change rooms at the same time as him on a couple of occasions, nothing too awkward. Several mornings in a row Ella would subconsciously race against his speed when her enthusiasm was waning. Then one day they were in adjoining lanes. Ella felt it would be rude if she didn't give a nod of the head when she was catching her breath.

Days later the Juggler was in Ella's lane. They didn't really need to share a lane. Ella swam faster that day. Over the next few days, despite how many other swimmers were punishing themselves at 6:00 a.m., the Juggler and Ella shared the same lane. He would swim up fast behind her, then drop back so he never had to overtake. She felt every slap of his hand against the water. At the end of the fourth day, the Juggler came up behind her and didn't drop back. They hit the end of the lane at the same time and she felt his arms on either side of her. Neither took off their goggles, as if they could argue intoxication, impaired judgement. Not a word had passed between them before this moment. Ella quivered.

When Ella had showered and dressed, the Juggler met her at the entrance of the building with a rectangular box of slightly undercooked chips and two coffees. Handing her one of the lattes he looked at the red oval imprints around Ella's eyes; 'Hi, my name is Miles.'

'Miles…' Ella put the coffee in her left hand and raised her index finger to the indent around her right eye, where she could see Miles focussing. 'Ella…' She held out the same hand to shake.

'My friends call me the Juggler, or Juggs,' Miles turned to walk with her away from the echoes of splashed water and humidity of chlorine infused steam.

'Really? 'Intriguing,' Ella said, 'There was a Juggler I knew back home in Melbourne. Always getting his balls stuck in all sorts of places he shouldn't.'

'It never happens to me Ella, I promise you, I know how to handle mine beautifully.'

Ella laughed. She knew this whole scenario should be awkward and shameful but it didn't feel that way. Ella refused the chips the Juggler offered her on three occasions as they spoke, but when he darted back inside the entrance of the swimming centre, borrowing a pen to write on the ripped off lid of the cardboard box, she accepted his phone number.

JODIE

Up at five o'clock on the morning of Christmas Eve I scrambled to pack two big bags: one for Sascha and myself and one for the boys. We had half an hour left before the hour drive to the airport to board a flight to Perth, followed by an hour's wait and then a plane up to Karratha. Majestic Mines had invited the families of workers up for Christmas and the kids and I were manic with excitement. Pete had missed last Christmas and the day had felt like a dress rehearsal of the real performance; the presents were all opened too quickly and the boys looked at me with sad eyes for the remainder of the day, sustained throughout a trip to the beach and a roast that overcooked our already toasted house. This year it was all going to be different. I had bought Bon and Gus mini high-vis outfits from a website for fly-in fly-out workers and made Sascha a light dress out of a yellow cotton high-vis shirt that Pete had been issued when he first started at Majestic, before many swings of eating deep-fried sweet and sour pork balls. I had sewed the high-vis strip around the bottom of the dress, which Sascha played with and tried to eat all the way to the airport, leaving wet streaks on the silver. The only vision I had of the mine was through Pete's descriptions and I imagined it would be very different through my eyes. Bon and Gus were buzzing on the plane from Geraldton to Perth; wiggling in side-by-side airborneness, no chance of either of them catching deep vein thrombosis. Sascha had fallen asleep resting on my right forearm so I held a cup of tea in my left hand. I sipped and flipped the pages of a free mining magazine I picked up at the airport, where the only other choice was a free Christian magazine prophesizing complete fucking destruction of life as we know it.

Perth Airport was chaos; lots of people returning, others heading home. I slung Sascha into the hiking backpack carrier I had inherited from a school mum who had shaken her head at me one day when I was trying to escape from the wrap-around straps of the baby sling. I growled at Bon to hold his brother's hand and not let go as I took slow steps, one bag in each hand through a security station and up an escalator towards the gate. The boys kept putting themselves in neutral, both still, eyes glazed, staring at all the action. Around them was more activity than those four eyes had seen in their whole lives at the farm. When they turned to my calls I could see how excited they were to be going and not left behind this time.

The plane to the Pilbara took just over two hours. By the time we were descending towards the red dirt beneath, Bon and Gus were ratty and Sascha was just finishing up nearly two hours of grizzling. My enthusiasm had been worn down over the flight to frazzled irritation. Perhaps I would throw Sascha (very gently) into Pete's arms and make a dash towards the horizon, rolling in iron oxide soils, never to be found again. Knowing that would not be very Christmassy of me, I bundled Sascha back into her carrier, swung her onto my back and herded the boys out of the plane. We were slapped by the heat of the air; 48 degrees of despicable.

'Welcome to Majestic, my name is April,' a smiley HR lady purred as we collected our baggage and were ushered into a bus standing outside the airport automatic doors; her teeth so white against the red hue. Three other families, four men in high-vis and one woman also joined the bus for the 100km drive to the mine.

'Been out here before?' the HR lady asked, professionally wiping dust from her forehead.

'Never. Not sure why…maybe because my daughter was too young and before her my son was too young. Wow, the heat. I hope you have a pool out there.'

'Luckily at Majestic, we do. Air conditioning is what saves me. Thankfully I'm in an office, not out in the heat.'

'Pete's told me how hot it is, but there is something different about it. More radiant – a wall of heat, like when you open up the oven.'

'Crazy temperatures out there but you won't be heading out to the pits with the kids. Set your aircon at twenty-two degrees and you'll survive.'

Sascha's yellow dress clung wet to her back from the few minutes outside and was now chilling down. Bon and Gus were hitting each other two seats in front of me.

'Hey you two, Dad will be meeting up with us soon and if I tell him you two have been mucking around on the bus he might not play indoor cricket with you like he said. And besides, you better not play up before Santa is due to visit,' I had momentarily forgotten the threat that trumps all threats during December. The boys immediately sat upright, eyes out the window, terrified of the lumps of coal Grandpa Jack had told them their dad received for Christmas one year after playing up on the school bus.

A weary hour of staring at rusty soil later, we arrived at the camp. There was a safety induction and jokes about our four-star accommodation (relative to other camp ratings). We were then led like little refugees of privilege to our demountable: a donga, three by twelve metres. A family room with two single beds and a small double. Around us there were rows and rows of demountables. I held on to my children. I hadn't expected it to be so quiet.

'Just try and keep your voices down to a dull roar please, boys,' the HR lady said, 'big miners who work through the night are sleeping in some of these now and trust me, if they are woken up early they're like angry bears. Some of those miners are ladies and they are the fiercest when awoken.'

'Excuse me, but how will Santa know which one we are in?' Bon asked, confused.

'Your dad will let him know, I am sure. I'll go back into the office and I'll check Santa's roster too if you like. I'll also see where your dad is – he might be letting Santa know right now. You get settled in and I'll see you a little later.'

'OK thanks, April. Can I ring the admin building if we get lost or anything?'

'Of course, all the details are in the booklet I gave you. You look tired, so have a rest and I look forward to seeing you in the mess later on.'

Pete's minibus pulled into the camp at five o'clock. His face was smeared with the red war paint of the resource boom.

'My boys, my boys!' Pete squatted down as both Bon and Gus launched themselves at him. Arms full, Pete closed his eyes.

'Jodes, Sascha, my girls!' Pete drew us all in, the four of us fitting inside his dust covered arms.

'Hi babe, we are so happy to be here.' I don't know if it was the heat, the flies or the long day but tears from my irritated eyes spilled onto Pete's upper arm.

'Cricket, Dad, let's play cricket. You said we could,' Bon demanded, no mind that his Dad had just arrived from hundreds of meters underground.

'Bon, there is time. Let me just give your mum some love.'

'Eww!' the boys squealed together.

'After that can we get carrots, Dad?'

'Are you hungry Gus, my boy?'

'For Santa, Dadda,' Gus replied, annoyed.

'Oh, I almost forgot. I'll take you to the crib and we can ask for some carrots. Let me just wash up first.'

It was predawn when Bon tentatively opened his small rectangular present. I could see he was concerned that Santa had only been able to deliver one gift to him and his siblings, with a note stating that the main haul had been left under their *Made in China* tree in Yuna. One corner of the wrapping paper had a tear from the journey revealing packaging inside so Bon's lips had already started to curl with hope. For the next half an hour we lost him to an electronic world and had to dress him while he sat on the edge of the single bed hunched over his gift. Gus asked five times per ten seconds whether he could have a turn of the device, ignoring the book on dinosaurs unwrapped on the floor next to his foot. Sascha stood with a baby doll in her right hand, gurgling on in a happy way, oblivious to the expectations we heap on the day called Christmas.

The boys wanted to see Pete off for the few hours' work he had to do before the rostered family time, so we insisted on accompanying him to breakfast. We were in the mess by 5:30 a.m. and started our day with hash browns, bacon and eggs. It was lovely to share the experience of shovelling down warm fatty goodness with him. Pete and I sat with the kids, scanning around the room of cranky high-vis-clad workers dosing themselves with caffeine and calories to last them until the first iced coffee break. Bon wanted to walk Pete to the bus so we followed him to the mine coach that was picking up Pete's crew. With the end of his swing so close and his family on site, I could tell that Pete's enthusiasm was heightened.

Michelle, the bus driver, was chirpy as Pete lunged up the steps and swung on to the first-row seat, waving out the window to the kids.

'What's up, Michelle?' we could hear Pete ask through the open door.

'The Aussie dollar has a permanent erection, it seems, which does not bode very well for any of us, Pete.'

'Well, I have my beautiful little family here and I'm going home tomorrow to deal with my permanent erection, so I couldn't care less what the Aussie dollar is doing with itself.' I looked at the kids who were picking up red gravel in their greasy hands, not listening to their dad.

'Ok, we'll commiserate on your first morning back, Pete.'

'Righto, Michelle.'

The other blokes were piling in, grumbling and cursing another day below the surface. The older men had crew-cuts and beards, blokes in their thirties had crew-cuts with scruffy facial hair, and anyone younger, a crew-cut alone.

Pete looked out his window to me and pointed as two blokes got on the bus. 'John and Chris,' Pete mouthed. 'The dickheads.'

'Looking hot, Michelle,' John taunted. 'How do you look so good after being up all night with me?'

'What a tool,' Pete mouthed to me through to the window.

'Anyone know where Mark is?' Michelle spoke though a microphone.

'Sing us some karaoke, Michelle,' John continued.

'Pete, Mark hasn't cut his swing short has he?'

'No mate, not that I know of.'

'Does anyone know where Mark is?'

'Gone to Mardi Gras I reckon, Michelle,' said Chris.

'For fuck's sake, shut the fuck up, you,' I heard Pete reply, irritated.

'Sticking up for your boyfriend, Pete? That must be a change from sticking it up him.' John smirked and the other blokes gave a loud grumpy morning grunt of approval. I knew I shouldn't be overhearing all this but I was fascinated.

'Michelle, give me five, I'll grab him,' Pete said and swung down the steps to the gravel outside.

'Come on kids, come and find Mark with me.'

'No more than five, Pete, my whole schedule will be thrown. Mark knows the deal. Not the first time his pay has been docked for lateness.' Michelle called out from behind the steering wheel.

Pete walked briskly back to the sleeping quarters and the kids and I straggled behind him. I was lost straight away in the rows and rows of dongas. Caravans going nowhere. A circus marooned in the middle of red dust and dirt. Pete knocked on Mark's door. There was no response to Pete's hard knuckles on the donga.

'Mate, are you in there? The bus is waiting. You've slept in. Open up.'

'Mark, are you there mate?'

Pete put his ear to the door. Just behind him, I could also hear what sounded like a muffled morning show and some strange groans.

'Jodes, keep the kids with you. I'll just be a sec. Mark, I'm coming in. Are you there?' Pete opened the door slightly and squinting in, we could see Mark on his bed.

'Mark, wakey wakey, the bus is waiting,' Pete called loudly into Mark's room.

I peered in behind Pete and could see that Mark looked groggy and was clutching his stomach. He was a young bloke who reminded me of someone I couldn't specifically recall.

'Mark, are you sick? You want me to call first aid? Bon, hold Sascha's hand. Jodes, Jodes, tell the kids to stay outside the door and come in quick.'

Standing above Mark I saw froth around his mouth and his eyes rolled back.

'What the fuck is going on, mate? You look fucked.'

Mark gurgled a bit more, both arms around his middle. Pete's eyes were hooked by a rectangular cardboard box on the bedside table. 'Zopiclone? Have you heard of these, Jodes? Have you had lots of these Mark? Is that what is going on?' Pete opened the box and saw two foil pill cards with each blister empty. 'Shit mate.' Pete looked back to the bedside table; strewn and smashed metal, plastic and glass. An electric toothbrush, a car key fob, a watch, a keychain flashlight, a portable clock radio and what looked like a banking security token. All items looked as if they had been slammed by a hammer. Pete picked up the toothbrush, confused. He looked back at Mark, who was writhing in his sheets, and then at me. Pete picked up the smashed watch. At that point I realised what was going on. The coin batteries were gone. Like Hitler and his cyanide pills, Mark had his little mundane instruments of death close at hand.

'Mark, Mark, just hold on mate, I'm going to get help.' Pete ran out the door for assistance. 'Kids, stay right here with your mum. Help! We need first aid. Hey! We need first aid here!' As Pete sprinted towards the onsite medical facility, I looked down on Mark. As gravel crunched below Pete's running feet in the quiet camp, I wondered what harm lithium batteries could do. Maybe it was just a matter of getting Mark to regurgitate them up and turn back time. Maybe by the end of the day we would still be singing carols.

The Royal Flying Doctors transferred Mark to Sir Charles Gairdner Hospital in Perth within hours of us finding him. As soon as the jet took flight, April, the HR lady rushed up and asked us to return to our dongas for an hour until they made appropriate risk assessments. Pete told us he knew the drill: there would be an investigation team chosen, interviews conducted of all relevant site hands, a thorough inspection of Mark's digs and a review of previously compiled risk assessments. A day of piecing together everything that had led to Mark frothing in his donga. Before the Christmas luncheon I heard coaches arrive and saw government workplace safety investigators and solicitors representing insurance companies walk around with cases on wheels not made for the gravel, all scratching around the camp interviewing relevant team members. April knocked on the door of our donga and said that the family Christmas lunch would still proceed but arrangements would be made as soon as possible afterwards to return us to Perth. Unfortunately Pete wouldn't be available to eat with us.

After Pete had cooperated in a day of rigorous interviews he returned to the donga, where we were lying low out of the heat, waiting for him.

'Jodie?'

'Hi babe.'

'Can I say hello to the kids before I…'

'Sure. Gus? Bon? Come here now. No, put that down. You won't be allowed to watch a movie on that device if you don't come now. I am serious, Bon. Put it down, now! Come on Gus.'

Gus pressed himself into Pete's leg, 'Dadda? I miss you every...all the time, Dad.'

'I miss you too, mate. What are you up to?'

'Mummy just made us have a shower.'

'What, she made you get clean?'

'Yes Dadda. All the time, Dad. And yesterday.'

'You were probably dirty, mate. You be good to your mum. She's a good mum.'

'Yes Dadda.'

'Bon?'

'Hi Dad.'

'Son, you look so old, what has happened? Has that device aged you already? I've only been gone a day and you look so grown-up.'

'Well, I do have lots of grown-up teeth so that means I am one hundredths grown up. Why didn't you come to the Christmas lunch, Dad?'

'I had to work mate, I'm sorry. But I'm going to play indoor cricket with you.'

'Good. It's much funner when you're here, Dad.'

'Yes, that's because Mum is so busy with you boys and your sister when I'm at work and not helping her. We get to head home tomorrow so maybe we can go fishing some time during the week.'

'Ok Dad. You want to see Sascha laugh? I've been practising tickling her.'

'Yes please.'

'Hey Pete. How did the interviews go?' I asked.

'I love you.'

'I love you too babe. What happened?'

'Want to put the TV on for the kids?'

'Yes, give me a second.' After I easily persuaded our three children to disconnect from us and watch a kids' show about designing a cubby house out of a wine cellar, I turned back to Pete. 'What's going on? What happened?'

'Well it seems definite that Mark tried to kill himself.'

'Oh no.'

'Apparently he did swallow lithium batteries and a whole lot of pills and that's when we found him all messed up this morning.'

'Why would that kill you – the lithium batteries? Wouldn't they just pass through?'

'No, they can be deadly. I heard today that lots of old people get into trouble from ingesting their hearing aid batteries by accident, mistaking them for pills. You survive if they pass through into your stomach, but if one gets stuck in your oesophagus, you are stuffed. Mark wasn't taking any chances possibly eating six of them. Apparently the battery acid starts to burn right through your throat. We don't know what time Mark took them. He has been flown to Perth so hopefully they will remove them in time. At least I knew straight away what had happened. If he'd been a neater bugger and cleared his bedside table I would never have guessed what he'd done to himself.'

'Will those guys be charged?'

'Chris and John? With what Jodes?'

'With bullying, for making someone's life so unbearable.'

'I don't know. The investigation has started. I am sure there will be a few reps in the firing line, with two grievances taken to them with no action taken. I've been with the workplace investigators all day. I told them everything.'

'Did you tell them about the wanking on the bus?'

'Yes, I told them. There is going to be a serious investigation. I think some heads will roll.'

'Good. That health and safety rep is as responsible as the bullies, in my eyes. He is meant to be the safety net and he failed Mark.'

'Hmm, we will see what comes of it all. I hope Mark is all right. I am shattered. If I'd known he was taking it so personally I would have done more to shut those guys up.'

'Will they let you come home tomorrow with all that going on?'

'I will sneak out of here in one of those massive bags of yours if they say I have to stay.'

'Deal.'

That evening I fussed around Pete like a housewife after singing 'Silent Night' ten times to get the kids to sleep. Nothing particularly holy about this night.

'How did we get here, babe?' I asked Pete.

'Huh?'

'Our family, in a tin box. Nowhere. As we sit here it is becoming more nowhere. Rock by rock. As they are working through the night taking what dirt makes up this place and taking it elsewhere, minute by minute becoming less somewhere and more nowhere; I mean, what are we doing here?'

'I thought you wanted to come for the site visit?' Pete looked at me deflated.

'It is awesome to see where you work; I don't mean about the visit. The kids are beside themselves with excitement. I just mean...I don't know...I always hoped life would be luscious. In my mind we should be somewhere with bursting life, life that is hard to tame, tall trees, fucking jungles of fertile life, not this. Just say Mark doesn't pull through? What kind of life has he had?'

'One a lot more privileged than most of the world's billions.'

'I know it's privileged because I sleep at night and never stress any more about feeding our babies, and one mum at the community health service told me that she can't stand it when FIFO mums complain because they have made their choices, but sometimes it feels like we sold ourselves short. I know you hate coming here. Today was awful – I don't want you having to deal with any of that…and where is it going? All that dirt?'

'Sit down Jodes, it's ok. Have a drink; it's Christmas night. I'm sorry you and the kids were here and that all happened. You should never have seen—'

'Let's think of another option, where you can be home with us, wherever we are.'

'Is this about the farm? Not just Mark? Not just the pits? I'm too tired, babe. I'm just trying to keep it all happening: feeding us, not letting the bank take the farm, trying to make the right decisions.' Pete sounded weary.

'I know…I just find it all hard, seeing those crazy monster trucks today, hearing them rumble, and the weeks you're away, having to fantasise about you rather than having you in front of me. Just say something happens out here to you and one swing you just don't come home. What if we mine the heart out of this country?'

I looked over and Pete's chin had dropped, his eyes closed.

My hand fell to the grey round table adjacent to the double bed. Four snuffly snoring mouths in a little grey demountable. I poured my pre-opened mini-bottle of semillon sauvignon blanc into a glass and looked to the suspended roof for some gratitude. I made myself remember how lucky I was that Pete had this job. I gave thanks that I wasn't at home taking a phone call from Majestic that something had gone terribly wrong for Pete today and he was lying in a Perth hospital bed.

LYLA

Lyla welcomed punters into Salacious as if they were long-lost family. Two sleeps to go. Lyla had suggested to Max that they go down south, have a coffee in a small-town bakery and test the quality of the old-school apple strudels. Too risky, Max had said; he couldn't chance running into anyone from Geraldton, from work, from his extensive family. Lyla was always forgetting that they were incognito, fornicating under a red radar. So they would stay in Forrestfield, hide and toast to street lights, blushing only when their powers of denial lapsed in between drinks.

'Ciggie, Lyla?'

'Sure Cherry, Barb won't mind.' Lyla beamed at Cherry and smacked her glittered lips together. Cherry looked at her suspiciously as they clattered out on the pavement.

'Have you got laid today? Fuck you have a glow. Not pregnant? You would have told me that was on the cards, wouldn't you?' Lyla put her non-smoking arm around Cherry and squeezed her close to her body.

'Oh my God, you haven't smoked some ice have you, Lyla? Please don't tell me...' Cherry was looking intently at Lyla through the smoke that was slow to disperse in the hot, still Northbridge night air.

'Bah ha ha! No, I haven't been smoking crack, just happy to see you.' Lyla wiggled her hips and bounced up and down on her heels. Cherry shook her head.

'Don't make me bring Lucy out to sit on you and squash all that happiness out. What is going on then?'

'I love working here but the prospect of a few days off is making me dance happy. How are you? Is York coming in tonight?'

'No, he has some work on. We might go down south for a couple of days later in the week. York has a friend in Rockingham.'

'Rockingham? I thought you meant Margaret River or Esperance. Going to Rockingham is not a weekend down south.'

'It is when you are both on a bike with a Great Dane riding side saddle.'

'Ok, fair enough. Does York have some meetings? Work meetings?'

'Yeah…'

'Meeting some associates?'

'Yes, sorting out some issues.'

'Issues?' Lyla pressed.

'Inside?' Cherry looked at Lyla, threw down her half-burnt cigarette and extinguished it with the clear tip of her platform stiletto. 'Time's up.' Lyla followed Cherry back into the building, thinking she might have pushed it a bit far this time.

Two hours of doof doof and a steady stream of business trade later, Cherry reappeared with a smoke for Lyla, 'Wanna come out?' Cherry put one hand in the air and stretched her spine, then hunched her shoulders, trying to realign.

'Sorry about all the questions before,' Lyla leant back until the painted brickwork grabbed the fabric on her dress.

'You're ok Lyla. Not an undercover cop, are you?'

'You think I seem like a cop?'

'I don't pick up a whiff. Always had a good feeling about you since you rocked up here with that fake Pommy accent.'

'I do not have a Pommy accent! I have a sexy Midwest accent,' Lyla protested. 'The questions are just because I'm just interested in your life. Mine seems so pale compared to yours.'

'Pale or safe?' Cherry laughed, shaking her head.

'I don't know anything about any of it – growing up in Geraldton…'

'There are bikies in Geraldton, drugs, skimpies…'

'I never saw them on the beach or at theatre classes. Then I left there at eighteen, followed my mum to Freo.'

'You don't want to know the nitty gritty, Lyla. There's no glamour in any of it. I thought it was exciting before I sobered up. Now York keeps me safe from the details. He prefers it that way – sheltered from the…'

'I want to know the details, how bad it gets.'

'Why don't you ask Honey?'

'No – fuck, thinking about what happened to her played with my head. I don't understand why she acted as if nothing happened. Why does she stay? Why does she smile to the world and not run fast for help?'

'What if she screamed for help? What comes after the help? After two weeks in a women's refuge? Who is going to protect her after that? You? Me? Barb? Honey's family hurt her worse than Jez did – they're not going to protect her.'

'She could move east. Start again somewhere...'

'Her family is over east. Besides, she's handcuffed here by the drugs, provided so easily by Jez. No one there to lift her out of the situation. I did ask her, you know, if she needed a place to crash for a while.'

'What did she say? She didn't take you up on it?'

'No, she said she was fine on her own.' The early evening air wore Cherry and Lyla like sparkly accessories: shiny lips, neon heels.

'I just want to rush in, sirens wailing.'

'I've got a nurse's outfit out the back Lyla, you'd look hot in it.'

'I just wanted to take her home, fix her up.'

'Can't fix someone who doesn't want to be fixed. If you took her on you'd never have a second for yourself. Honey would suck every bit of life force out of you and then when you have your own troubles you'll realise you've used up all your stockpiles of defence on her. That's a mug's game, trying to fight someone else's battles for them. Especially when they have already said, "No thanks." We all have our own days to deal with.'

'Yep.' Lyla agreed but looked down because she liked the idea of losing herself in the chaos of another rather than focusing on her own life. Much more enjoyable to focus on someone else's misfortunes, affidavits, and relationships that end in tears.

'Shall we?' Cherry stubbed out her cigarette and wheezed as she stepped back over the threshold.

JODIE

It was a heavy-hearted Pete Davey that returned with us from the Pilbara for his rostered time home; the gravity of rocks in his eyes, a layer of innocence skinned off him forever. Having taken separate cars, we were waiting inside for him when he walked up the path. When he opened the front door, I ran to him, placed my arms around his neck and held his head to mine.

'Oh Pete, how are you going?'

'I'm fine.' It was not a shock to me that Pete did not have the words to describe any of the stress in his head. As usual, I knew I would have to decipher his strange quiet like a wall of ancient hieroglyphics. However, life on the farm never allowed much time for quiet analysis and within minutes of Pete's arrival, we heard a sharp scream from Sascha, who had managed to wedge her head in between the heavy back of a sideboard and the wall, her scalp marginally swelling as she yelled, jamming her in tighter. After jumping to action and managing to shift the full sideboard forward a centimetre so we could pull her out, Pete and I held her to our bodies and rocked her. Dismissive of their sister's screams, Gus and Bon were yanking their dad's legs to follow them outside. There was cricket, footy, a boys' own cubby and a tree to climb. With nearly two weeks' absence to atone for, Pete bowled, kicked, crouched and climbed. By the time the sky was falling pink, Pete's other life of working under the ground and dealing with some egos that bash and some egos that bruise must have seemed months behind him.

During Pete's swing home, none of us felt the need to leave. Pete pottered around with his drill and wrestled the kids on the front lawn. We received a phone call from Majestic Mines confirming that Mark had been sent home from hospital after three lithium batteries were extracted from his oesophagus. They informed Pete that Mark had died a day later from stomach bleeding and the extensive tissue damage the batteries had caused in the unknown amount of hours in his body. They said there would be a coronial inquiry. It was not likely that John and Chris would be charged with any offences. Pete and I planted some Sturt Desert Pea in one of the garden's borders. When a fine specimen of Sturt Desert Pea flowers, I said to Pete, he would have to let his anger flow into grief. Pete walked around the farm in silence, for once not manically trying to fix and spray everything that needed his attention.

ELLA

'Hiya Juggler,' Ella answered her phone at the back door, where she was standing looking at plants that needed watering. The Juggler had been texting her but this was the first phone call.

'Hi Ella. I was just thinking about you.'

'About my thighs?'

'About your eyes.'

'Sweet talker.'

'No, really, I was thinking about your pretty green eyes and how much better they look when they are not behind goggles.'

Twenty minutes later the Juggler had arrived and laid Ella down on the bed gently. He whispered about her beauty in a lowered voice. Rhythmic, repetitive. Convincing. Her skin, her eyes, her hair, her neck, the dip between her breasts. Gentle kisses. Words. He had one hand on her belly as if she had their child inside.

'I want to make you feel better than you've ever felt before. Saturated. Intolerably good. Like you could open up and turn inside out. You are so gorgeous. I can't believe it.' Ella purred like a pussy cat.

Ella reflected that Max was always reluctant, not wanting to curse their relationship by talking it up too much. As if the words could weaken them. Not the Juggler. Ella and the Juggler knew their use-by date wasn't far off so they were reckless with their words. 'Forever' was probably only a few months away at the very outside. The Juggler had a knack of becoming a lady's soulmate. That was his gift. Sometimes he had four soulmates a week on the go. He was the multinational company that quickly slipped into a conflict-torn country after a peacekeeping mission had made it safe for them to come in and push their products on the vulnerable. Fly-in fly-out employment had paid him the jackpot. Women were sitting in houses everywhere, lonely and craving physical attention. He acted as if it was his duty to keep the home fires burning.

Ella had never meant to cheat on Max. In fact she hadn't really admitted to herself that she was being unfaithful. It felt more like a sustainability plan, so that things didn't fall apart when he was away. So when Max returned she wouldn't be twisted and punishing him for leaving her over and over again. This way, Ella would make the most of him. She would appreciate that he was back without fearing that her howling loneliness or a barrelling wave of tears was going to wipe him off his feet when he walked in the door.

LYLA

Lyla lay on her belly, scrutinising a victim impact statement that Matt had sent her that involved a perpetrator known by his associates as Fruit Cake. The statement was ninety-four pages long. It began when the victim was only nineteen years old and started a relationship with Fruit Cake when they met through her uncle who was also a gang member. As she read about Fruit Cake's tattooed hand punching into the victim's heavily pregnant stomach, Lyla turned over on to her back and winced. Mr Bang Bang raised his head from the floor where he had been spooning Lyla's leg, half out of concern and half due to the inconvenience as Lyla raised her knees and stared up at the ceiling. Lyla remembered her own mother flying sideways, kaftan fluttering, when she had dared to add some chilli flakes to a beef casserole. Lyla had seen her dad grab the spice jar, smash it on the stove top, hurl her mum towards the kitchen table and then open the fridge. Lyla had wanted to run to her mum and hold her head in her hands but she didn't move a millimetre until her father had pulled the ring on his can of piss and walked back to the living room. Lyla never understood as a child how her mum was meant to guess what would turn dad into a monster and trigger the words, 'What are you doing, you spastic?' Lyla had never even known what a spastic was, only that it sounded similar to elastic.

Lyla read that Fruit Cake forced his wife to participate in sex parties, where he stood over her and watched her suck another man's cock, then inflict punishment as if she hadn't been following orders in the first place. On one occasion, after she swallowed semen, Fruit Cake made her hit the man so hard over the face with a baseball bat that the bat broke.

'Yuck. That happened in a house not far from here, Mr Bang Bang. Come here. What a psycho – not you, Mr Bang Bang. Should we go for a walk? I'm sick of this.' Lyla placed one of her shoes on top of the statement to prevent the paper from flying all over her apartment when she opened the front door. As she put a lead on Mr Bang Bang her eyes rested on the photo frame of her mum she kept next to the door. Max had instructed her on how to mount the frame. Level. Lyla felt a sharp pain just under her belly button and her shoulders curled forward. With almost closed eyes she called out to her mum and the rough edges of all the memories scraped inside her skull. 'I'll save you,' Lyla mouthed as she rested her forehead on the closed door and let the sadness and night slowly fall.

ELLA

Ella held the phone to her ear with one hand, a handheld mirror up to her cheek with the other, and smiled to ensure her skin was maintaining optimum elasticity as she waited for Jodie to pick up her phone.

'Hello?'

'Jodie, it's me.'

'Ella, what's up?'

'Not much. What are you doing?'

'I just survived another meltdown hour. Arsenic hour...DSM hour.'

'What?'

'Diagnostic and Statistical Manual of Mental Disorders Hour...'

'What?'

'That's what it's like around here between five and seven. Every disorder on the spectrum. I just put the kids to bed, so now I'm having a red wine. We made playdough today so my lounge room looks like a playdough version of a Pro Hart painting. It can wait till tomorrow. What are you up to?'

Silence.

'Ella...? Ella...what's up, baby? What's wrong?'

'I cheated on Max.'

'What?'

'I mean I am cheating.'

'What? Ella, really?'

'Yep.'

'Oh shit.'

Silence.

'Who with?'

'Just a guy I met at the pool.'

'Oh. Has this just happened? You've been going to the pool?'

'Yes. Well, in the last couple of months there's been barely any surf. I wanted to keep fit. I'm mixing it up with the gym. You don't need to tell me – I feel fucked.' Ella dropped the mirror on to the couch next to her.

'Have you told Max?'

'No.'

'Are you going to?'

'Yeah, I suppose I have to.'

'Ella?'

'Yes, I am going to.'

'Ella, you have to tell him.'

'Why?'

'Ella, you have to tell him. He'll find out anyway. We have always been caught out with our lies. Not great liars-'

'I know, I know. The truth is, I don't want it to end.'

'Your marriage?'

'Well yeah, but being with this guy as well.'

'Shit, Ella – why? Why would you risk Max?'

Ella bowed her head over her knees and felt her eyes fill with liquefied guilt. 'Max is never here. I can't do it. I can't live like a married woman when I only see him for one week a month. You know me. I need to be told I'm loved every day. More than once per day. You know how needy I am. And not just with words, I want a body lying next to me at night. It's so fucked, Jodie. I sit in this lounge room watching shit TV, trying to be a good wife. I sit and I sit and I sit. I hardly ever go to the pub because married women in this town aren't supposed to go to the pub alone when their husbands are working away. It would be great if I could go out more. Talk to people. Hear some live music. That's what is doing my head in. I feel like I'm single but I'm not allowed to do all the good stuff single people get to do.'

'Sleeping around?'

'That's not what I meant.'

'Ella, you only got married a year ago.'

'Over two years ago...and I love Max, but he is never here.'

'So what are you going to do?'

'I don't know yet.'

'Who's the guy?'

'His name is Miles. Well, his friends call him the Juggler.'

'Great. Nice. A fucking juggler. And? Do I know him?'

'Don't think so. I don't even know where he grew up – Geraldton, I think.'

'Where does he work?'

'Um, he never really talks about work. I think he is a fisherman.'

'Shit, Ella – you haven't asked him?'

'It hasn't come up. You don't know what it's like, Jodie. Pete is home after two weeks, and your time when he is away is crazy with the boys and Sascha. For the three weeks Max is away I've done all my housework by eight in the morning, so I sit and think about having a cigarette and ask myself, what now? I swim before working at the shop, come home at five o'clock and ask myself, what now? How am I going to fill this evening? Turn on the TV, turn off the TV. Sit on the balcony, wonder how the fuck I'm going to fill in three hours before Max rings, the five hours before bed. If I could surf at night, I would.'

'I know it's hard Ella, but it's not forever. Have you told Max how lonely you are?'

'Yes, but he doesn't understand because he is never alone. He comes back here and catches up with all his mates if he wants to. If he can get off the couch we go to barbecues, go fishing, driving up the beach. He loves it, has the best time and can't imagine how I could ever complain when he's the one out at the mines. He doesn't understand that when he leaves, that good stuff goes with him.'

'But it isn't forever. You weren't going to do it forever, were you? Only a few years?'

'Well, it started off as two to three years to get ahead with the house. To pay off as much as we could. To pump money into the mortgage and then get out, but Max has started talking about doing it for five years.'

'Five years is a long time.'

'How long are you and Pete talking about?'

'I don't really know. Pete thinks there will be heaps of rain in the next couple of years...he might start seeding in eighteen months. If the gods don't give us rain who knows? I don't want my kids growing up only having their dad one third of the time – but Ella, it's not just fly-in fly-out work. FIFO alone can't break your marriage. I know women whose partners work in town and they disengage; don't interact with their kids, don't keep in tune; fly in and out without going anywhere. At least with our boarding passes and departure dates we regularly drop everything else, latch on to our partners when they come home and don't let go.'

'That's what I'm worried about, Jodie. Max and I don't latch – we fuck and watch movies. There's not as much warmth as there used to be. Things were definitely better before he went FIFO. I don't know, I think we've been sucked in by the money. I don't want us to be working until we're sixty-five, to only start really living then. I don't want to be a grey nomad. I'd rather travel without arthritis. Anyway, I have to get organised; I'm opening the shop in the morning.'

'Ella, you have to tell Max.'

'Do I? I don't think I can. It would break him. He would hate me. He'd leave me for sure. He'd rip up all our beautiful wedding photos that cost $5000.'

'Why didn't you think of your wedding photos before "the Juggler" if you are so worried about them? I'm sorry, Ella, I know you're upset. Why don't you come and stay the weekend with us? We can talk it over before you say anything to Max.'

'I can't, I have to work Saturday and Monday. Maybe another weekend soon.'

'Ok baby sister. Talk soon.'

'Good night Jodes.'

JODIE

I packed the tartan picnic rug, vegemite and cheese sandwiches, chopped fruit and four water bottles into a bag I could strap across my chest, smeared suncream over noses and sent Bon and Gus to find their hats. For one day out of a blistering school holiday summer I would find something wondrous on this vast property for my children. I drove the ute, loaded with us, for fifteen minutes towards the eastern boundary. There was some escarpment that I thought the boys would love to explore. Surely there would be some lizards, an emu, some roos. When I cut the engine the boys jumped down and ran across the rocky ground. I pressed the release button on Sascha's car seat straps and lowered her into the backpack carrier – an old-school one with a light aluminium frame and a pouch with two leg holes for Sascha's chubby legs to dangle below. The depth of the pouch had her chin behind the bottom of my neck.

I had forgotten to strap the picnic paraphernalia across my chest so I backed up to the back of the ute tray, lowered down the bottom of the aluminium frame and unhooked my arms. Finally sorted, I started the walk to the outcrop of rock. I wished there was ancient artwork on the rock walls, some handprints forever on cave walls, but this land preserved nothing. Bones, tools, artwork; all would have been made brittle or bleached out of existence long before Pete's family farming story began. The boys had run ahead and were ten metres away from the rocky ridge; rocks randomly piled by something other than hands, ledges for birds to breed amongst. As Bon and Gus started pulling themselves up, I listened to the chirping of bush birds swooping. It was hard to believe that a few short months ago there had been green in the landscape. There was only brown remaining.

As I moved forward, weighed down by a daughter and the picnic bag, I blew the flies away from my lips. They buzzed around, one under my sunglasses. Hot sun, sinking half-arsed moon. Sweat dripping in between my boobs and under all the various straps sashing me. Sascha grabbing at my hair, twisting a fistful. Before me, lizard tracks looked like BMX tread; two feet scrambling on both sides of their belly. There were roo tracks: a big long central track with two shorter parallel lines on either side. Sneakered feet, orange sand, rocks. My stomach felt a bit crampy. God, please no more gastro in the house. I wandered along wishing I could see stars during the day. It seems such a waste for them to be the domain of the dark.

In Melbourne, under the clocks at Flinders Street Station you can't even see the stars at night. Ella and I used to sit on the steps under the clocks looking at all the people move; down the steps in the mornings, up the steps in the late afternoons. The traffic of the city filtered through our young souls. What were they all rushing towards? Their homes must have been more exciting than ours. It was with no enthusiasm that we moved, always together, from those steps, after the rush had completely died down and the drunks and junkies drifted in and around. We never wanted their eyes on us. So many people back then, a moving river of mostly black outfits, umbrellas, cigarette embers falling underfoot.

'I see the moon and the moon sees me,' I began singing to Sascha as we moved towards the boys. 'Here we are, Sascha, see the rock, there might be some shade.' I would make sure my own daughter would never be able to relate to that isolation amidst a city on the move, flowing in, flowing out, never taking notice.

'Come and get some lunch, boys,' I called out to the open line of escarpment. I placed the carrier down on the ground and left Sascha in it, kicking the stones underfoot as I opened my bag and pulled out the picnic blanket. It looked ridiculous: one metre squared in an expansive landscape. A tile out of place in the mosaic. I yanked Sascha up and placed her sitting on the picnic blanket while I drank some water and pulled the other three bottles out of the bag. There were meat ants around us in minutes. I kicked them away from the blanket and reached into the bag to get the sandwiches.

'Mum! Mum!' I heard Bon yell. Pitches higher than usual. 'Mum… help…Mum!'

'Where are you Bon? I can't see where you are.'

'Over here Mum, up here.' I still couldn't see. I ran up to the bottom of the escarpment where I thought I could hear Bon's voice.

'What is it Bon? Where is Gussy? Are you hurt? Where are you?' I pulled myself up a rocky ledge, fingers in dirt and little balls of brown roo droppings. 'Gus? You better not be tricking me.' But I knew Bon wasn't joking.

'Here, Mum! Over here!' I reached one hand up to the top of the escarpment and felt around with my right foot to find a decent hold, trying not to think of the meat ants that would be circling Sascha. My eyes were high enough to rise above the flat top of the rock outcrop.

'Boys, where are…' My words stopped as my scanning eyes saw four legs and a small gwardar. The skinny snake had a black head, two little black eyes and an orangy brown speckled body. 'It's ok Gus, Bon, I'm here, I'm going to help you, just stay right there, don't move. Mummy's going to help.' My feet slipped back and I gripped the rock with my fingers. I steadied and then pulled myself up quietly. I locked eyes with the boys and put my index finger on my lips. My mind was racing. The western brown snake lay in between my sons and me. If I made any sudden moves, it might lurch at them, striking out indiscriminately and with an unmeasured dose of venom. 'Don't move Bon, I know you're scared. He's scared of you too. Be brave, my love.'

'Mum, he bit Gus, I saw him.'

'Gus, did he bite you? Tell Mummy, did he bite you?' Through a stream of hot tears, Gus shook his head.

'Mumma!' Gus whispered.

I grabbed a stick and slowly approached the standoff. I could only vaguely remember having been told once to throw a stick in the direction that you want a snake to strike. I couldn't quite recall whether there was another part of the strategy, but I crept up behind the snake and then tossed the stick to its right side, about a meter away. The snake struck out, it's skinny body flying up fast. I silently took five steps to the boys, turned so the snake was in my sights and picked one up under each arm. They turned their faces in towards my body as I stepped back as quietly and quickly as I could. The snake looked panicked as it retreated towards a big rock that could have only have been placed by the gods randomly on top of this line of Yuna rock.

'Gus, did it bite you?'

'No, Mum,'

'It did bite him, Mum, I saw it with my own eyes. Both eyes. That leg there.' Bon was brave but crying, distraught. Gus seemed less distressed. I squatted down and brushed Gus' shin. I couldn't see any blood. Placing one of my fingers on each of my closed eyes I strained to remember what

I should do. I grabbed the stick I had thrown at the gwardar, ripped my shirt off, tore three strips from it and tied the stick to Gus' left leg. All I could remember was to immobilise.

'C'mon Bon, let's get back to Sascha quickly. That's it, Gus, just lean right on me.' We could see Sascha lying on the picnic rug, crying, fists shaking in the air. I lowered Gus down the rocks gently, anticipating his slippage each time and holding on under his shoulders until his right leg stablised. Bon's descent was quick like his breaths.

'We're coming Sascha, we're coming.'

'I'll run down Mum. She'll be...' Bon slid down a rock face faster than he expected, 'don't come down that one, Mum, stupid rock.'

When Gus was on flat ground I put his right arm around my waist and told him to hold on tight as I walked, taking up some of his body weight until we got back to Sascha.

'Mum, why is Sascha's face all red?' Bon asked. 'Are they bites?'

'Fuck!'

'Mum!' Bon looked impressed. I picked up Sascha, placed her roughly in the carrier and instructed Gus to hold on again to the waist of my shorts.

'But what about the picnic stuff, Mum?' Bon grabbed his water bottle.

'Just grab the water, Bon, let's go.'

I powerwalked to the ute, Gus' body weight hanging on my arm as I moved, trying both to move him and keep him as immobilised as possible. As soon as we returned to the ute I lay Gus on the back of the ute tray on a dirty old towel that was hard from sun exposure and scrambled in the back seat for Pete's first aid kit. I quickly grabbed the compression bandages, heaving Sascha who was still on my back. I scratched at the plastic seal. I remembered Pete saying the rectangles on the bandage turn from rectangles to squares when they're tight enough. Taking Bon's word Gus had been bitten on his left leg, I bandaged from ankle to thigh. I removed the boys' car seats to the tray of the ute and lay him down on the two backseats next to Sascha's car seat. With Sascha strapped in I hurried Bon into the front passenger seat. No matter what physical pain his brother had to endure, Bon seemed ecstatic to be allowed to be riding in the front seat, and smiled at me as I turned the ignition.

Seeing Gus looking pale in the rear-view mirror, I panicked, grabbed the radio and turned to Channel 5, which I thought was the channel reserved for emergency response. I pressed the push to talk button and called out, 'This is Jodie Daley, calling for any emergency monitors.'

'I read you, Jodie. This is Len Fisher, just down the road from you. What's happening? Over.'

'I think my boy has been bitten by a gwardar, I can't see a bite, he's only four, I saw the snake. My other boy said he saw the snake bite him on the shin. Oh, over.'

'What's your location, Jodie? Over.'

'Yes Len, I am near our Eastern border, west of the Wandana Nature Reserve. Where all the pigs are. Near the rocky outcrop. Over.'

'Best to head into town. You could call an ambulance but they need a doctor to administer the anti-venom. You'll probably get into town quicker. Are you all right to drive, Jodie? Over.'

'Yeah, I'm starting to drive now. It will take me an hour. Do you know how long he's got, if he has been bitten? Over.'

'Are you sure it was a gwardar? Over.'

'Yes, I am sure. I've seen a few before in the sheds. Over.'

'Hard to say, Jodie. Best thing is to get the little bloke as quickly to the hospital as possible. Depends whether he copped any venom. Over.'

'Len, what should I be looking out for? Do you know? Over.'

'Nausea, headaches, vomiting, collapse. Usually within the first hour. Over.'

'Shit. Sorry Len. I'm going to get off the radio and drive with full concentration. Over.'

'Good luck, Jodie. I'll ring the emergency department so they expect you. I'll call you later to see how things are going. Over.'

'Thanks Len. Over.'

I drove with precision to Geraldton Regional Hospital. My focus switched from checking on Gus in the rear vision mirror to the road ahead. I drove as fast as I could, never tipping into speed wobbles but pushing my own limits. Everything blurred and slowed down. I didn't hear Bon or Sascha but my ears were monitoring Gus' breathing the whole hour. I was ready to swerve and resuscitate him. When we reached the hospital a stretcher was waiting to take Gus straight in for observations. I held my ripped shirt around my middle and moved the ute from the emergency department to a car park nearby. I closed my eyes. *Please let my boy be all right. Please.* I released Sascha's car seat restraint and held her close to me. Bon grabbed at my waist as we headed back to Gus.

'I'm hungry Mum, we didn't even get any lunch because of that snake. Can I have some money for the machine? Look, there's chips.' I looked at Bon as if he was insane. Sascha started grizzling, seeing the vending machine inside the front door of the emergency department.

'Ok, ok, here.' I found three dollars in my bag with one hand and adjusted Sascha on my hip before handing it to Bon. I felt like we were far from out of the woods but chips would probably make the wait easier.

'Will Gus be ok, Mum?' Bon asked with a mouth full of orange crunchy stuff.

'I think so, Bon. We'll get to go in and see him soon, I'm sure.'

For fifteen minutes the three of us stared blankly at a television attached to the wall in the corner of the waiting room showing news updates. Finally a nurse came, bearing an extra large white t-shirt she had located for me. She ushered us into an observation ward where Gus was lying, with a new compression bandage replacing the one I had wrapped around his leg in a panic.

'Hi, my beautiful brave boy. How are you going? Is anything hurting?'

The nurse stood at the end of Gus' bed. 'He was definitely bitten; we've taken a swab of the puncture site. At this stage there are no signs that he was envenomed but we need to keep him for observations for twelve hours in case there's a delayed reaction to the venom. But with all his observations being fine since admission it is very unlikely that will happen.'

'Thank you, oh thank God.'

When Pete rang up later from the Pilbara he turned off the TV to hear the details of Gus' snake bite. I told him the whole story as Bon and Sascha quietly snored in chairs next to Gus' hospital bed. The meat ants, the black snake eyes, the rectangles turning into squares. Pete listened quietly with few words and little response.

'I never knew about dry bites, but it looks like Gus might have been lucky today,' I whispered.

'Jodes, it sounds like you did all the right things. Well done. There wasn't anything you could have done better. Exhausted?' With that one question hot tears started to flow down my face; a slow flow, constant, grateful. A line of warm tears on my jaw line waiting to fall.

ELLA

Ella made sure that Whipits was the premier urban outfitter in Geraldton. Her peers in Bondi would be proud of the fashion creations she had displayed in the front window to lure in the shoppers who preferred to purchase online. Recycled t-shirts inside out with big words roughly printed on them: 'Offline is the new sexy', 'Misguided love', 'Let's stay in bed', 'Cute Convict Spawn'. Sexy and edgy was what she was trying to encourage in the youth. Mistreated floral. Ella's boss aimed for anything that was fashionable on the streets of NYC in the last three years. A blunt kind of cutting edge. Ella was patient, as she knew it was hard to be too edgy when it's 38 degrees celsius and you're heading down to meet your school friends on the beach to take turns riding a hot eighteen-year-old punk's jet ski way faster than your parents would approve of. Besides, the edgy should never override the sexy. She still had shudders thinking of the emo kids at Flinders Street Station. All that black. Smearing kohl around your eyes never made for a better day. She would travel back one day and sit under those clocks with her tousled hair, tan and fit body in an edgy charcoal dress with a big bottle of eye make up remover. She'd show her own scars and let the kids know life does get better. Sales were down at Whipits but that was to be expected without an online presence.

Max had been lucky to get an early flight from the mine site to Perth and had asked Ella to pick him up from Geraldton Airport at one o'clock. Ella would have to close the shop forty minutes early to go and get her car but that was fine as the midday heat wasn't good for Saturday sales. Ella and Skye, one of the junior sales assistants, had spent half an hour carefully selecting a loose smaragdine slip dress with lace trim for Ella to wear for the homecoming. After sending Skye home, Ella started closing up the shop when her phone blipped. It was a message from Max saying they were all disembarking back off the plane bound for Geraldton so that a mechanical error could be identified. He texted that he'd get a taxi home when he touched down. Ella touched her brow with two fingers and exhaled. She texted Max back and said she'd head home.

Ella pulled the security shutter down behind her and walked out. Her calves could take her home in fifteen minutes. Instead, she slowed her steps. It could be hours before Max dropped back into her life. Ella was always more distraught when the set plans changed. As if she only had oxygen rationed for the duration of the swing. Any more unexpected time and there didn't seem to be breathable air. At the corner of Fitzgerald Street and Chapman Road, Ella paused. One block up Fitzgerald, the Sandy Beach Hotel kicked back, paint peeling in the heat. She swung towards the pub and opened the glass-panelled front door. Fuck Max, she thought. Erect with anticipation, she had now fallen flaccid. Jimmy was the first person she spied as she entered the front bar. Even the back of his head was asymmetrical. Ella set sail towards him, through marine décor, tables that had not been cleared of lunch dishes and huddles of men having a flutter on the horses. Axl was sitting next to Jimmy, head hunched over what looked to Ella like a form guide, hands gripping his forehead.

'Hi Jimmy,' Ella said as she pulled up to the bar next to him.

'Ella, I never thought you'd come back. Axl here has been pining, hoping you'd return.' Jimmy slapped his hand down on the newspaper in front of Axl's eyes. Axl sat up tall in his seat and turned to face Ella.

'Hi Ella, don't listen to this old timer; she probably just wants a drink, Jimmy.'

'Yes, it's blisteringly hot outside. My delicate Victorian skin is no match—'

'Ella?' Ella flinched at the familiar voice.

'Juggler?' Ella stepped back to see beyond Axl.

'Fuck, of course you two know each other,' Axl shook his head, disappointed at his friend's territorial spread.

'Hi,' Ella blushed gossamer pink, 'I didn't know you were part of the family here.' As if she'd suddenly found out her lover was a second cousin.

'Ella, this is my deranged mate Axl, and my old fishing buddy Jimmy; and boys, this is the Ella I was telling you about.'

'It's hard to remember all the names,' Axl said, solidly unimpressed with his best mate.

'He said you should have been in the Olympics, love, for your swimming.' Jimmy was enjoying the young folk and their cracked communication. The Juggler walked around Axl and Jimmy and kissed Ella gently on the lips. She was thrown. She didn't imagine any of her friends or the girls from the shop would be in here but still she felt sick that she had been publicly exposed.

The Juggler pulled Ella in closer.

'I have only told them that we swim together and that I lust after you in my cockjocks, but that you are a married woman.'

Ella tried to exhale slowly so Axl and Jimmy wouldn't detect her deep relief.

'Let me buy you a wine, my lady,' the Juggler beamed at Ella, 'I'm stoked to see you.'

'Thanks, yes, a house white…please. How are you anyway, Jimmy?'

'Ella, that is the first time someone has asked me that in days, these pricks never ask, that's for sure.' Jimmy slapped Axl on the back of the shoulder and put an empty beer glass on the bar's mat.

'That's because we don't care how you are, Jimmy. I don't want you to get the wrong impression…that I care.' Axl looked at Ella standing in her heels and still looking small. 'Ella, you look beautiful today.'

'Thanks, Axl.' Ella's phone beeped loudly in her hand.

'Just one drink for me. Max has just left Perth. He's on his way home for a week.'

'So, no swimming this week?' the Juggler asked, handing her a wine.

'No swimming this week,' Ella said, feeling flattered but totally confused by all the orbits colliding.

LYLA

onday nights aren't meant to be dirty. Any other night can be stained, full of booze and mayhem, but Monday nights should be mundane, preoccupied with a focus on resolution, the highest road our souls can take. If we can't ride out the high road until Tuesday morning, the week is doomed to pass like all the weeks before. Lyla was dealing with loneliness in the reception booth at Salacious. She had a small spiral notebook and was writing down some goals for the new year. Lyla knew that if she articulated with words exactly what she wanted, there was a much higher chance of success. Now with her mum in the dispatch warehouse in the afterlife, Lyla was going to make a long list and pray to her mum to pull some strings for her. Number one was having Max by her side. Number two was never having another cigarette (starting next Monday). Number three was landing a role in a film funded by a government grant that was small budget but would gain cult status and catapult her into the national consciousness as a treasure. Not too much to ask.

Lyla's hour of power was interrupted by the entry of a big bloke with fat guts pushing out the fabric of a surf brand cotton dress shirt. A shirt younger men might wear to a wedding, smelling slightly dusty after sharing a couple of spliffs in a car, waiting for the bride to arrive. This bloke was tall; only half a Sherrin short of the doorway. Lyla took one look at him and put her pen down. He lurched forward with one big step, then stumbled back, clutching the doorframe. He pointed his index finger at Lyla, smiled, seemed to discuss something with himself and staggered forward towards her.

'You are fucking hot.' He put his hands up on the glass either side of the opening, one hand holding a plastic bag, and lowered his less than sweet face down to Lyla's sitting height. The stranger peered through the glass.

'Max? Is Max your boyfriend?' Lyla quickly flipped the pad over.

'Had a few drinks tonight have you, mate?' Lyla felt under the table for the button that would bring Barb and all her experience in ejecting alcohol-soaked patrons.

'I've had a few. I go back to work tomorrow so I'm here to sober up. Couple of soda waters, couple of dances and an early night for me.' Fancy Shirt looked like he'd been on a five-day bender. His vision looked slightly skewed and Lyla squinted towards him, looking at his lower left eyelid twitching.

'Work tomorrow, hey? I hope you work in an alcohol detox centre, mate.'

'Nah, beautiful, I fly in…fuck off…' With those words one of his big hands made a gesture like a bomb exploding rather than ascending into the clouds.

Lyla laughed, shaking her head, wondering if she should let this guy enter the club.

'That's why I have this,' the bloke said loudly. Lyla turned to see a big beige penis bursting out of the bloke's fly. Lyla stood up quickly and stepped back in her booth.

'It's the Donkey Dong – discrete synthetic urine device. I'd have preferred to have the tan or latino style but I'm as white as they come… you wanna try it on?'

'Wow. I've never seen one of those,' Lyla stepped closer, still behind the glass.

'It's all about the heat pack. If your piss isn't 33 to 38 degrees, you're busted straight away. You get tested here?'

'I haven't been tested yet, but I think the game would be up if I flopped out the Donkey Dong.'

'Nah, they make them for chicks too, don't you worry about that… something about Whizz or Piss. The Squirtinator?'

'That sounds disgusting.'

'I'd like to watch you piss out of a Squirtinator.' The bloke pushed the Donkey Dong up to the glass in a pathetic attempt at romance.

'Mate, I think it's time for you to go home. I don't think your dong is going to work if you're slurring your words.'

'Oh I'll be fine, like thousands before me.' Fancy Shirt grinned at Lyla and dropped a white plastic bag from one hand as the other slipped down the glass. 'That's just my hair strand detoxification shampoo…just saying that correctly should let you pass the test…fit for work…not pissed…I do want some hot chips though.' Fancy Shirt picked up his shampoo, shoved his Donkey Dong back into the plastic bag and blew Lyla a kiss as he backed towards the street.

'I'll come and see you when I get back, love. Don't miss me too much.'

'Holy heaven.' Lyla shook her head, picked up her pen and refocused on detecting her own defects.

JODIE

Two days after the snake bite I woke in bed with horror in my throat, having visions of the snake sinking its sharp teeth into Gus' shin, looking down the rocks to the ute so far away. I took calm breaths all day but by the time I was able to ring Pete that evening, I was distraught and wound up.

'Pete? Are you there? Pete?'

'I'm here. How's Gus?'

'I tried Pete, I really did. I thought I would transplant, you know, that I was hardy enough. But I'm not. I just can't do it. The farm...I...I must need more lime in the soil to thrive. It's not just the snake bite. With you away there are days when I barely survive.'

'Jodie, I know the snake bite has rattled you. That's understandable,' Pete sounded defensive, 'but Jodie, there are people living off piles of rubbish in Bangladesh. I don't understand why you struggle to survive on a Yuna farm with fresh water and electricity. Don't I provide? You have a town nearby where you can buy anything you want, which you do—'

'Cheap shot, Pete.'

'I don't understand what you need to be happy. Is it me? Are you unhappy with me? I know I'm a selfish prick sometimes—'

'I don't think you are.'

'Tell me, Jodes. Tell me, and I'll change what I can.'

'I don't like being on the farm.'

'Oh.'

'Are you there?'

'Yeah.'

'I just feel this loneliness here, even with our three kids, who I could not love more...with you away...'

'I'll leave the mines then. I'll come home.' As the words left Pete's mouth and travelled through the phone line to me, I knew Pete quitting his job was not the answer.

'This farm, it's in your blood. You know every tree, where the pigs like to run, which trees the roos sit under at noon, where the moon is going to rise. I know it's your perfect environment but I've realised that it...it is... not mine.'

'Oh.'

'Maybe when you were here I didn't notice. Maybe because the kids were so young there was no time to think about it all.'

'Where do you want to go? Back to Melbourne?' Pete asked quietly.

'No, I don't want to go back to Melbourne. There's a shack...in town...'

'A shack? That sounds shit.'

'I haven't been to see it yet but it's three hundred metres from the ocean. Just behind the sand dunes, I guess.'

'Three hundred metres to the ocean? Have you thought this through, Jodes? Can't we just keep going camping now and again? Do we have to actually have a house in the dunes? Fuck...'

'Maybe it will be beautiful...'

'And what are you thinking, that I'll keep working away forever? That was never the plan. What about when the boys are older? They'll need their dad. And the sandflies? Have you thought about the sandflies? Global warming? Three hundred metres closer to going under. Be patient, Jodes. Yuna might be beachfront one day as global warming ramps up...'

'Pete...'

'I get it. Well, I don't get it but I understand that you hate the farm. The snake bite must have been horrific, especially for a city girl. Jodie, I want to be with you. I love our family, it means the world to me, but what happens if we sell the farm, buy this dump, I mean shack, three hundred metres to the ocean and the southerly blows sand on your dream every afternoon. Daily sandblasting – what then? Where will you want to go then?'

'Cairns, near the mangroves,' I replied quickly. Pete laughed his warm laugh.

'What about the mosquitoes in the mangrove swamps, where then?'

'After the shack and Cairns I promise I'll try Yuna again.'

'But just say we can never buy back in, Jodes?' Pete's words as slow as tears. 'Can't we just go camping in the dunes, go on a family holiday to Cairns and stay on the farm?' I didn't know what to say.

'And what if I'm made redundant in a couple of months?'

'We could both get jobs in town. The boys are in school. I could work a few days a week. It wouldn't hurt Sascha to be in daycare. I just want to hear the ocean as the backdrop to everything I do. From three hundred metres away. I'll be happy then, I know it.'

'But just say you aren't?'

'But just say I am?'

'Go and have a look at it, take some photos and send them to me. Maybe it won't be exactly what you imagine. Look for corrosion.'

'Ok Pete. Thanks – and can I put the farm on the market?'

'Ha! Nice try. Good night my love. Go and kiss those kids for me, especially the snake wrestler.'

'Night Pete.'

ELLA

When Max came home, Ella had her legs firmly shut beneath the kitchen table, steam rising from a green tea. If nothing else, Ella would be anti-oxidising as this confrontation proceeded.

'Ella?' Max called out.

'In the kitchen.'

'Hey babe, what's happening?' Heavy drop as Max's bag hit the hallway floor.

'How was your flight?'

'Fine, when we finally got in the air. What's happening?' Max was puzzled at the lack of enthusiasm in his wife.

'Just thinking.'

'About what?' Max stood at the door kissless, trying to gauge the weather amidst the white goods.

'Want a cup of tea?'

'Nah, it's beer o'clock for sure...'

'Ok.' Ella sat. Max walked to the fridge and plucked out the last remaining beer.

'Have you taken up drinking beer?' Max asked affectionately.

'What do you mean?'

'I just thought there was half a case when I left, you don't usually touch it.'

'Life doesn't stop when you leave, Max. Maybe I have—'

'I don't care, Ella. My beers are usually there where I left them, that's all.'

'Your beers?' Ella tapping her shellacked nails hard on the kitchen table.

'I didn't mean it like that. Fuck, I don't care if you drink my beer, Ella.'

'Pete and the kids came around. I gave him some of "your beers" for the road when he helped me fix the bathroom tap that was dripping.' Ella was quick to lie. Well, they had been exchanged for services rendered by the Juggler.

'Gee, this is not the homecoming I was dreaming of,' Max flicked his beer bottle lid into the bin from a distance and turned to walk out of the kitchen.

'Where are you going?'

'To have a shower, I'm buggered.'

'Not yet; I have some questions.' Max's cheeks, as he faced away from Ella and towards the hallway outside the kitchen door, flared.

'Really? Straight away? As soon as I walk in the door?' Max turned to face Ella.

'You don't usually have a problem fucking me straight away, as soon as you walk in the door.'

'Much preferable.'

'What are your plans, Max?'

'To have a shower, go to the bottleshop, have some dinner, relax with my wife after three weeks away.'

'This is not working for me any more, Max.'

'Us?'

'Not us, you working away.'

'Oh.' Max's tense shoulders fell downwards.

'I am lonely, I, can't remember why we're doing this.'

'So I don't have to slave in a job here that pays a third of what I get working away.'

'I don't care any more. Let's sell the house and live in a bus shelter – at least I won't be so fucking alone.'

'Really?'

'And we aren't getting ahead. The money you're getting doesn't make sense for the time you're away from home. How can they expect families to make it work?'

'Well, how much are you making per week at Whipits, Ella? Could we survive if I pulled the pin on my job? Would it cover the house payments?'

'No, it would not, but what about us? We do not seem to be covering us. You don't even seem to care that we barely see each other anymore.'

Max rolled his eyes in response to Ella's cry for help. 'I'm here now and you're attacking me. It doesn't make me want to see you more.' Max's defensive was launched; drone strikes minutes away.

'What about when we want to have children?' Ella had her own drones.

'This is how you bring up *that* conversation?' Max's eyes looked sunken.

'Great contraceptive, to never be in town when I am ovulating? I have a twenty-eight-day ovulation cycle Max, and you are absent almost every time it falls.' Ella made a physical gesture as if she were placing something up her vagina and checking her fertility; 'Great, not home. Great, not home...'

'Stop it, Ella.'

'When should I stop it, Max? When we are completely detached and don't even care if we see each other or not because we've forgotten how to have fun together. I want you here.' The last four words popped Ella's tear ducts like releasing champagne corks. 'You don't even seem like you care any more.'

Max turned around slowly and started heading upstairs. Ella heaved in the kitchen, mascara splattered under her eyes. It was not the first time that Ella had begged for tenderness and Max had found none in his heart to give her.

An hour later Max came back down to the kitchen and patted Ella on the back. Ella always thought his comforting pats were vaguely disturbing.

'C'mon. Cheer up. We have one week together, Ella, I don't want to fight with you. Let's go and sit on the couch or up on the balcony. Make a plan for the week. Maybe we could go for a motorbike ride up to Kalbarri? You could have a surf at Jacques? I checked the weather; I think it will be cranking.' Ella crawled into the only embrace Max offered.

Before Max drove back to the airport seven days later he gave Ella a pep talk about not going backwards, not getting into strife or further debt, not losing focus of their goals. Ella did not want to go backwards, nor stand still, stuck. Coming to Western Australia had been commitment that she wanted to move forward. However, she could barely hold back from suggesting to Max that the money he made working away might be used up by IVF payments if they were never at the same coordinates to procreate. Ella didn't even care about children, she just wanted to have some fun with Max, not go through the motions once per month. To move forward, as if their love lived up to the promise of the wedding photos.

LYLA

On cue, before Lyla's resolution to quit smoking had kicked in, Cherry poked her head around the doorway.

'It's busy inside so let's go quickly. Time is money.' Cherry was barely recognisable in a platinum wig and designer trenchcoat. Thomas Burberry, in claiming the invention of the trenchcoat for military use, would have been delighted to witness Cherry further extending its usefulness.

'I think I'll only get half inhaled before the next wave of blokes come through.'

'Lyla, you drag so lightly and smoke so slowly, I'm guessing half a ciggie is five minutes for you, and I'll have smashed two in that time.'

'I didn't realise I was involved in a competitive sport, Cherry. Not long until I quit anyway.'

'Quit? What?'

'From the sport, not from Salacious.'

'Thank, fuck. You're the only sane one here, apart from Barb.'

'Cherry, are you trying to hit on me? You've never said anything so nice. Why are you so happy tonight?'

'York's out the back, I like it when he comes in and has a few drinks. I might give him a private.'

'No open leg work I hope, or I'll have to dob you in.' Lyla dragged her half cigarette across the brickwork to separate the ignited tobacco.

'Lyla, chuck it out! You are not going to keep a half-burnt cigarette. Yuck, that reminds me of my drinking days. I'll buy you a pack, hon. Not going to have you relighting a leftover. The global financial crisis hasn't hit us that hard yet.'

Beyond all the nicotine drags they shared, Lyla and Cherry could have kept burning oxygen for hours, generously sharing details and opinions about the night, the club, and the passengers of the Northbridge footpath.

They were building a bond but neither had yet stripped down to any real honesty about their predicaments.

Back inside reception, Lyla adjusted her bra and gave her hair a quick brush. Within thirty seconds the next customer was coming through. When Lyla looked at him, time seemed to slow down. His appearance was stock standard: crew-cut hair, beard, two sterling sleepers in one ear, rings on two different fingers, shirt tucked into denim on a medium build. But there was something very strange about him. His face was wet with sweat and flushed from too much heat.

'Can I help you?' Lyla asked cautiously, looking at his fixed grey eyes.

'What sort of kebabs do you have?' Lyla noticed that the little finger on his right hand drooped as if it had no bone inside.

'No kebabs here, I'm sorry.' Lyla felt wary.

'All I want is a fucking kebab. It said on the sign outside that you have kebabs and I am not leaving until you cook me up a kebab.'

'I am sorry sir, I am going to ask you to leave. There is a kebab shop two blocks down, if you go back out through the door and turn right on to James Street.'

'She thinks I'm an idiot,' the man said to the neon air inside the reception area, and he started flicking his little finger at Lyla, shaking off his rage. 'You think I'm an idiot, do you? Did you call me a goose?'

'No, I didn't—' Lyla's sentence was halved by York's appearance at the internal doorway. Lyla watched York stride fast towards the man, strike him sharply in the throat, turn him around and push him out the door. The man staggered and fell towards a parked car.

'You all right, Lyla?' York looked at Lyla, deeply concerned.

'Yeah, I'm fine. There was something freaky about that guy.'

'I know him. He's on PCP, smokes wet ciggies. It's a dirty drug, PCP. He's a lethal weapon on that shit. I thought he knew to stay away from here.'

'Will he be ok?' Lyla said, relieved that York had removed him.

'Until he slices flesh off his arm, mistaking it for a kebab spit.'

'Oh, yuck. Thanks York.'

'I'll be out the back if you have any other nutters.' York smiled a shy smile and backed into the ribs of Salacious.

JODIE

Ella met me at the surf club. I let Sascha out for a minute and she ran towards the little playground, partitioned off by steel fencing due to its state of disrepair. Ella's legs appeared out of her open car door a good five minutes before her body followed; laughing at something on her phone, checking her teeth, fixing her hair. I stood by my car waiting for her. Sascha shook the fence, happy, thinking the fencing was another extension of the equipment inside.

'Jodie, come here, help me with my bags.'

'Bags?'

'I just wasn't sure how long we'd be so I brought some stuff; a jumper, my bathers, a towel. Max has leathered up and gone for a ride on his bike to Horrocks so I thought we might have time to read some magazines.' Ella fanned three brightly coloured cheap magazines out of her beach bag.

'Oh my sister, you are gorgeous. I haven't had time to read a magazine in about six years, and you won't either while you're with us. Funny Auntie Ella!' Despite those words, I took Ella's beach bag and her hand bag and her sporty water bottle and carried them towards my car. When we had Sascha strapped back in with an array of snacks to keep her occupied, we dog-legged back up to the highway and turned right for the five-minute drive to the property. After waiting for an oncoming road train to pass, we turned right towards the dunes on to a narrow sandy driveway.

'We should have just met here,' Ella said.

'Does it look dodgy? Maybe Pete was right.'

'I hope we don't get bogged. Should we let down the tyres?' Ella looked to me for a finely tuned risk assessment.

'We'll be ok, I'll let them down if we get stuck.'

'I hate getting bogged, Max always manages to do it. It's always forty-eight degrees when it happens, on a track in the middle of fucking remote, fucking nowhere.'

'Child in the car, Ella. I don't want the F word as one of Sascha's favourites, thank you. As long as we're close to the ocean I don't mind getting bogged. Pete loves getting us bogged too. Thonging out the sand in front of and behind the wheels. Havaianas don't do the job. It has to be big male double-plugger thongs. Ones that could work as a flotation device for the whole family if you're stuck at sea.'

'I never noticed those double-pluggers in Melbourne. Do you think they've been banned by the mayor?'

'On behalf of the hipsters? Probably.'

A curve in the sandy driveway took us to the left gently and then the right sharply. Facing us was a house amongst the wattle shrub. The front door was boarded up and two out of the three window panels to the left of the doorway were shattered, with tape running along the lines of the main cracks.

'Nice speaker.' Ella laughed, pointing to the left eave of the shack where a big black box speaker was wired up. 'Who lived here? Maybe it was a bikie clubhouse?'

'I'd say bikers would keep the place in nicer condition than this.' We laughed; me with a touch of despair and Ella, at me. We got out of the car and I released Sascha from her car seat.

'Should we check for any syringes on the ground before we let her go?' Ella grabbed at her niece's food-smothered hand.

'We're not in Melbourne now, little sister,' I said, noticing the foliage mixed with white sand under my sneakers.

'Well, I think some West Australians have a taste for drugs too, Jodie. Come here Sasch, Auntie El will look after you even if your mum lets you play in the needles.'

We edged our way closer; huddled. It was not your usual home open; no coffee brewing smell here. We peered in the window. The kitchen cupboard doors were open, revealing a lack of plumbing under the sink, and some odd cups and plates. Through the salt crystals on the window I could see empty rum bottles and cleaning product containers on the benches.

'Why not have fun when you're cleaning? Three empty rum bottles explains why the place is still fucking disgusting, though.' Ella's nostrils scrunched up and she retracted her hands from the window pane.

'Obviously the price is just for the land value; we'd have to gut this place or knock it over.' Just as the words left my mouth, a swallow flew straight into the window from the inside. It fell stunned to the scattered floor, its wings leaving a beautiful impression on the glass, wings spanned upwards, its beak outlined on the pane.

'Shit!' I stepped back, heart beating like window bound wings. 'I wonder how it got in; it can't have been in there for too long. I wonder if there's an open window around the other side.'

'People might have come and had a look this morning, let it in by mistake.' Ella held on to Sasha's fat hand tighter.

'No tracks. Can't have. No tracks from the driveway and none around the house.'

'Wow, you're like one of those old bush trackers – not a city girl any more. Anyway, by the state of your fashion sense you are definitely a country girl now. Where did you get that shirt? Is that one of Pete's you've taken in?'

'No Ella, it is not, I love this shirt. I'm going around the back.'

'I'll wait here with Sascha.'

There was scrub right up to the walls of the shack; hardy scrub, lots of brittle branches and not much green. Conservative with its foliage. Tight. The salinity made the outside walls crystalline, a friction on my fingers as I hugged the wall as if I was being held hostage by the fibro cement. I peered around the back, relieved to see clearing and a raised deck above the sand. I stepped up and pulled on the balustrading, lifted one leg over and I was up. There was a wire security door underneath a rectangular window frame above with no glass in it. Swallow's entry. There was a boarded-up window ledge to the right of the door at waist height, so I put my right foot on it and gripped my fingers into the security door grating.

'It would have been easier to ask the agent for the key,' I could hear Ella yelling out.

'Can't wait to tell Pete I did a break and enter today,' I shouted back through shack and scrub. It was tricky but I managed to lodge the point of my left sneaker into the grating and heave myself up and into the empty window frame. With my upper body poking through, I realised that I was stuck.

'No wonder lots of kids do the break-ins around here,' I called out to Ella. 'Come and help me.' Ella squeezed herself, Sascha in her arms, around the side of the shack raising concerns about her dress, manicured hands and tanned arms all being scratched by shrubbery. By the time she arrived I'd managed to hold on to a ledge inside the house with my left hand and, with core muscles activated, flipped myself over so that I was sitting on the window frame, head in, legs out.

'What now, bat girl?' Ella asked, shaking her head at me. 'Jodie, get in quick, even that door looks crumbly. Any structure you built here would be three hundred metres close to complete corrosion.'

I swung one leg around to the side so that one knee was inside, then the other, holding myself in place with hands gripping the ledge. Scrunching myself up, I then jumped down to the hard, corduroy-style carpet, the colour of old brown wrapping paper.

'Open the door, Jodie, or I'll let your daughter try and climb up too,' I could hear Ella saying.

I had landed in a nothing kind of room. Not a bedroom, not really a living room. Empty apart from bird poo, little sticks, a phone book next to an empty clothes basket. I stood up and walked into the next room, the one to the back of the living room we'd seen from the front. I breathed in air quickly when I saw two words painted in white on the wall: LONELY LOVER. I breathed out heavily and crouched down, looking up at them. LONELY LOVER. Too much paint had been used so white drips, long since dry, ran down to the carpet. LONELY LOVER. The message wasn't for me but it was me, there in the musty salty smell of all the time I had been given up until now. There were cigarette butts on the ground, a couple of sheets in a pile and a few dockets. I had expected some driftwood, burnt-out candle stubs, and shells found at Southgates before any other feet had pushed into the sand. I picked up a docket that was so faded I couldn't see a date or shop name. I picked up another docket that seemed thinned by time or cockroaches. Probably from the bottleshop, I thought, fingering it as I stared back up at the painted words.

Ella bashed on the back door. 'Jodes, open up! Are you ok?'

'I'm fine, Ella, I'm fine.' I stood up, breathed in deeply and nodded at the wall. I walked back to the security door. It was snibbed from the inside and as I opened the door outwards, Ella and Sascha both lunged in and hugged me.

'Mumma!' Sascha called as she pressed her face into my knee.

'I'm fine, my girls, I'm fine.' I put one arm around each of them, 'I think I like this place.'

ELLA

Ella was lying on her back on the carpet, legs raised and resting on the arms of the couch when the phone she was holding rang.

'Hey Ella, it's me. Is your old man out?'

'Hiya Juggler. He sure is, left this morning. You want to come over and put me over your knee and feel how much I've missed you?'

'I am so horny for you. I've missed you so much. Been craving you like a crazy man. I am going to make you forget you've ever been lonely. Make you forget that it's been a week since I took care of your needs. Can I come around in about an hour?'

'I'll be waiting on my bed. I'll leave the side door unlocked. Sneak in and find me.'

Ella knew the Juggler loved sneaking around. Even when there was no one to sneak around; when there wasn't anyone who would care at all what he was up to, she was sure he still loved to look both ways and enter a side door, left unlocked especially for him. It was just on dark when he arrived. The light was leaking out of the edges of the sky and a black blanket was about to be thrown over the earth, sending it into darkness. Little solar lights were blinking along the path to the house. The grass had been mowed the day before.

Ella knew that within minutes of the Juggler's arrival, she would be giddy with happiness as he spread her legs wide and kissed her heartily. The Juggler opened the side door quietly and locked it behind him. He crept up the stairs with a smile on his lips and a tingling in his groin. Ella had struck a striking pose standing on her bed. Face to the wall, her naked body in an X shape, bum cheeks tight and glowing. Ella had pulled out the long auburn wig she'd bought on impulse when giggling with some young girls from the shop on the only occasion the owner had taken them to Perth selecting stock. Earlier in the day she had coloured her skin with fake tan and had removed every trace of hair that did not match the wig. The Juggler was surprised to look up and see a tanned redhead where he thought Ella would be. It only added to the tingle.

'Ella,' he murmured, 'Ella...' He approached her, gently stroked her back, stroked her left leg down to the ankle and gently bent her forward so that he could smell her skin. The red wig was so long it kept tickling his nose and making him laugh. Ella scratched her red fingernails down the wall and pushed herself harder on to the Juggler's face.

Watched in fast forward their lovemaking would have looked like a gymnastics routine. Ella was doing handstands, bending forwards and backwards, sucking the Juggler like a sea anemone. The Juggler was saying everything that Ella needed to hear to make her shine incandescent and stand above him six foot high, breasts bouncing. The Juggler took away her pain, her loneliness, her paranoia that her life had taken a very sad turn for the worse. And Ella made the Juggler feel like porn royalty. Eventually they collapsed on top of each other. The Juggler pulled out the pins securing Ella's wig to her hair and gently tugged it off. He kissed all over her forehead.

'Hi baby,' he said. 'How many days do we get to do this?'

Ella sighed. 'Max is back in twenty-one days.'

'And you're mine for all of them. Bad luck, Max. He doesn't know what he's missing and I have my very own twenty-one-day stocktake special,' the Juggler joked.

'What?'

'A twenty-one-day special? A limited time offer? A FIFO package deal?'

Ella's euphoria slowly fell down from the ceiling. A glacier of glittery happiness sliding silently into the deep water below. Ella felt herself spiralling down, her breath quickening, anxiety chasing happiness.

'Hey Ella? What's up? What did I say? Was it the stocktake special?'

Ella looked down.

'Baby, what's wrong? I thought we were having the best time? Weren't we?'

'It's just that...this is wrong. Don't worry, you make me feel amazing, it's just that the whole situation is...'

'You don't deserve to be lonely, Ella, you deserve to have a band around you playing odes to how awesome you are.'

'I don't think so. You know, I looked at my wedding photos the other day. I looked so hopeful – and now I'm part of a stocktake.'

'Shit, I knew it was that. Sorry.'

'It's not that you said it, it's that we are living it. I'm beginning to wish that Max made me feel the way you do, that he was excited to see me after three long weeks, rather than slumping on the floor in front of the TV. That he looked at me like you do. But maybe you're only looking at me like you do because Max isn't here. Maybe if I wasn't married and if Max wasn't coming back in twenty-one days you'd select another FIFO package deal.'

'I'm sorry I said that.'

'I mean, is this just skin deep? Is this all you want? I actually want my marriage to work. I don't really want this.'

'Should I go?'

Ella and the Juggler stared at each other, searching carefully for words.

'Please don't,' was all Ella could find.

JODIE

It was never going to be easy to convince Pete's dad, Jack, that a shack close to the beach, an hour from the farm, was a good idea.

'Jodie, has your stitching come loose? What are you thinking? You want to let down your tyres every morning to get the kids to school?'

'Let's be open-minded, Dad,' Pete said with an overload of sarcasm and smugness that made my mouth smile. Tough gig. Three generations of farm-lovers in my car.

'What do you think of all this, Bon?' Jack tilted sideways in the passenger side, turning his stiff neck to see Bon behind the driver's seat. 'Want to spend your whole life sunbaking at the beach? I'd get bored myself.'

'Well, I want to stay on the farm but Mum said I could learn how to surf if we move here.'

'My grandson, shark bait?' Jack would have eyeballed me but I was directly behind him.

'Open mind, Jack?' I requested from the back, knowing the worst would come when they saw the state of the shack. Jack's nose would scrunch as he walked around, thinking that May wouldn't even have considered it, would not have questioned her place on the farm, would have supported him through all the seasons of spraying, seeding and harvesting.

There was silence in the front seat when we pulled up in front of the shack. Pete turned around and raised one eyebrow at me. 'Your castle?'

'Snakes here too, love,' Jack said. Gus and Bon squealed in the back.

'I'm staying in the car then, Mum,' Gus said.

'I'll stay here too, Mum,' said Bon. 'It's my turn, Gus, I'll beat your highest score.' Bon stretched his hand towards Gus, who was clinging tightly onto Bon's device.

'Everyone out of the car; put it away,' I said sternly. This tour was not going to be cancelled by Grandpa Jack. I had suggested that we visit Jack after I'd taken Pete to the shack but Pete insisted that Jack needed to get out of his unit. We both knew the vote that Jack would cast: for the survival of his species, in Yuna, working the land.

I had organised a key from the agent as I didn't want to scale the back door this time. As soon as we entered Pete had begun knocking on the walls, feeling for structural stability, perhaps looking for some engineering flaws in my dream. His fingers pushed hard on the wooden window frames, feeling for rot. He reached up to push the plasterboard under the eaves, and I saw him shake his head quickly.

'Renovator's dream?' I looked at him sympathetically, nervously, 'What do you think?' I didn't want to plead, but it felt like he had the antivenom and I had the two little puncture marks.

'What do I think?' Pete entered in the doorway, cocked his head and sniffed the inside air. 'Hmm, what do I think...?'

'I'll tell you what I think, Jodie,' said Jack.

'That's ok Jack, I want to hear what Pete thinks.'

'I think the framework is probably sturdy,' I suggested.

'Hmm...' Pete continued his inspection, looking up at the ceiling, reaching one hand up to push the plasterboard, opening the kitchen cabinetry, laughing when he saw the absence of plumbing.

'Just a few surface problems, just superficial really,' I said as Pete bent down and pulled back the worn brown corduroy carpet to knock on the wooden flooring beneath. Pete's fingers touched a punch hole in the door leading to the lonely lover's room.

'Looney Lover?' Pete said with barely a second's look at the white paint on the wall. 'That's appropriate.'

I turned around, unable to watch any further. I returned to the living room, where Sascha, Bon and Gus were running around and Grandpa Jack was leaning against the frame of one of the front windows.

'What's all this about then, Jodie? The farm is a palace compared to this place,' he said.

'I just want to be closer to you, Jack. Sascha, come here! No, I get lonely, Jack. With Pete away, I've just never felt settled out there.'

'Just wait until your partner dies, your children grow up, your only purpose is to feed and shit yourself, love. You don't need to tell me about emptiness.'

'Exactly Jack. That's why I'm looking for a remedy now.'

'But Pete is still alive.'

'So Jodie, what are you proposing? I'm not prepared to sell up the farm for this place. All you're paying for is proximity; you'd just be buying a piece of sand dune. We're struggling to cope running the farm; how could we run two properties?' Pete looked at me, concerned.

'The only idea I have come up with is to sell off a bit of the farm, a parcel. Maybe that bit—'

'No one's buying now, it's a buyer's market, stupid bloody time to sell,' Jack piped up.

'The Chinese are buying.'

'Great, so you want to sell the farm off to the Chinese.'

'Just a parcel, not the whole thing. Chinese money is fine by me.'

'Tsk tsk,' Grandpa Jack's eyebrows scrunched closer together.

'Maybe we should talk about this later,' I said calmly to Pete. 'People in the cities are downsizing from a 700sqm block in the suburbs to small apartments in the city, surely you can downsize from five thousand hectares to four thousand? I'm not saying you have to sacrifice everything you want for me but I am asking you to be open to compromise, meet me halfway.'

'Meeting you halfway would mean pretty much at the Highway Roadhouse if you lived here.'

'I don't want to separate us, I just want a home I love. Couldn't you stay here with us when you're home? If you don't want to sell a parcel could we lease the farm out until you stop working away? I agree it would be hard to run both properties. When you stop working away you could commute from here to the farm for a couple of days at a time?'

'Would you still insist on going away all the bloody time if you lived here?' Pete smiled and looked down to the toes of his shoes. 'We'll see what the bank says.'

LYLA

Taking a break from reception, Lyla sat on the toilet, back arched forward, ankles high on stilettos, thinking about Max. It was two weeks since she had seen him. If he was in Perth she would have called him from Salacious and asked him to come down wearing different clothes, sleeves rolled up, showing the blond hairs on his strong forearms. He could pretend not to know her as she fumbled with the computer, blushing as she pushed his credit card into her eftpos machine. She thought the swings away would get easier, not progressively more torturous. Reaching for the toilet paper Lyla whispered to her mum.

'Mum, I love him. I love him so much: his arms, his fingers, his steady purpose. I love him so much, it stains my mind, my heart, my groin. Do I sound like a crazy stalker, Mum? He's probably only thought of me once to my billion. Why did I not get it, back then? Now I want to give him everything. Ok Mum, don't listen any more...really Mum, cover your ears,' she whispered to the back of the toilet door. *I want to give him everything, lie down in front of him, surrender to this constant irritation. I want him to come here and fuck me now...I want to kiss him behind a closed door, at the bar...in a supermarket aisle... My body is flushing hot. I want to have him inside me all the time, talk to him nonstop till I die, never running out of words. I want to kiss him, feel those arms around me, a finger in my mouth...* Lyla's lust was at full tilt when an impatient set of four knuckles hit the door.

'Hey, I'm busting, hurry up! What are you doing in there?

'Calm down, calm down. I haven't been in here long.' Lyla pulled up her knickers and opened the door within a minute. Standing in front of her was one of the dancers; a new one Lyla hadn't met yet, who looked like she was pinging or just about to have an accident. In either event, she raised her right eyebrow as Lyla stepped out of the grubby-walled cubicle. Lyla glared at her, not willing to be mowed down by an upstart, even if the upstart was earning approximately seven times more than she did weekly.

Walking back through to reception, where Barb was holding the fort, Lyla saw Cherry and York at the bar. They stood talking to a big lad who must have been hitting the steroids. York had a hand lightly held to the small of Cherry's back. His eyes darted around the room as he talked; always ready to fend off, take charge, protect. Cherry looked happy and was dominating the conversation, hands fluttering up and down. As York stroked from Cherry's shoulder, down her arm to her wrist, Lyla felt a bewildering sense of envy; not of Cherry or York, or their underworld, but of their freedom to stand and stroke each other. Thinking of Ella, Lyla dug her fingernails into her palms. A ridiculous situation she had soared towards. She knew that she only had herself to blame but felt a rush of resentment towards Max. Flooded by feeling limerence and annoyance, Lyla turned and walked slowly back to reception.

ELLA

Locking up the security shutters of Whipits, Ella knew where she was heading and it wasn't home to listen to the sound of rattling colourbond. She walked into the pub and made her way towards the bar, under the layer of fishing lures and through the overpowering odour of tradies, fish and chips. The Juggler was holding court as she approached the huddle 'Ella, my friend, welcome, I was just making an announcement.'

'You're pregnant, mate?' Axl asked innocently. 'About time!'

'No.' The Juggler looked very pleased with himself.

'Going to make Mrs Palmer and her five daughters honest women?' Jimmy asked, gesturing behind the bar for another beer.

'No.'

'You're going to bat for the other team?' Ella asked cheekily.

'No.' Axl winked at her.

'Your shout?' Axl asked with feigned disbelief.

'No, my friends, the news I have to share with you is that as of today, I have been left on the wharf and the ship has sailed. Unemployed!'

'Weeeehaaaa!' Jimmy did a jig around the bar stood.

'Well done, mate!' Axl slapped him on the back.

'So tonight the four of us shall drink and be merry! A toast – to being a sponsored member of the national Australian surf team!'

'Here's to hocking your box in the whorehouses of Kalgoorlie! I can see you in one of the Hay Street brothels.' Axl looked wistful, thinking of his hometown.

'Crying shame it is.' Jimmy shook his head, 'Once you've sold your boat, sold your pots and fired your deckie, it will be harder to catch the cockroaches when they start crawling again.'

'Cockroaches?' Ella looked at Jimmy quizzically.

'Crayfish, love. Cockroaches of the ocean.' Jimmy looked happy that he was able to teach Ella about his world.

'I tried to talk to my boss about leaving the whole business to me but strangely he wanted to sell it. He'll sell the boat and lease his pots. Anyway, not my problem now, Jimmy.'

'Juggler, I've seen you on deck since you were sixteen. You've never been without a job since. I'm worried about you, mate. I don't want to find you hanging from the rafters.'

'You know me Jimmy, too happy to be suicidal, mate. Besides, Jimmy, your mum's been giving me a shoulder to cry on all afternoon.' The Juggler was looking at Ella and they laughed together.

Axl turned to the Juggler. 'Really, what are you going to do?'

'I've got no idea. I could try and get another gig on a cray boat. I don't know anyone who's hiring though. The wet lining fishing industry is fucked. Apart from crayfishing, the whole fishing industry is rooted. The writing's on the wall. I don't want to be one of those old salty dogs, still fishing when they can barely walk, still cursing the fact that we've gutted the sea. Weekend fishermen don't give a fuck. Some commercial fishermen don't give a fuck either any more. They think the industry is dead so they're just looting while they still can. It makes me sad, my friend.'

'Well, the fish can't compete with 80,000 weekend fishermen using GPS systems to remember the exact lump of reef where the fish like to hang, can they?' Axl said.

'The old fishers have always known to leave the fish when they are breeding. These crew don't seem to understand,' Jimmy explained further to Ella.

'Yep, I think it's all over, so I don't know what I'm going to do. I'm thinking of walking away from fishing, but I've never done anything else.' The Juggler put his beer to his mouth and took a big gulp.

'I'm not sure that your fashion sense would be valued at Whipits...' Ella shuddered, looking at the Juggler's bait streaked boardshorts.

'Why don't you come out to the mines? I could have a chat to my supervisor, see what's available. You'll work like a dog, but it's good money. Start wearing the golden handcuffs like me,' Axl suggested.

'You can't go FIFO, we've only just started swimming together,' Ella said, tipsy from the heat and her single wine.

'I don't want to stop doing laps with you, Ella. Axl, what are you talking about, golden handcuffs? I don't think you understand what that means,' the Juggler loved to pull his mate up whenever possible. 'I think you are meaning that you are trapped by the big money. That's bullshit mate! Twenty dollars a night for a dorm bed at the Grantown Guesthouse? Too tight to even get yourself a single room. Lager is your only set of handcuffs Axl. Besides, not sure I could be that far away from the ocean. I've never been more than an hour inland.'

'You get used to it. After a while you don't even care about being down a black hole. It's like being back in the womb, mate. Apart from one year seeming like seven.'

'Yeah mate, dog years, don't think I could do it. Ok, ask for me. Otherwise I might be flipping burgers at a fast food joint with all those kids with pimples oozing out oil on to the hot plates.'

'I don't know that working at the mines is the job for you, Juggler.' Jimmy sounded vaguely paternal. 'Those mines sit like ladies of the night, legs spread, fanning themselves with a hand of money and all the blokes rush in. Then they can't leave, like dogs who get a knot in their cock when mating.'

'However, the high-vis would suit you, Jugs,' Ella squinted her eyes, thinking of the Juggler in bright orange and navy blue. High-vis was terrible for selfies though. She knew from experience. Max's high vis strips were so bright in a photo, no filter could salvage the shot.

JODIE

I didn't want to rub the whole thing in Pete's face, so I waited until he went back to work before I looked in the grey metal filing cabinet in our office for all the titles for the farm. There were a few adjoining properties that made up its boundaries, a patchwork of fields, some more arable than others. I would have to talk to Pete about what he thought he could let go of and what was the most valuable; what we'd have to keep for a viable working farm. I picked up a green cardboard divider with the separate titles and returned to the kitchen. As I put Sascha in her high chair for some morning tea my phone rang. It was the real estate agent looking after the shack.

'Hi Anne, I was going to ring you today. I've been talking to my partner-'

'Sorry Jodie, that's what I am ringing about, someone else has put an offer to the vendor so I am unable to receive an offer from you until we can clarify whether the property has been sold.'

'Oh.' Loneliness was back, like a soft bitch in my head.

For the next couple of hours I lay on the lino singing Elvis songs. Sascha wanted my full attention but I couldn't give it to her. Deep breaths, so deep my ribs lifted and my lower back arched. Sascha hovered over my face and I looked at her with dusty melancholy; *so beautiful, she is so beautiful, why can't I focus on her?* I thought. As the vision of the shack receded it black-inked my day; visibility temporarily lost. I should get up and wash the dishes, do a few loads of laundry, fix the fence on the western boundary that Pete had asked me to do three swings ago. I should get dinner started, think about school lunches for tomorrow, put away the Christmas tree and the curled-up Christmas cards. I had seen myself there at the shack, happily pottering inside, not worrying about Pete being so far away. Hearing a hungry ocean tearing up the shore. *It's just a shack,*

I reminded myself. The one that got away. I counted the curls on Sascha's forehead: thirteen in a bunch to her left side. She dribbled on my face and tried to eat my nose as I lay there.

'Sascha, stop it, that tickles,' I scrunched my nose and wiped the drool from the inner recess of my right nostril. 'Can you help me up, Sascha? Help Mumma up? Let's find something here to get up for. Should we go and watch the crows on the fence line?' Sascha lay on my chest with her face on my neck. I closed my eyes. 'Maybe tomorrow we'll find something to get up for? Bounce out of bed for? Maybe today we'll just spend a few more hours singing to Elvis?'

'No, Mumma!' Sascha scaled my lying form so that her face was over mine. 'Up!'

So, I got up. I took a frozen chicken from the deep freeze to start defrosting it, made Sascha a sandwich and stared out the window with a warm cup of tea in my hand. Pete would be happy, I guessed. He wouldn't understand this feeling in my stomach, a kneading of something in there. I was just thinking about finding the car keys to pick up Bon and Gus from school when my phone rang.

'Jodes, it's me...'

'Heya Jack, how are you going?'

'Good, love. Just wanted to let you know I sold some shares and have put an offer on that place you wanted.'

'What?'

'You said you wanted to be closer to me, didn't you? I thought you were probably dead right that life would be better for you there.'

'I thought you hated it, Jack.'

'Absolute bloody dump if you ask me but if you like it so much, you'll make it better.'

'We haven't even spoken to the bank yet, Jack; just say we can't sell a piece of the farm?'

'What's the point of me having shares sitting there and Pete selling off the farm in this market? No use in you getting the money in ten years when you need it now. You're family, love, whether you farkin like it or not.'

'Jack, I am...I don't know what to say ...'

'Well, that is one for the books! Jodie, speechless? I never thought I'd see the day.' My mind choked. I was walking softly in little circles, looking out the window, looking at my toes.

'You know, May always wanted to move to town. She didn't mention it much but she would have loved it. She even loved the lights at the wharf, the boats driving away. Signs of life. But then she passed before I had the chance. I always think about that…at night…'

'Have you told Pete, Jack? He won't believe it. We'll pay you back, you know we will.'

'We'll see. Alright, I'll let you go – just didn't want you to fret if you heard from the agent that the crazy house in the dunes had been taken off the market.'

'Jack, thank you.'

'You're right love. Family. Tickle those kids for me.'

'Ok Jack, bye.'

I grabbed Sascha out of her high chair and swung her above my face, through a pink afternoon galaxy of imaginary stars. 'What a day Sascha, what a day. Grandpa Jack? Of all the people. What do you think, Sascha? What do you think?'

ELLA

Max had been gone for two weeks already when Ella faced an empty weekend. Weekdays were never as bad. A Saturday and Sunday without anything scheduled were two big obstacles to overcome. Max told her that he didn't understand, the last week for him always flew. There was no chance of Ella filling some of her weekend with her big sister as Pete was home and they always seemed to fill his seven days home without any help from her. The Juggler had car pooled down to Perth with Axl during the week to get some basic qualifications so he'd have a chance of finding a job. Ella thought about ringing one of the girls from Whipits but they were all so young, they didn't even realise that Ella was actually still young herself. They all thought Ella was cool because she was twenty-six without kids. They all assumed they would be married and have produced, at least, a boy and a girl before they were twenty-five.

At 4:00 p.m. Ella's phone rang. *Great, Mum.* Ella shook her head and tapped her phone sharply hoping the call would divert to message bank quickly so she didn't have to feel so mean. Every time she felt depressed, her mum, without fail, would ring her in despair, as if the same angel had one hand on each of their heads, pushing them underwater simultaneously.

At ten o'clock Ella's phone rang again and as she fished around the back of the couch looking for it, Ella thought it might be Max ringing later than usual. It was the Juggler. Her lips curved up.

'Hi Juggler, are you back in town?'

'Yes, and I want to take you sandboarding on Sunday.' The Juggler always seemed to have a good hand of cards to play.

'I can't wait,' Ella responded, relieved, knowing that plans for Sunday would help her sleep tonight, would let her brain switch off.

Early on Sunday morning, Juggler, Axl, Ella and two other carloads of boys on their swings home headed south along the coastline. There was no other form of worship that could have tempted them more.

'Don't tell the rats about the good life,' Axl grinned over at the Juggler, who had stocked his car with two sandboards, a wakeboarding rope, four fishing rods, some cooked crays in a bag of ice and enough stubbies of beer for everyone.

'I'm not match fit for the rat race,' replied the Juggler. 'I wouldn't make it through the first heat. Years of being a deck rat is enough for me.' The Juggler turned around to face the back seat and smiled wide at Ella.

Living on the salty petticoat of Geraldton, they could fool themselves that the planet was vast and populated by few. Driving south along the dune tracks, they did not see anyone in the time it took to be sand blown and pumped full of happiness. Not a soul on those tracks, only the detritus of the cray industry thrown onshore by every swell since the industry began. A million white polystyrene cray floats like mutant bloated turtles' eggs nestled in every dip of sand.

'See out to the right, Ella, the Abrolhos Islands is out there. I've fished there my whole life. My dad had me scouring rocky ground there as soon as I could stand up by myself on the boat. He used to throw me out into the schools of fish above the purple staghorn coral when I could barely swim. I know that ground way better than I know the backs of my hands. In fact, the Abrolhos Islands have left scars all over these hands.' The Juggler glanced down at his blotchy hands, 'reaching into caves to pull crayfish out as they scuttle backwards towards safety, and chasing fish as they zip behind sharp reef lines. The fish over there know me when they see me coming. They say "Oh no, here he comes, look away from the Last Supper on the line, look away!"' Ella gave the Juggler a half smile, not really listening to him as she looked out the window.

As Axl drove onwards, Ella laughed more readily as the spirit of the coast infected her. Her eyes soaked up the rough, raw, jagged reef that prohibited swimming. Her eyes lit up as a thousand crabs scattered towards the water and disappeared into scratched-out holes. After about an hour of driving through soft sand, they arrived at the sweet spot, where the reef deviated away from the shoreline and the tide had left a span of firmer sand. The three cars pulled up and there was a frenzy of action as amped-up souls secured snap ropes to the backs of the utes, applied suncream, and threw sandboards on the sand. The Juggler gave Ella a feverish demonstration of his technique, then helped her up on to the back of Axl's ute so she could watch him closely.

The three utes took off one at a time, slowly at first so the boys could find their feet. After half a kilometre, this strange procession gained momentum. The Juggler yelped with excitement as Axl churned the ute through the sand, pulling him over seaweed lumps and eroded gutters. He flew, carved the sand and called out to the blue sky above. The boards skimmed out over the shallow water and zoomed back in behind the pull of the vehicle. Ella couldn't help but cheer and call out for the three sand boarders, who looked much more graceful than they had the last time she'd seen them at the Sandy Beach Hotel, full of beer. Ella laughed out loud when it was her turn and the rope pulled her arms hard and the wind took her long brown hair and whipped it brutally on her back.

The joy day raced by. There were cuts, sprains, perhaps even slight concussion but most of all, a delirium of happiness over the group. As the sun fell, Ella casually waded in knee-high waves between the Juggler and Axl, holding a fishing rod in her left hand and a beer in her right. There was little chance of catching a tailor, whiting or man-size mulloway but even less chance of Ella caring about the odds.

LYLA

Clocking on at Salacious, Lyla noted that it was four hundred and forty five days since her mum had died. Not even two years since she'd laid her in a biodegradable coffin in Fremantle Cemetery: 'A perfect choice for the environmentally conscious,' her mum had said. Minimal disturbance to the environment. A natural decomposition. For her final return she wanted to be unmarked, at peace under the kangaroo paws and kangaroo trails.

As she cleaned the counter with a disposable wipe, Lyla cast her mind back to her last road trip with her mum to Geraldton before she rode the clouds to London. They had felt like fugitives, not letting anyone know they were there. They wore sunglasses in their hire car and bog-lapped Marine Terrace. A Yamatji grandma in floral skirts corralled her grandies. Skinny young deckhands rolled cigarettes on street benches. An elderly man slowly made his way towards Cathedral Avenue with his trousers belted high above his waist. Lyla and her mum had wrapped towels around their shoulders and walked down to Town Beach, where they'd gone in her youth to escape domestic tornadoes and splash around amongst the seagulls. As a youngster holding a handful of hot chips, Lyla had always felt she had a dome of seagulls around her. Then, after one night in Geraldton, stalking their pasts, it had suddenly felt strange and the drive back to South Fremantle was easy, like there was a greater force of gravity on their side.

Two blokes walked into Salacious together, both wearing white shirts, ties and matching corporate hipster shoes. They respectfully paid their corporate money and wandered into the boom boom of the club. Lyla wondered what her mum would think of her job. She didn't have a lot of research to report back to Matt yet. He had emailed her to ask about deadlines for the research project. He had a screenwriter that was ready to be sent the information she had gathered.

Lyla saw that Cherry was not on the roster so her expectations of the evening fell. At least it would be busy later. Lyla looked up when she heard a female voice from the inside doorway.

'Hi Lyla.'

'Lucy?'

'I was bored – only a few blokes in there. Two are just sitting together talking about the indie music scene, not interested in any dances.'

'Gee, I don't know how they'll handle the playlist here then – not so indie.' Lyla was looking at Lucy with interest, as she hadn't really spoken to her in any depth before.

'Where are you from, Lyla?'

'The Midwest, originally.'

'Oh yeah, my uncle lives in Geraldton, but he only contacts us when he thinks he can get money out of us. Lied about cancer once so he could squeeze some money out of my nan.'

'Oh no.'

'Get bored out here?' Lucy walked in front of the booth.

'Most nights I don't get the chance.'

'Get many crazies coming in off the street?' Lucy's centre of gravity swayed from side to side with each step, as if her stilettos were a size too small.

'Yeah, a few. Cherry's man York sorted one out for me the other night.'

'York? Oh yeah, I wouldn't mess with York.'

'He certainly seems to know his martial arts.' Lyla leant back in her chair and watched Lucy.

'I guess you need those skills when you work in his trade.' Lucy connected eyes with Lyla as she pronounced the word trade.

'Yoga instructor in a day spa?' Lyla smiled back at Lucy, wanting to bluff that she knew York very well. Lucy laughed out loud.

'I only know about York's trade because it turned my little brother from a beautiful soul to a wastoid.'

'Ice?' Lyla asked, pretending that she knew the items on York's inventory.

'Dirty, fucking ice…you know anyone on it?' Lucy didn't wait for Lyla to answer, 'York walks in here, doesn't even look my way. He knows my brother. Mustn't care.'

'I didn't know about your brother.' Lyla sat forward.

'Of course, I'm sure Cherry wouldn't have mentioned it.'

'We don't really talk about York, just smoke cigarettes.'

'Just shits me that he's untouched and Kane is...well...I guess you could say he is well and truly touched – beyond repair.'

'You believe that? That he's beyond repair?'

'Fuck, yeah. He won't find his way back...always looks at me over his pipe and says, "Why would I quit and leave all this?" Kills me.'

'I'm sorry to—'

'Why should you be sorry? I'm not sorry. I used to be. Used to give him my dancing money so that he could keep a supply. To keep his sick off, he used to say. Tide him over until his next smoke. Not now. Detach with love, they say.'

'I've heard that – detach with love. I think my mum used to say it.'

Lucy walked up close to the other side of Lyla's counter. 'Please don't say anything to Cherry. I don't know if she knows about Kane. She'd kick me off the stage if she knew I'd told you. Not warm and fuzzy, that woman.'

'Mum's the word,' Lyla said uncomfortably, as if Cherry's toes were about to curl around the doorway to announce her arrival.

JODIE

After settlement I started transforming my shack. For the two weeks Pete was away, Sascha and I travelled to the shack during school hours. I set up a pile of art and craft stuff under the living room window and Sascha scribbled while I scrubbed. When she became restless I shamelessly let her watch her favourite kids' shows for a couple of hours. Back at the farm I sewed some neutral coloured curtains and lime washed old farm furniture. I found Pete's jigsaw and cut a piece of corrugated iron leaning against the wall in the shed in half to hang on the shack's living room wall. The oxygen had been digesting it slowly for ten seasons and left the most beautiful patterns; rust and flaws.

When Pete returned from his swing away he came into town to see the transition. He didn't give me much feedback, apart from a smart arse comment about how great our house at the farm would be if I showed it the same degree of love. Pete slapped both hands over his eyes in disbelief when I asked him to transport a few trailer-loads of dirt from the farm to the shack. He massaged his temples for a few seconds, squinting at me as if I was the most untangleable knot in the universe.

'Ok,' he said with his head shaking *no*.

'Just a bit of soil, that clay soil, so I can grow different stuff, a little oasis.'

'A lush garden in a sand dune?' Pete shook his head once, sharply. 'Ok. Jodie, have you thought this through?' Again, I had defied his sweet, practical country logic. 'Why would you bother, Jodie? Come back and live at the farm. Why can't we all just live at the farm? Why do we have to create an oasis in a sand dune?'

'Yes, a lush garden in a sand dune. I thought you'd be…"

'Impressed?' Both hands on the back of his head now, torso forward, eyes looking at my lime washed roof.

'Excited?' I suggested.

'I want you to come home.'

'Where? I don't know where that is. Not Melbourne, not Yuna. With you, yes. With my children centimetres away, yes. But with you away, this feels more like home.'

'What about the empty house at the farm?'

'What about it?'

'What about me? What I want?'

'What do you want? Talk to me, let's—' I stepped closer to him.

'I just wish I'd never gone to work away, you would have been happy.'

'I was lonely when you were harvesting, seeding, doing fences, shooting animals.'

'Animals that were eating up our livelihood.'

'Lonely.'

'Ok, so now you want some soil from the farm to grow the kind of garden you would be able to have at the farm without transporting the soil here?'

'Exactly.'

'Ok, babe.'

'I was thinking it would be gorgeous to bring some of those old jarrah sleepers here too, to make a little stairway up to a lookout. You could see the sea from the lookout. Check if it was fishing weather.'

'They would have to be planed so they weren't so heavy.'

'Could you teach me how to do that? I'd make it worth your while. I'd love a jarrah four-poster day bed on the balcony too, while you have the planer out.' My strategy was to hit up big and negotiate down.

'Gee I'll have to give Majestic a call and say I won't have time to come back to work.'

'And a little bath tub and that is all – one of the ones with legs – so we can lie in it together and look up at stars through steam.'

'So a connection to the hot water system up there too?'

'If that's what's needed,' I said flippantly, smiling as I turned my head away from him.

'Come here, Jodie Daley.' I turned around and reached up high, putting both hands around the back of Pete's eternally sunburnt neck.

'You know that even in that steam there will be sadness sometimes. Probably mostly when I'm away but also when I'm here.'

'I know. I know. Sometimes that feeling erodes me and I'm not sure what to do. I thought the salt water would be an antidote. I really did.

But that feeling is here already, two weeks in. I went for a walk along the beach on the weekend with the kids. I felt that emptiness…I searched each wave face, surprised to see her there…'

'You'll probably find that sex helps. Not with anyone else, just me.' Pete pursed his lips and blew some stray hairs away from my face.

'Should we see? I haven't read the current literature – are there any conclusive studies with positive therapeutic findings?' I leant in, my groin touching below Pete's.

'You know I do get those feelings too: missing you, the kids, the farm, fishing. Every time I think of it I feel shit, so I don't let my mind go there. Especially when I am at the start of the swing and two weeks seems never-ending. At least we get to talk. The phone calls make all the difference to me. Hearing all the details: stupid details, rainfall, milestones, what you had for dinner.' Pete scratched the front scruff of his hair, looking mildly uncomfortable.

'Even if the kids have a bowl of rice bubbles for dinner – twice in one week?'

'Especially then, so I can keep tabs on the malnourishment that occurs when I am away.'

'Should we go into the bedroom and have a quickie while Sascha is asleep and the boys are still watching that movie?' I made my play.

'How quick is a quickie? I thought you wanted me to go to Bunnings.'

'Are you rejecting me, Pete?'

'It's just I'm so exhausted, the kids have been driving me crazy, I haven't done any exercise today, I feel shit…' Pete said, mocking me in a stupid girly voice.

'Your loss,' I said, pulling my hair to the side and running my fingers through it to catch the knots. Pete leant in and licked me slowly from the base of my exposed neck up to the spot behind my earlobe. Holding hands, we quietly walked towards the room which would be our bedroom, over the original floorboards, which I had exposed at the first opportunity. Under the hard-worn carpet were jarrah floorboards, typical of the vintage of the house; a time where there must have been something in the water that made residents construct beautiful blood-brown floorboards and then nail coarse carpet over them. We lay together on the double inflatable mattress that had carried our happy bones through many nights of sleep. Under a sheet the colour of old pages, Pete and I kissed slowly. Eyes closed. He kissed my cheeks and I kissed all over his lips. He pulled my t-shirt up under my chin and sucked on one nipple, kissing it, holding it gently between his teeth. The back of my head pushed back into the mattress and I felt Pete's heaviness in between my legs. He kissed the skin over my ribs and the softness of my belly. My eyes moved from the ceiling to the wall. I would strike out the L and the E of LONELY and put an S at the end of LOVER.

'Mum, I'm hungry,' Gus complained, standing in the doorway, 'What doing under there, Mum?' I quickly pulled my t-shirt down and used my legs to flick Pete over so that he was next to me rather than on top.

'Um…Dad and I were just looking for my other sock, weren't we Dad? I think it might have got lost under the sheets last night…'

'What can we eat, Mum?' Bon now stood at the doorway too, looking down at his parents.

'There are some crackers in the hungry bag out there, boys, and some apples.'

'What are you doing?' Bon asked.

'We were just having a rest, mate,' Pete answered, looking at me, and subtly motioning towards his erection.

'Turn back over,' I said quietly, 'just don't pop the mattress.'

'I want to come under the tent, too,' Gus said, jumping up and down on the spot.

'I'll get up,' I said to Pete, one leg already out of the sheet, 'Come on boys, watch out, I'll get you!' The floorboards creaked as I ran towards my sons, grabbing at the back of their t-shirts, hearing them shriek sister-waking screams.

ELLA

Ella couldn't be bothered cooking so she decided to go for a stroll down Marine Terrace and buy some laksa from the Asian take-away. She pulled on her yoga gear to do a few poses en route on the grass under the Norfolk pines. She pulled a white silk tunic over the top and slid her feet into some teal bohemian flats. She rubbed some lip balm in between her top and bottom lips, making sure the shine was evenly distributed in the mirror in the hallway before grabbing her yoga mat, slinging it over her left shoulder and heading out. The southerly smacked the sounds of shorebreaks from the south to the north of town. Ella was still enjoying little doses of adrenalin from going sandboarding with the Juggler and Axl a few days earlier. She smiled involuntarily, thinking about an epic stack, when she'd lost balance but managed not to let go of the rope. She passed the football oval to her left, heading towards the foreshore. Boys were running around in the hour before dark, chasing the ball, families screaming from the side lines. Ella watched, a little confused, unable to comprehend what all the fuss was about. It always annoyed her when Max sat forward on the couch, yelling to the umpires that they were green maggots, falling back on the couch when the Eagles failed to kick the ball between the tall white posts. Ella scrunched her nose up and rubbed the smooth shellac nail polish on her left index finger with the pad of her right index finger.

When she reached the shady grass in between the yacht club and the new tourist centre, she took off her tunic and sat down cross-legged on her yoga mat. She uncrossed her legs, kicked off her teal shoes purchased with a staff discount at Whipits, and recrossed her legs, feet on opposing thighs in lotus pose. She closed her eyes and inhaled deeply. Fish and chips. Each inhalation smelt more strongly of fish and chips. Ella opened her eyes and around her, sharing the cool green grass, were families circling little mountains of deep-fried yellow chips and chunks of fish, laid bare on rectangles of white paper. Ella thought of hungry hippos swallowing white balls. Chomp, chomp, chomp. Ella had been given the board game in her childhood by a very fake-looking Santa Claus at the local community health centre's Christmas party. Arms reached for the chips and tried to fit a handful in a mouth, where the hands were bigger than the mouths they overfilled. Seagulls circled and screeched, biding their time, gathering closer to the children, who were more likely to bowl an overarm of hot chips their way. Ella glided forward on all fours into cat-cow pose before realising the ridiculousness of the situation. No way was she going to transition into downward dog with an audience of carb-loaders north, south, east and west. Ella sat back, flicked her legs forward, quickly threw her tunic over her head and her toes into her shoes, rolled up her mat and headed towards Marine Terrace.

Ella could hear the buzz of the Sandy Beach Hotel from a block away. It seemed perfectly reasonable to trade a yoga session for a glass of white at skimpy hour. As she placed her hand on the handle to pull it towards her, it was pushed out by a patron exiting.

'Axl!' Ella stepped to the side to let him past.

'Ella! Nearly wiped you out. Sorry,' Axl rubbed the back of his hair, elbow pointing upwards. 'You going in?'

'I was just walking past, thought I'd have a wine—'

'And do a yoga session at the Sandy Beach? Why not? Probably not the strangest thing that has ever happened in there. I was just going to have a look at the beach – would you like to come?' Axl looked intensely at her.

'Want to have a wine with me first? It's still really humid down there.' Ella self-consciously held her yoga mat behind her back.

'Umm, maybe we could try out one of the other pubs? We could walk down the other end of Marine Terrace.' Axl closed the door behind him.

'Axl, are you hitting on me?' Ella said, beaming.

'No, I mean, of course I'd love to but...' Axl was blocking the entrance, so Ella swung her rolled-up yoga mat in front of her chest and stepped so close to him that it was pushing into the length of his torso. She placed both arms around him, looked up at him with a layer of lust she had felt since they met, then placed one hand behind him, under the door handle, and pulled the door open. She rubbed her body around his side, smiled and said softly, 'They don't have skimpies at any of the other pubs though, do they?'

'Ella, wait…' Axl turned and followed Ella into the pub. Ella was strutting and laughing down the half-lit entrance hallway when the Juggler, with both his arms squeezing a woman, turned directly into the hallway from the main bar.

'Ella? Hi, beautiful.'

'Jugs?' Ella stepped backwards.

'Hey darling, this is my friend Jasmine.' The Juggler leant over and kissed Ella on the cheek.

Jasmine extended one arm out from beneath the Juggler's grip to shake Ella's hand. 'Hi, babe.' Jasmine looked back up at the Juggler and he pulled her in close again. Ella leant back against the wall, yoga mat falling on the dusty floor.

'Ella, call me tomorrow, love you.' Beautifully free, the Juggler and Jasmine stumbled a bit as they flowed down the steps and further into their story.

'Oh.' Ella looked across at Axl, who was looking up at the roof, unsure what to say, 'I guess it's just you and me then. Will you let me buy you a drink? Axl?'

'I tried to save you from that – didn't think you needed to see it.'

'What? Save me from what? I'm totally fine.' Ella didn't think that anyone knew that the Juggler sometimes kept her company. 'What? Come and sit with me, Axl. Tell me about your son. We never really get to know each other with Jimmy and the others around.' Ella was determined not to feel small as she entered the bar. She tried not to feel like one bait fish in a bait ball, the one picked off as prey. Finding where you stand with people is empowering, Ella had always heard herself say.

LYLA

Max generally called Lyla's phone at 8:00 p.m. She answered it when she could. Barb seemed reasonable about accepting personal calls but Lyla had avoided ever answering her phone when Barb was around, clearing the till or giving her some performance management advice, always delivered with her firm but fair tongue in cheek. The punters weren't keen on club personnel talking to their loved ones while they waited in an indiscreet line snaking out on to James Street. Lyla's phone was on vibrate and there was no one waiting to pay their entry fee when Max telephoned from the camp. He was walking from his room, on the way to the wet mess to have a mid-strength beer with a bloke he'd run into from home.

'Hi babe.'

'Lyla, can you talk?'

'Yes, there isn't anyone in here at the moment.'

'Many in tonight?'

'There was a big rush after work but things have quietened down now.' Lyla crossed her legs under the table and wiped some dust off the eftpos machine linked to the computer screen to her right.

'One more sleep until I get to see you,' Max said, which was about as romantic as he got before he slipped into sexy talk.

'I'm so excited; can't wait to see you. I am going to take you out and show you a good time. Maybe even ask you some big questions.'

'What sort of questions?' Max asked nervously.

'I've just been thinking, asking myself some tough questions. I was talking to Cherry last night and it made me face up to some—'

'Strip club counselling?'

'Yeah, Cherry and I have been tackling the big issues – at least for as long as it takes to suck one durry down.'

'Lyla, why would we mess with a good thing?'

'Why do you think, Max?'

'Is this all because I wouldn't go to Margaret River with you?'

'Would you be happy if we kept on going like this?' Lyla glanced towards the doorway to check no one was watching her: single, saintly Lyla.

'Um…yes? I don't want you to leave. Are you thinking of leaving again?'

'Oh Max. Ella, what about Ella?' Lyla was impatient, blocking the music out with one finger pressing her ear closed.

'I don't know what to say to you. Can we talk about it when I get there?' Max said as Cherry's knee appeared and a glow-in-the-dark stiletto heel rubbed up and down the painted wood of the door frame.

'Gotta go, Max, I'll ring you later.'

'Ok, babe, call me in a couple of hours.' Lyla shook her head at Max's opportunism, and the mirror it was to her own.

'I have ten minutes before the next group dance.' Cherry hurried Lyla as Lyla's mum had often done preparing her for school: hurry up, out the door, come on now, *quickly, quickly.*

'I'm over this place,' Lyla said, energy as low as the cigarette butts on the pavement, as they stood on the street.

'What? You've barely started. Salacious can't have worn you out so fast.' Cherry laughed.

'I would rather be in a beautiful knee-length red dress, hair curled, next door.' Lyla looked through the neighbouring window where couples swirled to percussion instruments, not coping too well with the complex beats of the salsa.

'It's all just a matter of costume, Lyla. They're no different in there: hungry people looking for a taste of something to make them feel good.'

'Is that what you see when you look in that window?' Lyla stepped in front of the glass, touching it with the tips of her fingers, not wanting to leave big streaks.

'Men leading, hairy arms touching made-up women…'

'I like the music better.' Lyla was not ready to accept that Cherry's meat-market world view was real.

'Forty-plus clumsy stumbling is all I see,' Cherry stood facing the Latin pulse, back to James Street, as the dancers behind the glass tried to find the one (beat).

'Cherry?' A male voice diverted their attention away from the Latin Club and cocked their heads towards the traffic.

'Yes, hang on,' Cherry said, taking a huge inhalation to last her for a couple of hours of house music and swinging her legs above her head on a pole. Lyla hadn't seen this bloke before and looked at Cherry to gauge whether she knew the face, framed by a hoody, eyebrow piercing above the left eye. Cherry was looking down, throwing her cigarette underfoot, when the man lunged towards her.

'Fucking slut, you can tell your boyfriend that he's fucked up. Tell him that his time is done.' The black hooded sleeves shot forward and grabbed Cherry by her ears, pulling her so she tripped forward over her now barely glowing heels.

'Stop it,' Lyla screamed. 'Leave her! Stop!' Lyla lunged forward towards the man and hit hard on the arm holding Cherry at his chest height as if she were weightless.

'Bitch,' he spat at Lyla and, holding Cherry up by one ear, he punched hard into Lyla's jaw. The force of the punch threw Lyla against the window pane; the couples inside stood still and watched with muffled sound as the man punched repeatedly into Cherry's glitter-sprinkled face.

JODIE

Pete led the kids and me towards the hardware warehouse as if he had bought a lottery ticket from a winning newsagency and was going to check if he himself was the winner; such was the excitement. When Pete was home and we were not camping, he had always taken the opportunity to transform our lives into an episode of a home renovation show. I was grateful that he restored order but it made me wonder if without him I would ever notice the bedlam that he did. I could live with dripping taps and stuck windows for years and they would become idiosyncrasies of my home, never causing the annoyance they did for Pete. Slung with power tools, he made our lives functional. I had flatly refused to go on Pete's epic hardware expeditions until the café section was installed with the play equipment for the little ones. Not even the fundraising sausages had previously sweetened the deal. The boys always followed their dad around, soaking up the sights of cheap hardware while I drank coffee and watched Sascha pull herself up on the slide installed in the primary-coloured play area. Now I was designing the layout for the shack, you could barely keep me away.

Pete trawled down aisle seven of the warehouse with Bon, Gus, Sascha and me lagging behind him. Pete was a good dad, taking the boys, but I could tell it was tricky for him to remember them when his attention was constantly being grabbed by cut-price 710W hammer drills and 185 mm circular saws with adjustable bevel and cut depth. He crouched down and picked up a modular soakwell, turned it over slowly in both hands then looked upwards, not focussing on the towering shelves above. If only he could only think of a use for it, I was sure he would buy two as they were going so cheap.

'Go and grab Dad a trolley, Bon.'

'Ok, Dad.'

'You know where they are, Bon.'

'Yes, Dad.'

As Pete grabbed Gus' hand, Sascha and I trailed off a few metres behind. One-on-one time, father and son. Gus would have all of his attention if it wasn't for the 25.4CC chainsaw for $135.00.

Towards the end of the aisle I heard him say, 'Right Gus, we need to make an action plan or else your mother is going to get to the end of her average coffee, grab what she needs and demand to know what else we came here for and whether we can leave. We have to position ourselves in an aisle quite a distance from the café section, preferably outside amongst the blocks of timber pieces. You know Gus, if we're bending down reading the tag stapled on to the end of a piece of timber, Mum might not even see us and we'll be good for another ten minutes as she does another circuit of the store looking for us. Gus, here comes Bon with the trolley. Let's go and look at the screw section; I need to get some screws to attach the shade sail I bought last time I was home.'

'What are these, Dad?' Bon asked, returning.

'Those, my son, are whirley birds, roof ventilators, you know for above the bathroom so that your stinky poo smells get sucked up into the roof and outside and we don't have to wear masks to breathe fresh air?'

'You mean Gus' stinky poo smells, Dad!'

'No, Dad, not my poo,' Gus protested, a little man trying to stand tall.

'Well maybe they are your Mum's stinky poo smells, what do you think, boys?' I rolled my eyes, still in earshot.

'Yeah Dad, we need more and more of those before Mum goes in there next.'

'Top idea Bon, well at that price, it can't do any harm to have a spare at home. In the trolley! Ok, the screw section...' Boys in tow, Pete was making his way to the screw section when some barrier plastic edging seemed to catch his eye. He looked like he was drifting off into a little visualisation of the garden beds around the farm house being neatly harnessed by this smart hardware product.

'In black, green or jarrah...' Pete mused as Gus unravelled some galvanised steel lawn edging from its cardboard packaging and dropped it on to the concrete floor.

'That's the beauty of big hardware warehouses,' Pete commented, 'there will be some very friendly team member who will sort that out,' and messily stashed the mess of lawn edging behind some bamboo screening. 'Now boys, a tip for beginners. See this edging here, it comes in all different lengths: six metre lengths for your suburban cottage, ten metre lengths for your upper income four by two, and thirty metre lengths for the likes of us who have land as far as the eye can see, and the disposable income at hand to chop it up with handsome jarrah-coloured barrier plastic edging. But what might not be obvious at first is that the lengths are only described in fairly small print on the circle of paper that is only loosely glued to the coils of plastic edging. So a flick of the wrist can result in one *almost* absentmindedly tugging the paper label off one coil and mistakenly attaching it to another of considerably greater length. Watch this, boys...'

In seconds, Pete had gently pulled one label off the thirty metre coil of jarrah-coloured barrier plastic edging and substituted the paper label from the six metre coil.

'Easy mistake,' Pete said to the boys. 'These labels are so poorly glued on to the coils, and it's very hard to tell, when they're all coiled up, which length is which.'

The boys nodded at their dad.

'The thing is, boys, if the team members at the counters were remotely interested in hardware, they'd pick up the error in a second. It's almost like a test; yeah, a consumer test, to check the vigilance of the team members. That's what we have to do, as often as we can, check out how committed the team members are to their products.' I choked, secateurs in hand, from where I was listening in aisle six.

'Dad, is that stealing? Mummy told me the other day when I put a car from the shops in Sascha's pram so that we could take it home that I was stealing.' Bon looked confused. I cringed.

'No, it's different, son. It's more like a loyalty system in hardware warehouses. A few extra lengths of timber here, a few more litres of deck oil there, it's just a bonus for our loyalty; nothing at all like stealing. Probably best if we don't ask Mum, though; she doesn't really know how it works in these hardware stores. Look, there she is now, looking through the shelves at us, shaking her head.'

ELLA

There was more than the normal amount of mayhem at the Sandy Beach Hotel on Thursday night, ten nights before Max was due to return. Ella walked up to Axl, who was four rounds into a discussion with Jimmy, the Juggler and four other big blokey blokes. To the right of the room was a gaggle of girls, screeching and stumbling around a bride-to-be in a white veil with unopened condoms pinned to it and a pink sash that stated the obvious. They were gyrating to the music and champagne was splashing onto the carpet. The skimpies looked shell-shocked, as if they'd never seen bucks as out of hand as these hens. Ella smiled sympathetically at one of the skimpies, whom she didn't recognise.

'Welcome to Geraldton!' she called out to the newcomer.

'Wow, what is going on here?' the skimpy asked with an accent that sounded vaguely Canadian to Ella.

'Women gone wild,' Ella replied, 'You wait until they bring out the penises; penis straws, headbands with two penises attached on springs so they bounce around, inflatable penises,'

'I might not make much money tonight if they start flashing their tits and hugging blow up cocks. Thanks for the warning. Anyway, I'm Carly.' Carly held out her hand to Ella.

'Nice nails Carly, I'm Ella,' she said as she gestured to her own chest then shook Carly's hand. 'I wouldn't worry, I think they will scare the blokes off. I'd be scared if I was male in here tonight. Especially looking at all those pin pricked condoms on the hen's veil. I love your glitter pumps, are they really Hello Kitty ones?' Ella cocked her head to one side to look down at Carly's footwear.

'Yes, I found them in Tokyo recently, aren't they divine?'

'Gorgeous. Although, style is fairly wasted in the Sandy Beach Hotel I would have to say. Carrying around a tray of beer is probably the most attractive thing to the guys that drink here.'

'Thanks for the local knowledge.' Carly looked at Ella as if she would much rather keep talking to her than work the room for gold coins.

'Good luck, babe.'

After grabbing a wine, Ella tuned into what Axl, Jimmy and the others were talking about. One of the blokes had made a comment about 'the Aboriginal problem.'

'Yeah, mate, I have a few problems, like why your ancestors collected my ancestors' ears for sport,' Axl was staring hard, arms angling back, chest pumped up.

'Yeah, but what about those Aboriginal kids that cruised in today and just stole our Emu Exports out of the fridge at the Grantown?' a Steve from somewhere asked.

'Well, all I can say is that they have very poor taste, mate. I wouldn't drink that shit if you paid me FIFO wages to,' Axl responded.

'Yeah, but what about the fact that they think they can just come in and take what they want...'

'Ever heard of Terra Nullius, mate?' Axl held a beer with one fist, his other arm crossed over his chest now, hand restrained under his own armpit.

'Some of them looked about eleven years old on the CCTV footage. Who's supervising them?' Unknown Steve asked.

'I was one of those "unsupervised kids" people always whine about. No one really wanted to get involved when I was little.' Axl looked through Steve. Ella was finding this conversation difficult to listen to, and images of her mother passed out at the hands of a random boyfriend flashed between her and the conversation. 'That's got nothing to do with me,' replied Steve defensively.

'No, of course not.' The Juggler entered the conversation. 'You have every right to sit here and sink your piss and not give a rat's arse about anyone but yourself.'

'Luckily for me, I had an uncle who remembered stories of what it was like before you fellas came along.' Axl said as the Juggler inhaled, nodding at his words, and the other boys murmured uncomfortably.

'The main "Aboriginal problem" I can think of is colonisation. Within eighteen months of those colonial bastards setting up, an area stuffed full of kangaroo and emu was depleted of food sources. A year later, the area had nothing. People were forced to steal. Potatoes and sheep.'

'Not to mention all those dirty STDs brought over the high seas.' The Juggler shifted his weight from one thong to the other, hugging his beer into his chest.'

'Yep, the white pus of the white man,'

'Well there might be a bit more of that tonight. Don't pick up any condoms from the floor that might have fallen off the hen's veil.' Ella wanted to show her support to Axl but wasn't sure how to do it.

'Don't worry I'll wear two at once, which I usually do with chicks I pick up from here anyway,' snorted Steve to Ella's distaste.

'And the drink…suddenly we had grog to deal with. Drinking became a problem. No mystery there my friends. They drank, like I do now, to wipe it all out.'Axl had not finished.

'You're not alone there Axl,' Ella said, reapplying her lipgloss.

'There are stories of my people fighting back but we were fighting against mongrels.'

'Civilised mongrels?' Steve said.

'Civilised? Mate, you are deluded: my people were dying in large numbers after eating flour that had been treated with arsenic…civilised? "Sweet damper," the settlers called it…sick bastards. Funny that we were the ones named savages.' Axl lowered his gaze.

'But what about all the kids that are running amok?' asked Steve, the random tall bloke.

'Fuck, man…where have you been for the last ten minutes?' said the Juggler.

'I tuned out as soon as he said the word colonisation,' the bloke said, looking around the front bar.

The Juggler put his beer hard on the bar behind him and turned square on to face him. 'Mate, I don't think you're welcome here anymore.'

'Forget it Jugs, don't waste your breath.' Axl rolled his eyes. 'Same fucking story. Three strikes and you're out, sorry I forget what your name was. Steve, was it? Is that what you'd like? Lock them away so your Emu Exports can continue to chill in the fridge?'

'Can I get you a drink, Axl?' Ella asked in a gesture of solidarity.

'I'm good thanks, Ella.' Axl turned his head back to the newcomer. 'Steve here, he obviously doesn't see the ghosts of settlers. Probably denies the lot. Pretends there's a clean white slate for history to start again; image of the First Fleet sailing in on the milky seas of their clean white slate...'

Ella looked at Axl, transfixed. Without thinking too deeply, Ella wished he'd been there when she'd needed someone to stand up for her in her own painful history.

LYLA

Max flew in to Perth Airport from the mine site at 5:00 p.m. as per the usual schedule. If he hadn't been so masculine he would have skipped through Perth Airport towards the car park. His steps were always light as he gravitated towards the far right-hand side of the temporary car park. As he approached the area where Lyla usually parked, he turned his head around scanning the grid of cars. He couldn't see her. He drew in quick breaths. Max tried Lyla's phone, which went straight to message bank. Dumbfounded, he just stood and stared at the car in Lyla's usual spot. The sun was setting and Max was not sure where to find her. He didn't think she'd chosen not to be here; he trusted that she would be if she could. He walked back towards the terminal to grab a taxi and head to Lyla's apartment. It was out of character for Lyla to not have contacted him to let him know she was sick or unable to meet.

After waiting in a queue, Max lowered himself into the front seat of a taxi and asked to be taken to Forrestfield. He checked his message bank. No messages. No sign of any missed calls. Max's fingers tapped on his bag. He was worried; Lyla was reliable, unlikely to just not show up. Max ran up the side pathway of her apartment block, up the three flights of stairs and knocked loudly on the door. Scuffling paws on vinyl floors but no sign of Lyla. Max opened the fuse box and grabbed Lyla's spare key from inside a little box that looked like an old-school fuse; a security system that relied on an intruder being fairly stupid to not be able to work it out. Max opened the door and Mr Bang Bang pushed his snout out and lunged towards his legs, knocking him on the left shin.

'Mr Bang Bang, my mate, where's your mummy? Where's Lyla? Where is she?'

Mr Bang Bang cocked his head to one side. No sign of Lyla. Max looked in the fridge. The fridge contained some milk that was off, but that was not a rare occurrence in Lyla's household. It did mean that she probably hadn't been home this morning. Max tried her phone again. He wasn't sure what to do next. He didn't have any numbers for anyone in her family. None of them were close at all. Distant. They might not even know she was back from London. Besides, he had no phone numbers.

'Salacious, Mr Bang Bang, I will call Salacious. Fuck, it's poor form that I ring a strip joint before any family or friends, looking for her.' Max searched for Salacious and dialled their number. Barb answered.

'Hello, my name is Max. My girlfriend, I mean my friend Lyla, works for you. I was wondering if she was there, if I could talk to her.'

'Max, hey?'

'Yes. My name is Max Bennett.'

'I haven't heard Lyla mention you, Max.'

'Yes, I work away; Lyla was meant to meet up with me this evening and I'm just trying to track her down.'

'Lyla is in hospital, Max; Royal Perth. There was an incident last night and Lyla was hurt.'

'What? Is she ok?'

'No, she's not great, Max. You better ring the hospital.'

'Thanks.' With trembling fingers, Max called the Royal Perth Hospital.

'My name is Max Bennett; I am ringing to talk to Lyla Evans, a patient.'

'Just putting you through to the floor.'

'Could I please speak to Lyla Evans, my name is Max Bennett.'

'Hi Max, are you family?'

'I am her partner.'

'Ok Max, I'm just going to check for you.'

Max waited, frozen.

'Max, we don't have you down on any paperwork as a next of kin but Lyla was admitted last night in a very critical condition. Are you able to come down to Royal Perth?'

'Is she ok?' Max asked.

'She is still in a critical condition. She's had some severe facial trauma and minor cranial trauma.'

'Oh my god...Lyla...'

Max called another taxi and patted Mr Bang Bang as he waited. He was at Royal Perth within a thick hour of traffic. As Max ran towards the ward, in his mind he was fighting the urge to run away so he wouldn't have to see Lyla in pieces. Max choked when he opened the door. Lyla's eyes were slits enclosed by purple puffs above and below. Below, her face was purple and swollen.

'What happened? What happened to you? Who did this to you? What the fuck?' Max was hyperventilating, spiralling up in anxiety. Lyla was heavily medicated and far from lucid. Max had no sign she knew he was there.

'I'm going to take care of you. I will never leave you. I'm sorry. I'm sorry. What happened to you?' Max was bawling, unable to really see any of Lyla except her purple blur.

'Oh my god, oh my god, oh my god.' Max took Lyla's hand and rested his forehead on it as he gushed sadness. A nurse came in and checked on Max. She didn't have many answers for him: an incident in Northbridge outside a club, Lyla caught in the crossfire. Photographs of the injuries had been taken as a matter of course but the police hadn't been able to interview Lyla yet. No other witnesses had been forthcoming. Max stumbled out to the hallway and telephoned Salacious' number. Barb answered again.

'Max, as far as I know, it was a drugged idiot in Northbridge – crystal meth possibly.' Barb knew more but would not lead people into the fire. This Max especially; he could be anyone. She hadn't heard Lyla mention him before.

'But what happened? I don't even know what happened.'

'Lyla and one of our dancers were having a smoke outside and a man walked up and started assaulting them. Lyla fared better than our dancer, who was holding her face in her hands when the ambulance arrived.'

'Who was this guy?'

'Unidentified male, early thirties, Caucasian appearance. The CCTV caught the whole thing.'

'And no one at the club recognised him?'

'The police interviewed all the witnesses and no one said he was familiar.'

'Would they say if they did know him?'

'I imagine they would, Max.'

'What animal does this kind of thing? How could it happen? I don't understand.'

'I am really sorry, Max. I really have to go now. All the best, love.'

Max sat and looked at his phone. Maybe, if he'd had balls, he would have followed Lyla to London and this kinked chain of events would never have happened. They could be in Soho, tucked away in a courtyard accessible via an alley, in a rustic, Andalusian-themed bar dedicated to sherry. Now he had a wife who deserved so much better than the sham he offered her and a lover who couldn't open her eyes.

Max hesitantly re-entered Lyla's room. He stared at her enlarged face, her matted hair. He wanted it to be his face that was purple, his cheekbone shattered. He wanted his soul to pay the price for the life he was leading; not for Lyla's face to be bloodshot from his lack of penance.

'I am so in love with you, Lyla. My life would end if you weren't around. You are the cement between the bricks, my cyclone-proof bunker, my perfect partner on the dance floor. If I didn't have you in my life there would be…sadness…nothingness…a punched hole. I'd be lost. If only I'd been here, if only I hadn't been working away, if only I could have protected you.'

'What could you have done?' Lyla whispered through blood-stuck lips.

'Lyla, Lyla. What did he do to you? Are you ok? Should I call the nurse?'

'Shhh,' was all Lyla could say before drifting away again.

Three days later, Max had barely left the beige vinyl chair by Lyla's side. Mr Bang Bang was being cared for by a neighbour and there was nowhere else Max wanted to be.

'Lyla, I just booked us a dinner reservation. Homemade Mediterranean recipes handed down through three generations of family, originating from the Province of Livorno, Tuscany, and conveniently now served in a family-run cafe two streets away from Royal Perth Hospital. Sounds like it was made for you. Come on, you must be tempted,' Max ribbed.

'Can you tell them to keep my *linguine ai gamberi* in the bain marie while I have my cheekbone repositioned and held in place with small metal plates and screws?' Lyla winced and spat as she spoke.

The doctors had initially thought that her left cheekbone would heal by itself but a CT scan the next day had shown it needed surgery.

'I can't have my eyeball displacing and sinking backwards at the restaurant just for the sake of a panna cotta.'

'Ok, you're right, I'll cancel the reservation.'

Max kept his eyes on his phone, avoiding eye contact, as he asked, 'Lyla, are you ready to tell me what happened?'

'Max, it still hurts to talk.'

Max raised his eyes to meet the five millimetres of Lyla's eyes visible in between the swelling.

'I stupidly walked into an ambush. Eyes open. Tits pushed up. It was Cherry he was targeting. I thought he was going to kill her, so I jumped in without a second's thought. Max, is Cherry all right?'

'Let's talk about it later, Lyla.'

'Or now? Max, is Cherry all right?'

'I think it would be better if we talk about it later.'

'Now.' Lyla was grimacing from the bleeding in one eye and her swollen green face.

'Lyla, I really don't think it would be a good idea to talk about it now.'

'Max, stop fucking with me. Tell me now!'

'It's not great Lyla. It's really fucked up. I am sorry because to hear this will hurt you again. Cherry got really fucked up.'

'So she is alive?'

'Barely. She's here. I haven't seen her. I rang Barb to let her know you'd stabilised and she told me what happened. I'm not really sure you could say she is lucky to be alive. Sick fucker. He smashed her so hard in the face she lost...'

'Lost what?'

'She might have lost her eyesight.' Max's voice followed his head falling downwards.

'Ohhh.' A wail of horror pushed out of Lyla's swollen lips. 'Oh my god, oh my god. Mongrel! What a mongrel!' Hot tears were streaming down her face. 'What the fuck? Why is life so cruel? So fucked up and cruel. Max, how could this happen?' Lyla's breath was smashing in and out now, her stomach burning. 'What kind of sick world do we live in? Max, tell me.'

'They think they'll find the prick. It was all on CCTV. He had a hoodie on but he pushed one sleeve up out of the way after he smashed you, revealing a tat. They will find him, Lyla.'

'And what about Cherry? Will she even be ok?'

'I don't know, babe,' Max's tears were flowing too. The last three days had given Max hospital-grade clear perspective on his own well-intentioned but despicable nature. Two hours later he was on the phone to Ella.

ELLA

Ella was sitting on the upstairs couch, nibbling on a bowl of cucumber and carrot sticks, posting a photo of herself in front of a gigantic Moreton Bay Fig in Dongara, when the phone rang.

'Max!'

'Ella?' Max kept his voice down as he stood with the cigarette smokers outside the entrance to Royal Perth Hospital.

'Max? What's happening? I was worried when you hadn't phoned for days and I couldn't get on to you. I was about to ring that emergency number you gave me ages ago. What's going on?'

'Ella, I've been a terrible person.'

'Max?'

'No, really. You will hate me when I tell you what I've done and I want you to know before I tell you that you're an angel, and deserve much more than a prick like me.'

'Max? Tell me. You're making me nervous. What have you done? Have you slept with someone?' Ella pulled her legs up on the couch, crossed them in front of her and placed one arm around her shins.

'Yes Ella, I have, and even worse, I've been lying to you for a long time now.'

'What? What the fuck? Max, don't tell me...don't tell me...not Lyla?'

'Yes, Lyla.'

'I thought she was in London.'

'No, she came back, her mum passed away. We first met up about a year ago.'

'Oh you dog. You white dog...a year? I thought you said you didn't have feelings for her anymore. You've been seeing Lyla for all that time?' Ella's mind time travelled back over the past year, feeling the outrage mount. Lyla's name had blotted out any thought of her own lack of fidelity.

'How have you even seen her? Did she get a job at your site?'

'No Ella, I'm so sorry...'

'When did you see her, Max?'

'I'm sorry.'

'When?'

'The week before I come home.'

'What do you mean?'

'My swing is still two weeks on, two weeks off.'

'What? No...' Ella stood up and slowly walked towards the bathroom. She shook her head as if to break the moment. As she entered the bathroom her arm slowly lowered until the phone fell down onto the tiles.

Max only heard the soft bump of the phone, and not the bottle opening. Ella ingested twenty-three pills before she slumped back against the wall.

In the minutes before sedation arrived with strong arms, Ella wistfully mused that she was totally alone. Out of all the minutes that had built up to this moment, she hadn't managed to put anything in place, no safety net, no one to save her from the pain. This was the white light, the white out, the absence of anyone to hold you back, the white tiles of a bathroom floor. This moment was not poetic or spiritual, it was cold. As Ella lay down, she found herself in the way of the southerly wind as it cascaded down from the bathroom window.

'Not Lyla,' Ella whispered.

Twenty minutes later, the downstairs side door slid open, and the Juggler called out.

'Ella? Ella, where are you, babe?' He bounded up the stairs and saw the opened bathroom door.

'Ella? Fuck, Ella, what have you done? Why would you do this?' The Juggler looked in disbelief at the little white plastic bottle and the line of saliva joining Ella's mouth to the bathroom floor. 'You are not fucking dying on me Ella. Ella? Wake up. You are not fucking dying with a big dirty hicky on your neck. Ella?'

The Juggler pulled out his phone and called an ambulance. 'I've just arrived at my girl's house and found her on the bathroom floor. There's a bottle here. Yes, it looks like...alprazolam? Is that right? I didn't actually know she was on any. No, I can't see any other bottles. Yes, she has probably had a few drinks this time of night. No, I doubt she's had any other drugs, what? Like cocaine? No, I don't think so, mate. Nah, definitely not methadone. Looks like just these pills and probably a few drinks. She's glazed over, not really responding.'

In ten minutes, the ambos were at the house, injecting flumazenil into one of Ella's veins. It gave Ella a cold slap in the face and reversed her sleepiness. By midnight Ella was far from alone, with Jodie crying at her side and Pete, Bon, Gus and Sascha sharing a bag of salt and vinegar chips, sitting at the foot of her hospital bed. The Juggler had made a discreet exit when Jodie arrived.

JODIE

Back at the farm, Pete was stuffing the last items into his bag before shoving it in the back of his car to drive to the airport and catch the clouds away from us again.

'Did you need a new tube of toothpaste?' I asked, hovering.

Pete was crouched over his navy-blue duffle bag and didn't respond.

'Pete? Are you listening?'

'Yes, sorry, what was it?'

'Toothpaste? You had one that was running low last time you went back to work?'

'Yes, please. Could you get it? A new one?' I did a quick barefooted loop to the bathroom cupboard and back, dropping the unopened rectangular box into Pete's bag, and then flopped onto our bed, watching.

'Jodie…'

'Yes, Pete?'

'Promise me you won't get too sucked in by Ella and what she's going through?' Pete looked up, looking as if his mind was actually half in the car, the airport, or the campsite.

'Sucked in?'

'I'm not criticising you, I'm not saying you would be easily…anyway, I just think that you have enough on your plate while I'm away.' Pete zipped his bag, left to right.

'That is a bit harsh isn't it, making out like Ella is a drama queen or something?'

'Well, she is hard work sometimes, isn't she?'

'Hard work?' I echoed the words that punched.

'Unstable? Less than happy…unhinged? A bit off the chain?'

'Off the chain? That doesn't sound nice.'

'So I'm not allowed to comment after your sister tries to kill herself?'

'Not if it's going to be slanderous.' Tears welled in my eyes.

'I just think maybe you survived your childhood better than she did. Maybe it will take a few generations—'

'For what? What are you hoping will happen in a few generations?'

'Not you, you're fine. I just think Ella didn't come out of it all so well.'

'It was Max's fault. Ella would be fine if Max hadn't followed his dick. Max is the bad seed. It's all Max's fault,' I stood up from the bed, arms folded over my t-shirt.

'You think it's a normal reaction, to swallow – however many pills?'

I wasn't prepared to answer.

'Have you said goodbye to the kids? Isn't it time for you to leave?' My eyes darted around the room, making sure there was nothing that would delay him.

'Yes, I was meant to leave ten minutes ago…see you next time.' Without a kiss, Pete shook his head, picked up his blue bag and strode towards the door.

When I heard the country rumble of Pete's engine, I ran towards the door.

'Pete, wait!' I jumped over a bike standing up with training wheels, an old tennis racquet and Sascha, tummy down, watching ants on the pavers. 'Pete, don't go!' Pete stopped reversing the car and depressed the window control to remove the glass between us. 'Don't you remember that May used to say to sort fights out? Pluck the splinters out from the wound as soon as you can? Were you really going to drive away and let the Southern Cross set on our argument?'

Pete smiled his big, white-toothed smile. 'Jodes, whether you're here on the farm or at your new dream home, the Southern Cross never sets.'

'What?' I leant in close and placed both sets of fingers over the window slit.

'It is circumpolar. It will never set in-'

'Circumwhat?'

'Circumpolar, if you look out your window, the Southern Cross never sets below the horizon, but it does make a circle in the sky…like a ferris wheel…' I must have looked blank, as Pete continued, 'Imagine Bon and Gus holding sparklers, in the dark, dressing gowns tied tight around their middle, making an arc, a circle with the sparkler as it burns, that is what the Southern Cross does in our skies; it tips and traces a big wide circle in our sky.'

'I don't get it, but you probably really do have to go…'

'Ok, so you get that we are south side of the planet, below the equator?'

'Yes…'

'So you know where the South Pole is?' Pete's tone was part genuine, part really fucking enjoying giving me this tutorial.

'Yes…'

'There is a South Celestial Pole as well…'

'Whoaa, hold up Stephen Hawking…' A fly was buzzing around my right eyelashes and I could hear the boys bumping things loudly in the living room.

'Imagine there is a big bubble around us that contains the stars we see…'

'Hmm…Pete, you are going to miss your plane…'

'Well, the Southern Cross circles the South Celestial Pole-'

'Ok, I'll take your word for it…' I motioned my index finger in a circumpolar gesture for Pete to wrap up this astronomy lesson.

'Jodes, I'll take you out one night and we'll take our camp chairs, a couple of blankets – better out here than in town – to see the stars.'

'And have a couple of wines?'

'And I'll point out the constellations I know.' Pete looked deep into my eyes. 'Have we made up?'

'As long as you say you adore my sister.' I leant in so our noses were only ten centimetres apart.

'Yes, deal. I adore your sister. Promise me you won't get lost in her chaos. Now, kiss me before I start talking about the Carina Constellation.'

I hadn't told Pete that I had worried non-stop over the three days since Ella tried to kill herself. Despite feeling exhausted, I had not been able to sleep at all. Pete had been close to the truth; I was twisting inside with anxiety about Ella, queasy from the hospital kiosk food, and tension over wanting to be there for Ella but having my own responsibilities. 'Stay with me,' Ella had pleaded the day before. Holding her hand, I explained that I had to take my kids home. Ella had pulled her hand away from mine. 'Can't Pete take them home? I need you.' It didn't matter that Pete was about to leave for another two weeks away. Ella did not care about my wish to spend the last night with him. 'I thought I was your everything?' Ella asked, cheeks wet with nonstop tears, her body and mind recovering from the overdose. 'You have grown up so beautifully,' I said to her. 'A credit to yourself, you are always in my heart.' I gathered my boys and my girl and walked them out of the fluorescence of their auntie's self-harm and into their car seats, where even Bon had placed a soft toy for the long ride home.

LYLA

Being in hospital reminded Lyla of her mum's last stand with cancer. There were smells, hitting like cruel hallucinations. During the day there was a buzz in the wards but as the evening set in, the smells were more frequent than sounds. Lyla lay, eyes closed, totally awake.

'How are you going, love? You ok?' A nurse rostered for the night came and stood by Lyla's bed and tucked the thick hospital sheet covering her under the side of the mattress.

'I don't know...can't sleep...I thought that with all the meds I'm on, something would have knocked me out.'

'You want something to read? The nurses have some magazines at our station – are you up to reading yet?' The nurse looked at Lyla with compassion.

Lyla wondered what the nurses thought of her; victim of an assault, a strip club employee. 'Yeah, I think I could read a bit, I'll give it a try.'

The nurse came back with two magazines and a newspaper from the UK that Lizzie, one of the nurses from Leeds, bought each week for her Sunday shift. Lyla thanked the nurse and selected the newspaper.

'I'll come back and check on you in half an hour. You can tell me about the page three girl,' the nurse said cheekily. 'I'm not sure why Lizzie doesn't just look at the UK news online – said she likes the feel of the paper, it smells different to newspapers here, she reckons. Sounds like she should just go home, if she's that homesick. Are you comfortable, love?'

'Thank you, yes.' The nurse left Lyla to the dark oil slick of her insomnia.

The front page ran two main stories: fear mongering about the financial viability of the European Union, and a national swimming legend who had just been found guilty of paedophilia. Lyla skipped pages two and three and paused on page four, where one headline read, 'Complaints as another stowaway falls from space', Lyla's eyes were stinging but she persevered to read about an unidentified twenty-five-year-old man who had fallen on to the rooftop of a commercial building from the wheel well of an airplane as he attempted to make it to Heathrow Airport. It was reported that he would have fallen, frozen, after hours at minus sixty degrees celsius. Lyla held her zygomatic bone gently with her right hand as she read on. The article focused on the frustration of some constituents of West London who were losing patience with people falling from the icy undercarriages of planes on to their pavements and rooftops. One grumpy resident, referred to as Russell, had previously been greatly inconvenienced by an unidentified man who had fallen, almost vertically they guessed, onto the hood of his car.

'Shit.' Lyla laid the paper down on her lap and rested her head back, eyes closed. At 18 000 feet he would have experienced light-headedness. At 22 000 feet, Lyla hoped, he would have lost consciousness. Sooner or later his body temperature would have dropped dangerously; a premonition of his fall. Lyla wondered how she was going to crawl out of the undercarriage she had designed. She pictured on the back of her swollen eyelids an image of the frozen man in the wheel well. 'Apparently he was travelling without a ticket,' the newspaper had observed, without a shade of grace. Lyla knew she had been a stowaway in Ella and Max's marriage; a parasite under their matrimonial skin. She had been frozen in the wheel well of Salacious, riding without a ticket, losing blood flow to her extremities. And she had smuggled herself into the flight path of the fists meant for Cherry alone. It was time, Lyla realised, to choose strategies less bound for complete disaster.

ELLA

Ella lay back on the crisp white linen pillow case and held her phone up with one hand above her face. Pouting her lips a little, she took two shots, one landscape and one portrait. She checked whether she had a flattering shot, which she did, especially with the contrast of the nurse's call button adjacent to her head, her slightly haunted eyes and her white, over-laundered gown. The filter she chose thrust her eyes into the forefront and smudged the hospital bed behind. After uploading the shot she pressed the home link so she could see what her friends on Instagram were doing. Ella had never fooled herself that she was following 1020 friends; probably only twenty-three were friends, but often the photos of the ones she'd never met hooked her in more than those whose lives had actually touched hers.

As Ella lay back, she found comfort in the photos of a thirty-one-year-old who was travelling from Brisbane to the Kimberley, around the bottom, in a 1957 Skyline Junior Bondwood vintage caravan. Ella smiled as she looked at a photo of a white horse eating a carrot out of the hand of the woman, who glamorously stood beside the whipped-cream-white door of the caravan. She scanned through shots of healthy, long-haired women on the crests of Byron Bay waves, toes curled around the front of slide boards. She gazed at a photo of a young mum riding with her baby in a sling on a motorbike along a Balinese road with rice terraces stepping down on either side of her. Ella gazed with increasing craving at shots of women with big sunglasses and skinny legs pouting crazily with red lips as they celebrated a big night out with their yoga wives.

As she scrolled down the feed of twenty-four hours in the filtered lives of her abundant Instagram friends, she started to feel a sickness creep into her stomach through the images flicking in front of her #nofilterneeded green eyes. She flopped her phone arm down next to her body and stared up at the boring hospital ceiling. Tears obscured the room as Ella recalled

Max's words: that he had walked out on their marriage for Lyla. She knew that she herself had ducked out of the marriage for short periods, but those sojourns outside vows were more like weekend getaways, never with any plans of total defection.

'What now?' Ella whispered the question to herself. 'What now?' Ella could feel herself disconnecting; from Max, from their house, from Geraldton, her meagrely paid retail job, her allegiance to the Fremantle Dockers Football team, the rough allure of being a sandgroper. As the images of her life in the Midwest pixelated out of focus, Ella started to drift into other imaginings; of retail in Bondi, lattes and yoga, raw gluten-free chocolate cakes.

'Why would I stay?' Ella asked herself. 'The Juggler? I could never rely on him. Jodie? She's the only thing for me here...Jodie and the kids.' Ella heard a soft knock at the door and Axl was standing there with a bunch of green and red kangaroo paws.

'Jugs told me – I hope you don't mind.' Axl stepped inside the room.

'How embarrassing – I feel like an idiot.'

'I've tried before, ended up in hospital too. My ex, she wouldn't let me see Zack because of my drinking, before I started working away. I didn't know how to handle it.'

'Oh,' Ella sat up straight. She had never really spent time with Axl alone, without punters, skimpies, the Juggler or Jimmy bouncing around. Just them.

'Is it ok if I sit down?' Axl gestured towards the vinyl chair to her left.

'Please.' Ella motioned for him to sit at the tucked in end of her hospital bed.

'Need a hug?' Axl said cringing a little at the words as they came out. Ella nodded. When his arms wrapped around her she held on tight.

'It's going to be ok, everything is going to be ok.' Axl spoke into her scalp, words travelling into her history and her future. He spoke in a voice she had always craved to hear, from an unknown father, from a kind stranger at Flinders Street Station, from Max, and from the Juggler. A voice that let her unwrap, be flawed. When Axl stood to leave, Ella did not need to say a word. She felt barrelled. Full.

JODIE

The weekend after Pete flew out I started packing up things from the farm to take to the shack. I didn't want to empty the farm house, knowing we would always move in between the coast and the paddocks, but I wanted to skim half of our clothes, books and toys. Take them with me. I knew I was taking the best bits: my favourite clothes, Pete's swiss army knife, the few photo albums I had created before having children.

I started rummaging around quietly for the kids' commemorative birth certificates, which I knew were deep in a heavy chest of drawers in Sascha's room. I was trying to be quiet as Sascha was having her morning sleep, when I heard the dusty grumble of a car accelerating up the driveway. The boys raced outside into the Saturday morning, the aluminium door slamming unmuffled into the steel door frame. I looked over to Sascha who lay, two arms outstretched above her head, unfazed. My heart raced when I saw it was Jenna's car. I had assumed that she had struck me off as incompatible after her previous visit for morning tea. I ran to the bathroom and looked in the mirror. All I saw through sleep-deprived eyes was a high level of dishevelment: an under-showered, bewildered woman. Jenna knocked on the door with a firm fist. I quickly brushed my hair and completed one circulation of my toothbrush around my mouth. I answered the door to Jenna's smile, a lasagne, a muffin tray with something other than muffins on board and a freshly baked chocolate cake.

'Jenna? Hi, how are you?'

'Oh Jodie, I heard the news. The CWA ladies and I just wanted to show our support.' Jenna's shoulders were rounded down by the wheat-based weight of her kind offerings.

'Heard the news?' I was unable to think of any other lasagne-worthy incident besides Ella's attempt to medicate herself away.

'Sorry, Jodie, we heard about your sister.' The edges of Jenna's eyes looked like they had been touched by precious, perpetually light Yuna rainfall.

'Wow, yes, it was just a few nights ago…I didn't think anyone would—'

'I hope you don't mind, Kristy's mum works at the kiosk at the Regional Hospital and she tends to see all the comings and goings. She likes to know that people are linked in to all the support they can get.'

'And a lasagne? You must have started making that as soon as you heard.'

'Yes, I did. I wasn't sure what else to do and I know a lasagne is always useful, especially with the little ones. Kitty made the bread lilies.'

'Bread lilies? What are they?' Jodie squinted at the tray, which appeared to hold meat in a ball in the centre of a piece of white bread, which was gathered together to loosely resemble the petals of a lily. No stamen.

'We thought the kids would like them – basically it is just a meatball in bread that has been puckered in to resemble a lily.'

'Oh, Jenna, I don't know what to say.'

'We just wanted to do something. How is your sister, Jodie?'

'Would you like to come in, Jenna?'

'If that is all right with you, Jodie. I didn't mean to arrive unannounced; I tried your phone.'

I took the lasagne out of Jenna's hand and led her into the farm house. 'Sorry, I didn't hear it. I might have forgotten to take it off silent, I always mute it overnight. Sascha is…' I placed my index finger on my lips and motioned towards Sascha's semi-closed door. I led Jenna into the kitchen, which looked decent, as I had extracted half its contents and placed them in a tower of banana boxes in the hallway beyond. I placed the lasagne on the bench and flipped the switch on the kettle. Jenna carefully lowered the bread lilies and chocolate cake on to the kitchen table and stood, both wrists covered with wooden bangles, fingers holding on to the back of a chair. Her jeans had neat little rips and her white t-shirt with lace neck trim was tucked into her brown braided buckle belt. She looked softer than last time, like the history of country music had moved through her since I'd last made her a morning cup of tea.

I cleared my throat and brushed the back of my head with my hand. 'I think she's going to be fine. I think she's glad that she was found…that she didn't succeed…'

'Oh Jodie, it's terrible, did you see any signs beforehand? Was she struggling?'

'I don't think she'd mind you knowing that her husband had just broken up with her. She literally dropped the phone and swallowed some pills. I don't think she saw it coming. I don't think anyone could see that kind of thing coming or they'd surely have time to prepare, somehow.'

'Like the warning we get from emergency services when a fire is approaching?'

'Exactly. I don't think she had the heads up, so it just wrecked her when he said he didn't want to be with her.'

'You know my brother did it.'

'Broke up with his wife?'

'No, killed himself.'

'Really?' I passed Jenna her cup of tea. 'I'm sorry, I didn't know.'

'He was only nineteen. He knew about guns, had been shooting since he was five. Mum still says it was an accident. Dad and I know it wasn't. He had a big fight with Dad two days earlier. They hadn't said a word to each other and then Hugh was dead.'

'Oh Jenna, I'm so sorry. How old were you?'

'Five years younger; I'd just turned fourteen.' Jenna quickly wiped away a few tears. 'Jodie, I am sorry, I didn't mean to come here and talk about Hugh. You don't want to—'

'Jenna, it's fine. My little sister...the doctor told us that it is really difficult to die from an overdose of the pills she took unless you are mixing up different drugs. Luckily for us, she didn't know exactly what she was doing.'

'The CWA ladies said if it was needed, they would rally around and make sure someone was with your sister for the next few weeks.'

A mouthful of hot tea sipped down my trachea and I choked involuntarily. I looked over at Jenna and she looked small behind the double-layer chocolate cake baked by the CWA President Mrs Joyce Knightly. 'You mean like a suicide watch? The CWA ladies would do that? For Ella?'

'Well, yes, for Ella...and you...not watching you, I mean watching Ella for you, if Ella was happy for the company.'

I smiled with genuine amazement that out of the busy dry days these ladies managed with art and graciousness, they would find the time and heart for my broken sister and be willing to make sure she had a net, lest she fall again. Of course, I knew being babysat by the CWA would push Ella closer to desperation, so I looked at Jenna with true tenderness and said, 'The offer is so gorgeous. Thank you so much – will you tell the ladies? But I think she's going to be fine.'

ELLA

Ella had been home from the hospital for one day and was cleaning up her kitchen when the Juggler telephoned.

'Hi, baby.'

'Jugs, when are you home?'

'Well, it has taken me approximately twenty hours to arrive here from the Grantown so I guess once I pack up my bags I could be home in about twenty-one hours?'

'Don't tease me.'

'Axl, Eggs and I took turns driving and sleeping throughout the night; it was bearable. We arrived at Perth airport at 5:00 a.m. It wasn't like one of our typical road trips to Kalbarri or Lucky Bay; no beautiful ladies and no piss. A few smoko breaks but that was all. Bet you're glad to be out of hospital.'

'Yes, I feel much better. Hey, thanks...I probably owe you this cheap life of mine.'

'You're ok, gave me a shock that's for fucking sure. I always expect to walk in on you spread-eagled, but not like that.'

'What's it like up there? If you see Max, smash him for me.'

'If I find him I'll throttle him in his sleep. Don't you worry about that low-life. It feels like I've worked away for years already. I guess hanging out with Axl and the other blokes at the Grantown...for all the shit I've heard the other blokes talk around the table...I already knew the names of heaps of their workmates. Especially the slack ones. I'd heard those guys whinge about the heat, the long hours, the dust, heard them talk up the food, so it all seems familiar.'

'Strange to be wearing a uniform other than board shorts?'

'Yeah, that is probably the strangest thing. I guess the work itself will be very different from working on deck. For one thing, there will be no more pissing over the rails.'

'Strange things happen at the mines.'

'I'll ring and let you know. The airport was chock-full of men in yellow and blue shirts standing looking half-asleep. The biggest beards you've ever seen. Groups of men at the café buying big double-shot coffees. Bored. Already in work mode.'

'Max used to tell me about the beards.'

'The hostess blushed slightly when she saw me board – took one look and confirmed with the other hostesses that I was BOB: best on board.'

'I have no doubt, Juggler, no doubt.'

'You'll be right, Missy, especially when I get home and lick up your tears.'

'Bye.'

'Bye...'

JODIE

I ran my fingers over my beautiful new repurposed, distressed wood dining table (seven nights of sanding an old shed door, which had fallen out of the trailer whilst we were transporting it between Yuna and Geraldton). Sascha knelt on one of the classic retro chairs I had picked up at an antique show in Greenough; the boys had only agreed to attend when I threatened to put a price sticker on them and sell them as cheap grandsons to the old timers making their way into the event. The chairs had old sailing ships etched in glass in panels at the back and after the lime wash treatment they looked fit for a shack three hundred metres from the ocean. Sascha and I were eating three crackers each, a slice of cheese and a chunk of cucumber, a banquet that would not have sufficed if Pete was home. He liked cooked lunches or at least a dish that was sophisticated in some manner. Something a bit exotic. Mango chicken or Thai beef salad, not trio of crackers. One cracker in, I heard my phone ringing in the bedroom.

'Hi, babe.' Pete sent the words gently into the phone.

'Hiya Pete, what's happening?' The mid-shift phone call had me on high alert.

'The bosses called a meeting today. Due to the "falling price of iron ore" the mine is shutting.' Pete waited for my response.

'What?' My eyes covered over with a gauze of confusion. The farm? The shack? 'How soon?'

'They are calling for immediate voluntary redundancies and then they will slash with forced redundancies as they wind down the mine.'

'Will people be offered jobs elsewhere?'

'They said there will be no redeployments.'

'Wow, I'm shocked. We knew it was on the cards but I thought they'd reduce the operation rather than close it...'

'There has been chaos in the wet mess. Lots of young families will be stuffed.'

'Like us?'

'A geologist in his fifties was panicking about supporting his wife who has breast cancer.'

'Oh Pete, that's—'

'Some guys said that their wives would have to go to work until they could line up another job. Everyone knew it was a possibility but most were shocked that it's happened so soon.'

'Would we cope if you took a voluntary package, Pete?' I walked back out to the living area where Sascha was kneading cucumber into the table top.

'We'll have to sit down when I'm home next, look at all the figures and work out whether it's the right time to start back on the farm.'

'We could juggle the kids between us and I could get some work in town.'

'Yes, we might have to. We'll have to work out whether we can put a crop in, talk to the bank.'

'It must feel like the rug's been pulled out from under you.'

'For sure. It would have been great to have another couple of years of steady income. Now I don't know exactly what we'll do.'

'How much is the redundancy package if you accept it? Would it help get a crop in?'

'Not really but it might be doable. I'll look around to see if anyone is even hiring. If no one is, then we'll have to seek other options.'

'I wish I was there with you.'

'Jodes, trust me, you would not want to be here, there's a black feeling in the air.'

'You're ok though?'

'I promise I would never do anything stupid. I don't want my children growing up on rice bubbles for dinner.'

'Hey, we had eggs on toast last night.'

'You're a good mum, I'm just trying to rev you up. I'll be fine. I think we have options.'

'Become bohemians? You could grow a long beard and I'll smoke skinny cigars and we can hide from society in our shack. The pigs and crows will take over the farm; we can let them have their reign while we make sand sculptures and sew our own kaftans.'

'Sounds like a five-year plan!'
'Do you have to go back to work?'
'Yes, the bus is coming soon.'
'Talk to you later?'
'Yep, talk to you later.'

I pressed the 'end call' button and sat down, feeling shipwrecked. I looked down to the ground and breathed a deep breath. There was an uncomfortable feeling in my belly. A metallic taste in my mouth. What was it? If Pete came home, I would be ecstatic, wouldn't I? Wouldn't things finally be able to slip into a lovely, predictable, continuous routine? Conversations, fights, kisses could run their course without the quick clapping hands of the roster, rushing, running riot over our rhythms. Breaking the flow. So why was there a sick feeling in my gut? What did I gain with him gone? Crackers? Spread eagling the bed when he was away? No more nightmares? An ability to unilaterally direct time? A closing down of the boundaries of my body with no one else inside for the swing away? Domination of the remote control? No one observing my body, my moods, how I filled my time? A release from the standards of cleanliness? Snippets of solitude? Being off duty from love?

I would leave the decision to Pete: to take the voluntary redundancy or stay and take the chance that he'd get a bit more time on site as the operation dwindled down to an empty mass of displaced infrastructure in a barren place.

LYLA

Lyla was sitting in her courtyard watching barely existent clouds, wisps of white on their way somewhere better, when Mr Bang Bang started barking at the door with excitement. Max had been gone for two weeks, ringing more than usual, checking she was managing to eat, take fluids, and avoid falling face-first into the horror of it all. The earth seemed to have slowed down its rotation in the courtyard as Lyla contemplated her assaulted future. She heard the door lock click and raised her head to see Max letting himself in. He dropped a branded bag at her doorway and took his boots and thick socks off. Pushing them against the wall, he hesitantly walked towards the courtyard, teeth clenched, mouth in a frown, scratching his coarse blond hair, reluctant to look at her bruises. Max sat on the ground next to her cheap banana lounge. She turned her head and smiled at him.

'I told Barb I wasn't going back to Salacious. I was just lying here thinking I would go to some auditions, get back into some acting work.'

'For road accident ads?' Max suggested. He had not yet transitioned back from the onsite banter. Lyla held her cheek, trying not to smile.

'You're a prick, Max Bennett.'

'I know.'

'How was the flight?'

'Fine.'

'Reckon we should go somewhere new? Surely we could work out a way to purchase a little apartment in Buenos Aires? We could tango and let that sexy city creep under our skin?'

'Naaah.'

'What do you think, then?'

'Lyla, I want us to live here. We don't have to hide anymore. We can let the sexy city of Perth creep under our skin.'

'I might already have a little asphalt from Northbridge under my skin – not so sexy though.'

'I just want to stay here, not go anywhere.'

'Yeah, me too.'

'I want to sit here until we remember all the stuff we planned when we were seventeen.' Max shifted his weight from one side to the other on the cement.

'With all those joints we smoked on top of the town lookout, I wouldn't have remembered the plans we made the day after we made them, let alone ten years later.'

'You wanted to be an actress, I wanted to get a motorbike and drive us both across the Nullarbor…start a family…'

'Leave the kids with my mum while we escape to Indo for a week?' Max nodded in the silence of impossible, mislaid plans.

'Mum's not here anymore, and please, no motorbikes in our lives for now.' Lyla's scalp still felt unnaturally tight and pressure pushed into the back of her eyes.

'Should we get some take-away instead? For now?' Max crossed his legs and took his phone out from his back pocket to scroll through all the options within a 10 km radius.

'Yeah, I think I'm just starting to get my appetite back.'

JODIE

It was a week after Ella's big swallowing that we got the news that Mum had died. Blood alcohol level of 0.24. I doubt it was just the alcohol because 0.24 would have been a normal weekday for Mum. The love I had for her was fictional; a bundle of coping mechanisms I had cobbled together. Usually I was releasing a rope in my mind, with her on one end and me on the other, increasing the distance, setting her out to sea. I have anger for all the times I had to tell Ella it was going to be ok when it clearly wasn't. My mother's crazy red words had made me want to run away; take Ella's hand and get on any bus that rumbled down the Northcote roads. I dreamed of us boarding a plane and flying to a little island village where we would be adopted by villagers who would make us work hard and fish for our dinner but never screech at us so loud we wanted to die because we didn't know where else to hide from the sound. I didn't have any friends because I was too ashamed to bring them home to a house that never provided afternoon tea. Back then life had been a battle, to not let her suffocate the small amounts of genuine happiness I had over anything: a new hat, a nice teacher, a cloudless day.

Ella and I met at a café down the west end of town and stared at each other blankly. I had left the kids with a school mum; I knew my parenting would not be spectacular today.

'Remember we used to pack a bag of clothes and go and sit at the corner of Separation Street and Victoria Road, near the petrol station, really believing that a guardian angel would come and pick us up and take us to her home?' Ella asked, starting to cry.

'She never came, did she?' My eyes were dry.

'Lucky we had the good sense to not get in the car with anyone who did offer us a lift home.' Ella had worn waterproof mascara since she first smothered her long lashes in black.

'Maybe that guardian angel was looking over us.'

'Nah, I don't think so.'

'Me neither.'

'I thought I'd stop hating her when she died. That I'd stop wanting to kill her. But I still feel it.' I looked at my beautiful little sister in front of me, the only person who knew what we'd been through. Ella's head was bowed and I remembered that same head when it was smaller, bowing in a corner of our mother's room, quietly sniffling as I got a bucket and an old towel from the laundry floor and started wiping up piles of vomit from the carpet. Our mother snoring, so I knew she was alive; no need to open the front door and nervously walk to the neighbours, up the concrete path, up three concrete steps to knock and ask for an ambulance to be called. I never understood why she wanted to kill herself rather than cook us dinner, read stories and hear about our day. Mum liked to drink. I know now it is a disease but it always felt like insanity. Glasses of insanity; my childhood washed down her selfish throat.

'At least she didn't follow us when we did leave her.'

'What mother doesn't check up on her kids when they are that young, Ella? You'll realise when you have kids.'

'Jodes, I do not need to pump out some kids to know what basic human needs are. I remember the night before we left, she was screaming right into my face and I could see two blackheads on her nose. The words were a loud blur but I looked at the skin craters filled with a dark plug. I remember swearing to myself that I would never ever have blackheads – or kids.' I looked across at Ella and the grief hit me. Not grief for my mother. Grief for the precious young girls we were, hoping the police would take us, not leave us with her again and again and again.

'We're ok now Ella, we made it. She can't hurt us anymore.'

'You can probably feel like you are ok but seven days ago, if you remember, I tried to top myself.'

'It's all going to be ok, I promise you Ella. We will get you some professional support, you know, to help if you are in that dark state again…'

'Well, hopefully I won't have another husband who cheats on me for a year with his childhood sweetheart. I'm not planning on being in that ole dark place again.'

'You know what I mean. Fuck, I think I need professional help too. I have just found out that the woman who brought me into the world has died and I don't care. I really don't care. Don't want to go anywhere near her, even dead.'

'Me neither.'

'I don't want to go to a funeral service, don't want to have to organise one, I don't want anything to do with it. I don't even want to tell Pete she's dead because he'll think I don't want to go away when he gets home next weekend and I do. I want to go away and not think about her blood alcohol content, brown paper bags, the torture of her. Screwed up or what?'

'Yep,' Ella said gratefully. 'That is screwed up. But I hear there's a hot psychologist in town. One of the anorexic girls at the shop told me about him. Said she starves herself for a few days before her appointment because she wants to look extra skinny.'

'Maybe we're not doing so badly after all!' I put my latte glass to my lips and tipped my head back to drain every last drop.

ELLA

Ella saw Max approaching through the skimpy happy hour crowd. He had asked to meet up for an hour to discuss the logistics of finalising their lost marriage and their financial relationship. He hadn't asked to stay with Ella in their house so she assumed he had organised some accommodation elsewhere. Ella was glad as he would only be close for an hour. She was not sure if he would make her feel homicidal or suicidal. Why Lyla? That was all she wanted to ask him. Early on in their relationship Max had talked about Lyla and their high school days with a fondness she immediately envied.

'If he tries to kiss me on the cheek, I think I'll vomit,' Ella said quietly to Jimmy.

'That would be a mongrel act, to try and kiss you. Want me to whack him if he tries?' Jimmy was hunched over his beer, facing the bar.

'Thanks Jimmy, I can handle it, I don't want you to risk knocking your beer over.' *Don't kiss me on the cheek, don't kiss me on the cheek*, Ella thought as Max approached.

He came up to the bar and stood in front of Ella. He moved closer and then pulled back. He must have seen her recoil.

'I'm so sorry, Ella,' Max looked right into her red face.

Ella shrugged. Jimmy leaned into her from behind, giving her some support.

'Can I get you a drink?' Max pulled out his black wallet.

'If you want to wear it.' Ella was putting her fighting gloves on.

'I'm really sorry, Ella. Not sure what I can do.'

Jimmy shook his head, picked up his drink and walked over to a table where a few blokes he knew from the Abrolhos were raving about the wind direction and where the crays were running.

'I'm going to buy you a white and if I wear it, I deserve it.'

'Ok, deal.' Ella wouldn't waste a white on a foe. Beer or bourbon of course, but not a semillon sauvignon blanc.

Ella looked at Max's shirt. Thankfully she hadn't bought it for him. It would have made it impossible for her to sit, skimpies swirling, marriage carnage scattered around him if he'd been wearing a shirt she'd picked. Max handed her a sweating glass of white wine and they sat awkwardly on their bar stools, facing out, as if they were on a first date and not at the end of the line.

'What are we going to do about the house, Max? Do you want to come and get your stuff?'

'Maybe next time I come up?'

'I'm pretty keen to move it along,' Ella said looking out at two blokes laughing so hard they were bent over.

'I've had some legal advice…'

'What? Fuck you.' Ella stood up and placed her glass on the bar behind her. Jimmy stood up at his table five metres away.

'Ella, I just want it to all be fair.'

'Fair?' Ella's eyes were swamped with tears. 'Fair? Fuck you and Lyla… fair? There's nothing fair about this situation.'

Max looked down. Ella looked over to Jimmy, saw his concern, paused, then motioned to him that she was ok.

'What did you want to talk about, Max?'

'Well, the house – what do you think we should do about it, then?'

'I'm not sure I'm ready to have this conversation. Is that what the lawyers advised? To kick me out of the house?'

Max shook his head.

'Why Lyla, Max? Why did it have to be Lyla?'

'It would never have been anyone else. I didn't go out looking for someone new.'

'I guess you didn't have to when she even came to our fucking wedding. Was she ever *not* in the picture? Did I ever stand a chance?'

'I loved you the moment I met you.'

'So you just loved her more?'

Max looked as though one of the Sandy Beach Hotel's antique fishing lures had fallen from overhead and lodged squarely in his throat. To his credit, he nodded.

A nod of the head can change a life. It can show agreement to try for a child, to accept a proposal, to show readiness for a coffin to be lowered.

On this occasion, Max's nod set Ella free. The mystery was solved and the foreman of the jury had delivered the verdict. Ella exhaled a breath that filled the Sandy Beach Hotel, swept up the old staircase and exited out unused balconies.

'I want to stay in the house.'

'You want to stay in Geraldton?'

'I want to be near Jodie and the kids.'

Max nodded again.

'Please tell me you and Lyla don't want to move up here?'

'No – I'm going to move down there.'

'I guess you've already moved down there. How long ago was it?' Ella remembered, but she just wanted to see his face when he said the words. 'Also, Mum passed away so there's no reason to return to Melbourne, not that she ever was one.'

'Your mum died? What? When? I'm sorry to hear that, Ella.'

'Yes it's been a massive couple of weeks…epic…' The sarcasm felt warm and delicious in Ella's stomach.

'Ella, I have no problem with you staying in the house. Of course, there's not a huge amount of equity in it but the repayments aren't ridiculous at the moment.' Ella's eye's widened to hear Max talk dollars and sense.

'I'm not going to fight you for the equity; I'll walk away, start again.' Max was trying to make some headway against wind levels that were dropping but still threatened an unseaworthy vessel.

'You make it sound like I've won the meat tray.'

Max closed his eyes. He had always found words difficult. It was hard to pick ones to put together that were not instantly smashed down. The words that randomly rolled out of his mouth were usually vulnerable to Ella's scorn.

'I'm so sorry, Ella, but I'm not sure this is getting us anywhere. Should I email you? Maybe it would be better to communicate that way?'

'No, don't go Max. Let's talk. I was seeing someone too. Just a fuck. Well, not really just a fuck – a funny, crazy, hilarious, heart-warming fuck. No one you know. I was doing it for the survival of our marriage though. I actually thought it was making things better between us. Anyhow, an even score?'

Max dropped his head on to the rim of his beer glass.

'What? You were seeing someone?'

'How do you think I coped with you absent for three-quarters of my life? He was soothing my loneliness.'

'Soothing? Is that what they call it these days? Fuck me, here I was feeling like the most evil person on the planet.'

'Max, I still think you are the most evil person, not for leaving me, not for having sex with another woman, but for marrying me as Plan B.' Ella flicked her hair over her right shoulder and looked calmly at Max. 'Maybe if I had really loved you I would have noticed you were missing in action.'

Locking eyes, they both saw tears and their joint future receding. It would have been nice, like a warm cup of tea. There would have been kids, a few car upgrades, camping holidays and supporting each other while time took toll on their joints. However, it just hadn't worked out that way.

LYLA

Mr Bang Bang was scuffling forward, tension on his lead, nose to the ground as if he were tracking rabbits on the wide, empty suburban streets of Forrestfield. Lyla pushed her oversized sunglasses up her nose but the humidity of the late afternoon made them slip downwards again straight away. Her bruises were hidden under thick concealer and the shades but she hoped she wouldn't be in eye contact with anyone other than Mr Bang Bang. Mr Bang Bang hadn't been out of the house much in the last month and was riding low on his four shortarse legs. As he pissed on nature-strip shrubs, Lyla looked at him and saw herself earlier that day attempting a yoga pose on all fours, hands shoulder-width, knees hip-width apart, lifting one knee directly to the side. The roads seemed too wide, as if Forrestfield had overcatered for a party. Lyla passed shops with 'for lease' signs in their windows, soliciting for someone, anyone.

The Forrestfield Police Station sat back from the street; more like a suburban house with solar panels, a brief grove of trees at the front and to the right of the car park. It looked quiet, orderly, grass mown millimetres from the brown. Lyla took a big breath and exhaled through pursed lips. Her sore eyes squinted as she thought about her previous statement to the police. It had all been accurate except for one omission: the comment the hooded psycho had directed at Cherry as he lunged towards her. The assault was a warning to York. Lyla hadn't intended *not* to say anything to the police at the hospital. She hadn't wanted to cover up *or* be a participant in any bigger pictures. It would have been easier if there was no pointed motive, if it had been a random, brutal act of violence, but she knew there was nothing accidental about the assault. She knew that Cherry would not have told the police that her partner was implicated in any way.

Mr Bang Bang yanked Lyla towards the bunch of gums to the right of the car park. The eucalypts were about fifteen years old, not new and fragile but not yet mature and established; still in the danger zone. After sniffing a silver-barked gum with a cock and balls knifed into the trunk, Mr Bang Bang left his own territorial mark. Lyla wondered briefly how he had any urine left in that small keg of a body, then turned her face back to the entrance of the police station.

'Come on, Mr Bang Bang.' Lyla pulled the lead and headed towards the police station, 'we'll just go and tell them what the bad man said, hey? Here, come on.' Lyla led him across the grass, holding her left jaw, which still didn't feel exactly right, even after surgery. Crossing the bitumen driveway to the right of the police station, Lyla felt her stomach contract. What would it mean for Cherry? How would it affect her if she waltzed in and sketched York Stanz into the picture? The police would ask Lyla what else she knew; why would the perpetrator want to target York Stanz's wife? What was York Stanz up to? Lyla pulled her phone out of her pocket and dialled Max. No answer. It felt like an hour until the dial tone handballed to message bank. She didn't leave a message.

Lyla stopped ten metres in front of the entrance. She stood, swallowing saliva. Mr Bang Bang sat down at her heel. Frozen by all the unknown consequences of her actions. She knew she did not want to protect the man who had smashed her jaw and she didn't want to protect York from the karma he was constantly trying to evade with yoga classes, cold-pressed juices and the protection of his chosen few. She did want to protect Cherry but did that mean taking action that would draw York into the spotlight? Twenty minutes must have passed as she stood there, thoughts flickering, Mr Bang Bang now lying flat on the road. Not a single car had turned into the car park. Night was falling slowly like a hit song down the charts. Knowing she'd censored her police statement, Lyla felt awkward and dirty. She took one step forward. Mr Bang Bang raised his head then lowered it, not needing to move. If she kept her mouth shut, was she enabling the same violence she had read about in the violence restraining order transcripts; that Jez had inflicted on Bambi after close at Salacious, the grievous bodily harm dealt to Cherry? Ten more minutes passed and Forrestfield's street lights were taking over from the sun. Lyla flinched as the thick glass door of the police station opened outwards.

'You ok there? Can I help you with something?' A policeman with an Irish accent stood in the doorway, holding the door ajar.

'No, I'm fine, thanks. I was just—'

'Would you like to come in and have a chat?'

'No, no, I'm good, thanks, I was just…looking for some water for my dog.'

'We just noticed you on the camera. We thought you might want to…sure you're feeling ok? Would you like me to get you some water?'

'Yes, I mean, no, thank you…no water but I'm fine.' Lyla pulled on Mr Bang Bang's lead. 'Come on Mr, let's go home.'

The constable retreated inside and closed the door, accustomed to human beings who didn't make sense.

JODIE

I sat outside one of Geraldton's main pubs on Marine Terrace at a little round table on the street. The street lights looked blurry; just big balls of yellow shine, bigger than the smaller, whiter balls of light that spread out from this centre of the universe up to Kalbarri and down to Dongara. The school mums were all looking glamorous; unleashed for the night and spraying out all the grown-up words they swallowed in front of their kids. I had blow-dried my hair and my lips were Red Wiggle scarlet. One mum called Kate came out to check I was ok. I told her I was just getting some fresh air; I struggled to concentrate on whatever else she was saying. She turned on her high heels and went back to the bar, leaving me to sit with my mother's foe: alcohol. I had gulped wine after wine, probably an inflated, hotel-priced bottleful by now. My hands felt a long way down as I opened the clutch Ella had given me for Christmas in a last-bid attempt to stop me from being so unfashionable. I pulled out my phone to call Pete.

'Jodes?'

'Yes baby, it is me, *Jodee.*'

'Wow, you sound shitfaced.'

'Could be…'

'Did you end up leaving the kids with my dad?'

'Yes, I wasn't sure if my beautiful little sister could hack three extra lives on top of her own at the moment, to you know, keep alive.'

'Where are you now? Sounds like you've had a good night.'

'Never heard the word "cunt" so many times.'

'What?'

'These school mums are good fun. What are you doing?'

'Damn! Not mine…not mine…nope…shit! I'm trying to find my clothes.'

'Have you been drinking too?'

'I cannot blame two mid-strengths for this. I'm running around twenty-odd laundry blocks, trying to find my orange and blue high-vis shirts and three pairs of work socks and Jodie, every single block has about fifty washing machines and guess what is in every one?'

'I can guess, babe – orange and blue high-vis shirts and three pairs of work socks? Aren't the laundry blocks labelled? I remember seeing them.'

'Yes, it's not the system that's flawed. I was probably thinking about you and the kids.'

'Yes, let's blame the kids.' Jodie drained her glass. 'I miss you.'

'Me too. Are you going to go dancing tonight?'

'I might not be allowed to go home until Monday; there's a bit of peer group pressure to party going on already.'

'Ok, I better keep going, there will be a stopped machine somewhere with my gear in it.'

'Good luck with that. Night babe.'

'Good night Jodes.'

ELLA

Ella was rushing out her front door to open Whipits when her phone rang.

'Is this Ella Bennett's phone?'

'Yes it is, I'm just rushing to work though, so if this is a telemarketing call…'

'I really need to speak to you, Ella.'

'Ok, can you hold on a minute?' Ella turned the key of her front door with two hands as she held her phone with her chin to her shoulder. 'This sounds important. Who is this?'

'Ella, my name is Constable Jennifer Cotts; I work for the WA Police Coronial Investigation Unit. I have to inform you that Miles has been involved in a workplace accident at the Pilbara Birdfellow Site this morning.'

'Jugs? Involved? What? Tell me.' Ella looked up at the glaring morning light.

'I'm sorry Ella, Miles has been involved in an accident.' Ella's head bowed, brown hair falling out of place.

'Is he ok? Please tell me he's ok.' Ella fell to one knee, then hunched over on the grass.

'Ella, I'm really sorry. He was airlifted out of the site but was pronounced deceased upon arrival in Perth.'

'That's not possible…'

'We're not exactly sure what happened yet, Ella. There will be an investigation.'

'You must have some information.'

'Preliminary investigations suggest that he may have been involved in an accident with a loader.'

'Was he driving a loader?'

'It appears he may have been pinned in between the pit wall and a loader.'

'But he only just left, he only just started...'

'This must all be a terrible shock. Do you have family you can contact for support?'

'Yes, Max, I mean, no... Yes, I have a sister. How did you get my number? From his phone?'

'Miles put you down as an emergency contact...apparently he nominated you on induction papers as his senior next of kin.'

'Senior next of kin?' Ella turned this title over in her mind like a three-dimensional shape.

'I need you to have a think about whether details can be released to the media or whether you would like twenty-four hours to let family members know.'

'I have no idea about his family...how to find them. What should I do? Yes, definitely twenty-four hours.'

'Does Miles have a relative or close friend that might be available to travel to Perth to identify his body?'

'Yes, I mean, should I do it?'

'That's up to you, Ella; you may find it very distressing. Is there someone else you had in mind? Sometimes partners feel that they have to be the one.'

'We weren't partners.'

'Sorry.'

'Well, his best friend, I know where he is; he's probably still out at Birdfellow.'

After Constable Jennifer Cotts hung up, Ella sat down on the grass and looked blankly at her phone. She shook her head in disbelief. Ants started crawling over her sandalled feet and up her calves. She replayed the last conversation she'd had with the Juggler, over and over, looking for a sign that she should have picked up on. Some intuition. She cursed herself that she hadn't been on the lookout for misfortune happening in threes.

LYLA

Lyla sat across the table from Cherry. Wall-to-wall blue epoxy resin flooring underfoot led to windows that magnified the expanse of Indian Ocean beyond. Shorty and Snoop lay protectively close to Cherry, jowls as foamy as the white wash below. Lyla had purchased two take-away coffees en route to Cherry's Scarborough apartment, which sat on the shiny white surface between them.

'I can't say it's nice to see you,' Cherry said after one barely warm sip.

'Do you want me to go? I wasn't sure…when you said it was ok to come…'

'Lyla, it's nice to hear you. I just can't fucking see you.'

'Oh shit, yeah, sorry, fuck, I wasn't thinking.' Lyla winced as she shook her head from side to side.

'Best fucking view this edge of the continent and all I can see is black.'

'Well, you're not missing anything with me in front of you: fifty shades of yellowy green still.'

'York is giving me a daily update on my colour scheme too. Royal purple at seven o'clock this morning, apparently.'

'Yes, I think you might have a bit of Shiraz there.'

'Lyla, don't tease, I would die for a Shiraz right now.'

'At 10:00 a.m.?'

'Yeah, that's my favourite time for drinking and I wouldn't even have to draw the blinds anymore.' Cherry's laugh turned quickly into an inhalation of grief before she was heaving with deep despair.

'Oh Cherry.' Lyla's hot tears, lying in wait since Cherry opened the apartment door, obscured her vision and fell towards the epoxy floor. Snoop and Shorty stood up with some level of difficulty on the resin and licked Cherry's face. Lyla sat, hands only unclasping to pull another tissue out of her bag, until Cherry's breathing had returned to a chain smoker's norm.

'Cherry, do you remember what happened?'

'I remember the guy's face, when he first approached us.'

'Do you know who he is?'

'The police asked me to watch some CCTV footage.'

'And?'

'Not so easy with no eyesight.'

'They can't save your sight? I thought they might be able...'

'No.' Cherry's face turned up towards the roof. 'The surgery didn't help. York says-'

'What does York say about the attack? Remember the guy said—'

'I don't remember what he said.'

'I remember he yelled at you that your boyfriend had "fucked up" this time.'

'I don't remember that.'

'C'mon Cherry, don't bullshit me...'

'Don't bullshit you? Lyla, you have bullshitted me since your first day at Salacious. The nurses told me you had your boyfriend there at the hospital. They thought he was cute. Told them he'd been in love with you since puberty. Are you married?' Cherry pushed her chair out from the table and walked towards the window, using her two hands to guide her.

'Well, he's married, I'm not. What about you? Crystal meth? York is obviously not a street dealer, looking around this apartment.' Lyla raised her voice to reach Cherry.

'I told you about his big money. I never lied. What? You thought he made it coding? That he created an app? Saying he was in Northbridge when he was really in Silicon Valley? I never lied to you. Anyway, so what? We don't know each other, we just shared a few cigarettes.' Cherry faced the ocean and adjusted the bandages covering her eyes.

Lyla's shoulders hunched. She could not think clearly.

'Cherry, I wasn't expecting to make any friends at Salacious.'

'And who did you make friends with, Lyla? It seems it wasn't me. What do you mean, he's married and you aren't? You're having an affair with him? For fuck's sake.'

'He works away. Spends one week a month with me. Not really what I would have called my partner.' Lyla drank the remnants of her coffee in one bleak gulp.

'So you just hang around waiting for him? Work at Salacious to fill in time?' Cherry's words were patronising.

Lyla was weighing up whether she should let Cherry hate her for observing her without consent or scoff at her for thinking she was a kept woman.

'Lyla? I never could understand why you were there.'

'Well, I might as well tell you.'

'Tell me what? What are you talking about?' Cherry spread her fingers on each hand out on the cool glass wall in front of her.

'I was commissioned to gain some insight into bikie women and why they put up with violence.'

'Lyla, you are kidding me, aren't you? Tell me you're fucking pulling my leg…commissioned by who? Who wants to know?'

Lyla looked down in violet shame. Cherry soundlessly smashed her fists against the window and screamed, mouth open wide, close to the glass.

'I told you about my son, Lyla. You did not deserve to know about my son.'

'Cherry…' Lyla stood up and moved hesitantly towards Cherry's anger.

'What, are you going to report this too? Let me get you a pad of paper and you can take some notes. I'm going to ring York, he's going to kill you. He's going to want to kill you. Do you understand that? This is not playtime, Lyla. Not standing in the wings waiting for your man to swing in and fuck you for a week and go back to his wife. Do you live in a fucking fantasy land? York is going to kill you.'

'Cherry, I haven't written anything up. I won't…none of it means anything now…it was just for a screenplay. It doesn't even matter.' Lyla stood facing Cherry, arms by her sides, palms forward.

'Why are you still here?' Cherry, composed, turned away from the Indian Ocean's blue, never-ending promise.

'Because I love you…in a real, *you're one of the only people who knows me, even if you don't know me* way.'

'That's true; I don't know you Lyla, not at all.'

'When my mum died I realised she was the only woman I have ever known, that has ever known me. Through all the years there are only just fragments of people, bits I took and made something more in my mind. I don't have any other women in my life who are real.' Lyla lowered herself down on the ground with tears that stung her grazed cheeks.

'Lyla, you've done it again; you don't love me.' Cherry guided herself to the ground and leant back on the glass.

'When that guy lunged at you, I wanted to get in between—'

'It's natural to want to stop someone being attacked, no prizes for that.'

'Cherry, it's fine if you don't feel the same way, I do really care for you…despite…despite everything. I want you in my life.'

'York is going to kill you,' Cherry said with a little bit of warmth.

'I know,' Lyla said with a tear-logged smile.

'Get me a fucking cigarette, will you, and stop staring at the woman who can't see.'

JODIE

Ella lay curled up on her bed and I stroked her life-worn head. She was tattered by what had been far from mundane days. I opened the curtains and slid the balcony door ajar with my foot. The easterly and southerly were battering each other outside. No clear distinction between the brutal wind dropping off and the southerly arriving. I am sure there used to be a gap. Maybe I wasn't paying attention. Sascha started to totter towards freedom so I slid the door shut.

'I'll make us a cup of tea, Ella.'

'I'm ok, you make one if you want. I know you're here to talk about Mum, I just can't...'

'I understand. I can't think straight myself, even just not knowing what Pete is doing with work, let alone having a loved one die.'

'I never said I loved him.'

'I thought you were going to say we both had a loved one that died.' I smiled.

'We loved her, if you think of a definition of love that fucks with the boundary in between love and the wasteland outside of love. That is the love we felt for her.'

'Yes, exactly,' I picked up an empty white wine bottle next to the doorway and looked up at Ella. 'Got a piece of paper and a pen up here?'

'Hmph,' Ella, unimpressed that she had to move her body, flicked her bag over towards me. 'Maybe in there.'

There was a flyer for a discounted pedicure and a pen in Ella's bag. I uncapped the pen and started writing on the back of the flyer.

'Dear Mum, this is all you get. An empty bottle and a note on the back of a pedicure flyer. A message in a bottle. We just wanted to say thanks for a few things...'

'Thanks for not knowing who our fathers were?' Ella called out, half sitting up for the first time since I had arrived. 'Thanks for possibly giving us foetal alcohol syndrome?'

'Speak for yourself, Ella.'

'Even though she ruined hers, I am grateful to her for my looks. She was gorgeous before the grog got her.' Ella was sitting upright now, crossed legs, slapping her knees as she used to do when we played Monopoly. She was always stealing money from the bank when I was looking away.

'Thanks for my big sister who I would follow almost anywhere, even that sandfly-riddled dune humpy she lives in now.'

'Thanks for teaching us more swear words than the boys at school knew,' I added, my writing running all over the place.

'Thanks for familiarising us with the Collingwood Soup Van, TABs...'

'Yeah, we used to love those big strawberry jam white bread sandwiches.'

'True, those kids in functional homes probably never got many of them – thanks Mum!'

'And Jodes, what about how I am so fearless in the waves? You don't get that without a fair amount of damage in your upbringing!'

'Thanks Mum,' Ella and I chanted in chorus.

'If Mum hadn't been so screwed up, I wouldn't have been on the lookout for something better. I might not have met Pete.'

'Can I blame her for when I met Max?' Ella and I looked at each other. I put the pen down.

'Hug?' I offered.

'No, let's keep going, I love this memorial, let's not let Max stuff things up again,' Ella wiped one eye and flicked her hair back over her left shoulder. It's still a good thing I met Max, and the Juggler. I've found what's left when you're left alone.'

'Ella, should I add that one to Mum's list too?'

'Yes, but I always had you, whenever she was out of it, I had you. Anyway, I don't think Max ever had the power to hurt me. Maybe that's why he was never really committed. We probably jumped into marriage too fast.'

'You can admit that Max hurt you, Ella.'

'No way, not even to you.' Ella smiled and held out one bangled wrist to me in a noncommittal offer of a hug. 'At least Jugs adored me. I really felt that. Not in an adult way – he had other girlfriends. I didn't care.'

'Well, being married, it would have been a bit tricky to care, wouldn't it, Ella?'

'Yes, yes.' Ella looked at me, annoyed. Same routine as always, Ella swept up in some fantasy and me popping all the bubbles. Ella planning how to run away with the circus and me working out where our dinner was going to come from. I wasn't going to go along with today's story that Max didn't matter and the Juggler was doing more than spreading himself around as thinly as he could.

'Jodie, he probably saved my life.' Ella looked beautiful but put on this strange expression I remembered from our teenage days when she slept with a man too old for her and didn't want me to disapprove.

'I only met him for one minute at the hospital, he seemed lovely. I am sorry he's not here having a midday beer with us.' I watched Ella's face transition back to authentic and then travel further, onwards towards sadness.

'Love you Mum, love from us. That will do, won't it?' I started rolling the pedicure flyer like a dodgy homemade filter for a joint and reached for the bottle to seal it inside.

ELLA

Ella watched Axl inhale on a cigarette. She watched his lips purse before he self-consciously changed his hold from index and middle finger, palm facing towards his body to bowing his head forward, cigarette held between thumb and index finger, the rest of his fingers masking the bottom third of his face. They sat outside under the skinniest of moons with strangled hearts. The multi-coloured Chinese lanterns that Ella had mounted above the outdoor furniture a year ago had been bleached white by the blistering coral coast sun. The thin paper had shredded off corroded wire and only a few lanterns still flicked off light. Ella looked up and could barely remember the woman she had been, happily attaching little lanterns, dancing around in excitement, with Max about to come home from his two weeks away. She picked up her white wine and let the coolness fall inside her. A year embedded with much more than a year is designed to contain. Ella watched Axl as he dropped his cigarette into the open mouth of a drained beer bottle. There was a little hiss and then silence.

Ella pulled out two tissues from a box on the table between them and wiped her eyes. Night-time tears didn't have to hide, they just followed gravity. Axl folded his arms and stretched his ribs forward to take the pressure off his back, then sat forward, elbows on bent knees. He turned his head to look at Ella, worried. His loss was different to hers. After identifying the Juggler's body the day before, Axl's loss would haunt every one of his breathing days. Ella's loss would blur and fade like old ink under aging skin.

Ella looked at the garden beyond the rectangle of paving under their chairs. It was six months since either she or Max had put any effort into nourishing it. Max had only ever found the energy to mow the lawn when he was home. Couch grass had formed tight rings around the native rose and the grevillea olivacea was struggling to grow in the harsh conditions. Ella maintained the front garden as a minimum. It was a long time since Max had seemed to care about the ants, the weeds, the little white snails that sucked other plants' moisture. Old man saltbush was the only plant that thrived and it rose ghostly under Ella's gaze.

Ella stood up, went inside and returned with two head torches, a pair of women's gardening gloves and a pair of pruning shears. She silently handed one of the head torches and the shears to Axl and walked to the rear of the garden. Axl stood, amused, and carefully began clipping at the old man saltbush. The couch grass was tough. Ella began yanking with all her weight against a weed perfectly adapted for survival. Tug-of-war style, Ella grasped two handfuls of grass, one hand in front of the other, core activated. It did not give a millimetre. Its roots were fused in the ground, a thousand anchors that Ella was trying to pull simultaneously.

'Are you right there sister?' Axl asked, a smile on his face as he watched Ella shout angrily at the grass.

'Why does everything…' Ella panted, 'have to be…' She was going red in the face. 'So hard?' As the last word exited her mouth, one line of grass broke and Ella fell backwards onto a patch of itchy couch behind. Axl looked up, and shaking with laughter, walked over to offer Ella a hand.

Ella and Axl wandered back to their chairs, choosing alcohol over midnight gardening. Ella looked at Axl, garden shears by his chair.

'Axl, I want to touch you but I don't know how to do it like this.'

'Trust me, we do it the same.'

'What? Not, because you're Aboriginal.' Ella shook her head and laughed.

'Like what then? I'm confused – tell me.'

'I've only ever been with someone where the attraction was physical.'

Axl bowed his head, then held his chin up, chest out, proud.

'I can't help the way I look, Ella – my mum's head on my dad's body.'

'Sorry, I'm not saying it right. With Max and the Juggler the attraction was just physical. That's what I know how to do. I don't know how to do this.'

'Oh,' Axl looked over at Ella with an expression that would stick in her mind.

'You're just grieving…must be just grieving.'

'Please, come to me.'

Axl slowly rose from his chair and knelt in front of Ella, with her fistful of tissues, watery eyes, feet tucked up under her chair. She stretched her legs out nervously. Axl picked up one of her ankles and bowed his head to gently kiss and rub the skin. He rested his forehead on the top of her foot. His fingers touched her toes. He sat down cross-legged in front of her, not moving any closer. Axl looked down and tears fell from him in the dodgy lantern light. Ella pulled two tissues from the box and leant over to wipe Axl's face, softly, across the cheek, under the jawline. Axl looked down at the limestone beneath him. Ella put the tissues down and placed her fingers under Axl's eyes, letting his tears wet her. She touched her bottom lip and tasted him. Axl placed one of his hands over his face and breathed her in. Ella raised her other hand so that one rested on each side of his face. Axl looked up and closed his eyes to the stars of the damp night. Ella pushed his bent knees apart and sat down with her back to his chest. She pulled his knees back up so that she was surrounded by him. Axl placed his arms around Ella, clasping his own hands together, the strength of history and sadness within him.

'Waxing crescent moon…seventeen percent full.' Axl spoke into Ella's hair. Ella snuggled harder into him and away from any other thoughts. Axl dropped his head next to Ella's cheek. Time passed. Ella kept her eyes closed as the fabric of space shuddered.

'Now?' Ella asked softly and tilted her head back to Axl's left shoulder. Axl placed his lips on Ella's neck. He gathered her long brown hair with his left hand, wrapped the ends loosely around his fingers and pulled gently. Axl licked close to the edge of Ella's impossible. Her body arched as she guided Axl's right arm over her chest to curl around her back. His hand turned her around, still within his crossed ankles. Ella looked up into Axl's face. Things passed through her mind: her mum, Max, the Juggler, the form of a perfect wave. When their lips met, everything else fell away. Face to face, crazy bugs flew into the light of their head torches.

JODIE

The late afternoon at the farm was mild. Still. Not so overbearing. Not so desperate. Where had the flies gone? Empty, like the quiet after a nuclear disaster when the world breathes *what the fuck?* The sun looked like it sizzled as it fell, radiant heat seen even from here. Pete had taken Bon, Gus and Sascha in the ute, driving the farm's boundaries to give me an hour to shrink back into sanity. Knuckles gripping the roll bar, the boys would be loving the adventure of everything that happens when Dad is back in town.

Step by step, I walked down the driveway to the grain shed. The shed walls were corrugated, painted, blistered, repainted, blistered. Modern art: green, rust, and lupin white. My hand traced the corrugations, little bumps of absentia, daydreaming. Next to the grain shed was an empty grain silo. I held my hand to the warmth of the day stored in the metal. Hard and silvery blue. I walked around it and stared at the manhole; its lipped circumference and space beyond. My shirt hung where it should, not blowing west away from my skin. I placed one hand above its rim and lowered my eyes inside. Right foot first, then the whole right side of my body. Head ducked, my left side followed. Inside was dark and cool. Only a light beam from the grain hole above penetrated down on to the skin above my left knee, below the line of my shorts. I lay my head back and looked up. Days like this, when they are numbered, steal parcels of your soul.

Being here, away from the shack, which had become home with a velocity that had been alarming to Pete, I felt relief. Now the farm had become the away, the breath of space, the pause. As the storyboard of the past few months flashed in front of my eyes, I tried to follow the logic of the episodes and found grains of meaning. A scatterfire of moments where experiences had blown bits of me away. I sat up and held my bent knees closer to my chest. Sounds rose out of me that were part grief, part bewilderment, part acceptance. The sound grew in the silo into something much more than the one from me, as if I was not alone. They weren't words but they were song and they sang of my unknown dad, and at the last minute, before the boys blustered back home, they sang of my mum.

LYLA

A week before Lyla would drive to Perth Airport to collect Max and take him back to her cocoon, she lay on her bed looking up at the cracks in the paint she never noticed when he was there. After Max told Ella the irreversible facts of his unfaithfulness, he swung into Perth; two on, two off. Contemplating the ceiling and thinking about her time with Max, Lyla felt like she had upgraded her monthly plan but hadn't really felt any benefits yet. Max had travelled up to Geraldton last swing home to try and talk to Ella about how they might be able to make a clean break. Of course, Lyla knew there would not be a clean break. Ella would now live as a ghost in their relationship, the collateral damage of their covert conspiracy against her. Lyla had doubled her time with Max but Salacious had been subtracted from the equation, so the net effect was a familiar loneliness.

Looking sideways at Mr Bang Bang, Lyla realised she had to snap herself out of it. 'Get up and walk it out,' had always been her Mum's advice through schoolyard bullying, the onset of oestrogen, through phases of the moon where the gratitude diary remained blank. Lyla sat up and brushed her hair, pulled a hand-dyed blue shirt dress over her head, and reached for her favourite vintage fringed tan ankle boots. She tucked some money in the side of her right boot and forced herself out the door, grabbing her bruise-covering sunnies and Mr Bang Bang's lead. The air was still balmy.

The vibrant heart of Forrestfield was quiet as Lyla's fringes swung around her boots. She let Mr Bang Bang sniff every metre of cement, not rushing towards or away from anything. She walked past gabled patios, Balinese water features and low-maintenance synthetic turf landscaping. She heard metal hitting metal in home workshops at the rear of properties and the clink of wine glasses penetrating from alfresco areas to the footpath. In one window she saw a man with a face washer on his head reclining in front of a television. Kids screeched as they cannonballed into fully fenced below-ground swimming pools. In one suburban block Lyla's eyes took in a mini smiling Japanese Jizo Bosatsu statue made from volcanic ash, a Greek column and a letterbox-high version of the Lady of Guadalupe made from grey resin.

Lyla scuffed her soles as she wandered towards the shopping centre. Vacant trolley bays and empty numbered car parks signalled that it was probably time all good boys and girls should be at home. Lyla strolled ahead, past a closed bottle shop and discount store. Mr Bang Bang pulled his lead following his nose to a cardboard cup of hot chips discarded in the gutter.

'Disgusting,' Lyla said absentmindedly to Mr Bang Bang, wondering at the same time who had taken her place on reception at Salacious. A few metres closer to the supermarket, Lyla saw a little parcel in the gutter: plaited palm leaves containing frangipanis, sunset-coloured carnations, a red geranium and some crackers. Lyla bent down to look at the offering sitting near a stormwater drain in the carpark. She lowered her sunglasses and touched a frangipani petal between two fingers.

'You like?' A female voice sounded behind Lyla's crouched body. 'Some people around here, they kick my *canang sari* if I leave it on the footpath so I put it there.'

Lyla forgot to hide her bruised cheek as she turned around quickly.

'Did you make it? It's beautiful.'

'You haven't been to Bali?'

'No, I haven't made it to Bali – too many people from my home town are there. More West Australians in Bali than here.' Mr Bang Bang sat down and looked at the lady, who had a roundish face, beautiful dark hair pulled back under a hair net and a smile with wattage. The lady's laugh spread out over the empty car parks.

'You live here, in Forrestfield? I am from Indonesia. I lived in Bali for a long time so know lots of English language.' The lady nodded her head with every sentence. 'Bali is set up for you, you should go there and have massage, relax, eat beautiful food.'

'Leave Forrestfield? No way.' Lyla blinked her puffy eyes and quickly covered them, smiling back at the offering.

'Your man, he treats you no good?' the lady asked. 'I had an Australian husband. He hit me too. Luckily I left him, now I cook beautiful food at the Noodle Bar. You want to come? I cook you some pad Thai...you like naked chicken sushi?' Lyla looked at the lady, who was already talking to Mr Bang Bang. 'Come over here, mister, I get you some water. Quiet night tonight, I get you some food.'

Lyla followed the lady into the door of the Noodle Bar and fished the twenty-dollar note out of her cowgirl moccasins. 'My name is Lyla. I just live down the street. I haven't been here before.'

'Lyli, that is a sexy name, Lyli, yes? My name is Gemi. What do you do Lyla? Do you work?'

Lyla cringed. 'I just quit a job.' She tried to think how she could explain her research project, Salacious, the attack. 'I am going to have to find myself a new job.'

'Ahh, ok. Now, you sit down and I will make you some beautiful food. After that I can show you how to make *canang sari*. Lyli, read a magazine, relax, have a drink.' Lyla selected a flavoured mineral water from the glass fridge and sat down at a little table near the counter.

ELLA

Finally the coroner released the Juggler's body. The morning of his funeral was fishing weather. At dawn the petrol stations were chockers with people fuelling up their dinghies. The water in the harbour reflected the silos, the industrial collar around Geraldton. The trees were still, the Australian flags around town flopped down. Through Polaroid sunglasses the water looked Mediterranean. Patches of reef were clearly visible and the flat bottom of flippers could be seen as blokes snorkelled around to see what the crayfish were doing. The sky was empty of clouds. Ella knew if this had been anyone else's funeral the Juggler would have made up some excuse for not attending and been kilometres out to sea at African Reef, hooking mulies on to a line and reeling a big fat dhu fish out of the see-through water.

Ella sat in front of a mirror. Concealer, foundation, powder. Fifteen minutes later and she started on her eyes. Eyeshadow, eyeliner, mascara. Fifteen minutes later and she looked like a dark junkie version of herself. She stumbled into the shower and lay down crumpled under the cold water, watching it surge down the plughole. Pulling herself together, she sat in a towel on the balcony and stared at the ocean through red, puffy eyes. Her night had been long. She'd got up a few times, watched some television, made a cup of warm milk, had more pills than usual, sat on the balcony and looked at the patchy starry sky. She'd howled back at the wind. But in the morning the cold front had passed and the wind had gone with it.

Ella wasn't sure what she should wear. Sunglasses definitely. Massive sunglasses to hide what others would think was a gross overstatement of grief. She would tell anyone who asked that she always found funerals emotional. And a funeral where the deceased is so young will be particularly sad. That's how she'll carry herself. She will bite the inside of her mouth so the sharp little pains distract her from bawling.

Ella decided on a black dress with squares that were slightly transparent. She pulled out her special-occasion black stilettos and flashbacked to the Juggler lifting her high-heeled legs above her head as he thrust himself into her core. Could that have been only a couple of months ago?

The mood at the Sandy Beach Hotel was dark. Bowed heads and silence. The Juggler's drinking buddies had drunk to his honour the night before. They had taken the piss out of him as if he had been sitting there with them and not cold on a bench somewhere. A Canadian backpacker who had only met the Juggler a few times played the blues on a guitar that had been all over Asia, South America and now, Australia.

Ella ordered a wine and listened to the murmurs.

'Bastard, who's going to roll all our joints now?'

'What a prick, he owed me fifty bucks.'

'Funny bastard.'

Jimmy and Axl were the slurriest and messiest, having drunk way too much, too fast. Ella thought the Juggler would have wanted it that way. The management of the Sandy Beach Hotel had cooked up a barbecue of sausages and pork spare ribs in the Juggler's honour, which were devoured immediately by drunk, stoned, sorrowful mouths.

As the blokes talked, Ella heard that the Juggler had brought a stream of women to the Sandy Beach Hotel and the Grantown Guesthouse. Women he'd hit on at the beach, the petrol station, the pub, the supermarket. He had famously even got a lover the one time he had got his shit together to go and vote. Ella was told he had asked the pretty young lady to show him how to fill out the voting forms and one thing led to another.

'Who's going to give me free fish now?' one of the blokes at the bar said, shaking his head.

'What a shit thing to do, to go and get killed,' another fishing buddy commented.

The flattened mood at the Sandy Beach Hotel could not last long in the heat of such a glorious morning. The bar staff put on some loud music and most of the blokes went outside for breakfast cigarettes. Ella sat with Jimmy feeling empty under the fishing lures when women started turning up. Like the Juggler's last brag to the boys, *Here you useless pricks, even though I'm dead, I'll still bring the women.*

'Hi, I'm a friend of Miles.'

'Hi, I'm Ella.'

'I was wondering if I could come with you guys to the funeral?'

'Hi, my name's Jessica, I didn't know exactly what was happening with the funeral so I thought I'd come down here.'

'Hi Jimmy, remember me? I came here one night with Miles after he took me out for dinner and drank with you guys.' Stunning women in black. Big black sunglasses and big sunhats. The Sandy Beach Hotel looked half like Melbourne Cup Day and half like the funeral of a Melbourne underworld crime figure. There were definitely fashions on the field. Axl put some money on the bar: champagne for the ladies and rums for the boys. FIFO money well spent. The procession of ladies continued. Make-up running everywhere.

At 1:00 p.m., Axl announced that they would leave for the funeral. They walked together; Ella, Axl and Jimmy, surrounded by gorgeous girls. A black swarm of beautiful-smelling sadness. And some fishermen. They walked all the way on the road. Axl held a bottle of whisky to put in the casket and held out his other hand to Ella. The Canadian kept strumming his guitar.

LYLA

Three Noodle Bar dinners later and Lyla and Gemi were laughing like sisters. Gemi had made vegetarian noodles and mee goreng tonight and Lyla was eating it with a plastic fork, lips shiny with oil, when her phone rang.

'Max, I hope you are coming home soon. I am going to be double the size if Gemi keeps feeding me a sweet and sour pork ball every time she fills an order.' Gemi laughed, face raised so high she noticed the air vents were choked with dust and fat.

'Wow, you've really moved into the Noodle Bar, haven't you?' Max sounded a galaxy away.

'Gemi promised she'll dim the lights when I bring you here for a romantic dinner – Wednesday?'

'Yes, I can't wait. Should be 5:30 p.m.'

'I make Lyli some oysters with chilli and ginger,' Gemi interjected, giggling.

'You don't need oysters when your partner works away,' Lyla responded from the other side of a steam wall from the hot plate.

'Lyla, are you going to talk to me? I'm spent.' Max spoke as he walked wearily back through his door to lie down.

'Yes, I'll go outside.'

'You go talk sexy to your man,' Gemi said as she dunked thinly sliced spring onion in ice water to curl.

'How was your day, babe?' Lyla stroked Max with the tone of her voice.

'Long, tedious, I'm over it.'

'It's been a slow two weeks, that's for sure.' Lyla's healing face felt itchy in the warm air that parked around the shopping centre.

'I think I might say good night, leave you to it; I don't have anything interesting to tell you.'

'I don't need news, Max, just the sound of your voice – a dose to get me through another day.'

'Won't be long now.'

'Good night…Max?'

'Lyla?'

'I might even meet you at the airport.'

'Well, I hope so.'

'I mean, I might even meet you at the gate.'

'Wow – that would be amazing.'

'Night, Max.'

'Good night.'

Lyla patted Mr Bang Bang on the head and walked back into the Noodle Bar. Gemi had cleared Lyla's table and was laying out the *canang sari* components for the next day's offerings. Lyla sat down and picked up strands of palm leaf to make into a little rectangular plate under Gemi's instruction.

'Can I make one to take home?' Lyla looked down at her fingers on the pale green.

'Of course. Any time. I am teaching you. I hope that you can make *canang sari* every day, pray and have joyous life.'

'Things are getting better, but I am heavy inside.'

'Why? You beautiful, helpful, sexy girl – why heavy?'

'I've done some shit things.'

'And you've had some shitty things done to you?' Gemi looked pointedly at Lyla's puffy eyes.

'You know, this was an accident, it wasn't my boyfriend Max.'

'Oh ok, a motorbike accident?'

'No, a guy, in Northbridge.'

'He got you good?'

'Yeah. They haven't found him yet. The police told me to do a compensation claim; I'm looking into it.'

'Is that why you are heavy, because they haven't found him yet?' Gemi clipped a saffron-coloured carnation off just below the bud.

'That is something I think about but…well, this is embarrassing… Max is married and I was having an affair with him. I stole him away from his wife.'

'Lyli, you naughty girl! Married man can't be stolen though, not like a television.'

'Worse than stealing a television.'

'You know her?' Gemi placed a frangipani flower carefully atop woven young yellow palm leaves.

'No, not really.'

'Maybe you have balance now, maybe balance is restored.'

'Max told me not to link our dishonesty to the assault. I'm not sure if I believe that the ripples of one action cause another.'

'In my village, we always pray for things to be fixed up, to learn from our mistakes then let them go – every day.'

'What? Just let them go and move on as if you haven't done anything wrong?'

'Exactly! Lyli, you have got it! Such a beautiful girl.' Gemi leaned over and put a frangipani behind Lyla's ear. 'But you must learn; don't forget to learn from your mistakes. Then go and be joyous.'

'Sounds good,'

'Ok, you come and eat here and we can make *canang sari* and I will tell you more and you can go home and learn. Your mum, growing up in your village, did she say you need to be sad your whole life? No one says this. Adjust your mind, live joyously.'

'You are a guru, and you can make dumplings – you are a keeper.'

'What this means, keeper?' Gemi looked at Lyla with Bali eyes; lovingly, patiently waiting for her Australian friend to catch up and learn the most fundamental laws of the cosmos.

ELLA

Ella had called in sick for work and she lay with Axl on the couch, squares of silver insulation in the windows to keep out the morning light. They had already been to the lighthouse to check out the surf at Hell's Gates but it was blown out. Being Saturday morning they had seen teenagers with flippered feet on shark biscuits throwing themselves into the barrelling waves on the right side of the limestone groins at the foreshore as they had driven past in a loop home.

'Want to move in with me?' Ella asked, passing Axl a latte that had been cooling on the coffee table.

'Are you kidding?' Axl accepted the coffee as he considered the proposal.

'You don't have much to lose. You'll always be able to book a bed at the guesthouse, won't you, if it doesn't work out?'

'Are you for real, Ella?'

'What's the big deal? You're here now. It's not like you really have anything to move in — do you? It's like you are here now and then tomorrow you'd still be here and then you might fly out to work and then, guess what? You'd come back here. Well?'

'What do you mean? From when?' Axl sipped his coffee and looked across the couch at Ella and the future she was casually suggesting.

'From now. Why don't you call the guesthouse? Tell them to give your bed to someone else.'

A tear swamped Axl's eye, which he wiped quickly. 'You're not going to rip me off, are you?' Brown eyes happy.

'What do they charge for a single room at the Grantown?'

'I don't know – $70 per night or $350 per week.'

'Ok, what about $100 per week, considering the whole *terra nullius* thing? Maybe I should be paying you.'

'Today? Were you thinking today?'

'Totally. It's no big deal.'

'Yes it is, for me.'

'Me too. Reckon your ex will let Zack come and stay if you're not living in a whorehouse any more?'

Axl looked at Ella with the warmth of a thousand candles at a vigil. 'I can only ask.'

'Sorted!' Ella sipped her coffee and looked over at the lines of light streaming in the room around the edges of the insulation.

LYLA

There are some moments that are holy even when they are the most commonplace. They are remembered forever, burnt into the circuitry. Lyla knew she had been the one to throw her future off track. She had been young and seeking the ultimate of arousals but just didn't know where the fuck to find them. Standing at Gate 12 in Perth Airport on Wednesday felt to Lyla like waiting at the altar for the bride to arrive. Heeding Gemi's advice she had been praying like a motherfucker in the mornings, in her car, in the bath, before sleep. Her practice of penance was changing her, shaving down her shame. Not punishing herself freed up some time. As the bruises faded, she realised there was a way through the muck.

Max stepped out of the jetbridge, sunnies resting on top of his self-cropped hair, bag slung over his right shoulder. He nodded at the air hostess who was helping the passengers disembark. His eyes scanned the lumps of people clotting the way to the baggage claim area. He found Lyla. His steps slowed and he looked at her face, with its oversized sunglasses and her hair pulled back in a messy bun. People pushed past, anxious to return or arrive, but Max and Lyla held their gaze. When Max was a metre away, Lyla took her sunglasses off and held them in her shaking hand. Max inhaled quickly when he saw how well she was healing. He would never forget those first steps towards her hospital bed. Lyla stepped forward and they came face to face, closer, faster than they expected.

'Max—'

'Lyla—' Max leant in. A kiss as common as ants and as holy as heaven.

JODIE

Even on calm days here, three hundred metres down from our shack, the ocean has spittle and a trim of ferociousness. When I see the waves hiss on the reef I think of my mother's spit as she drenched us in her rage. I had felt uncomfortable as I opened the envelope and saw an interim distribution cheque inside from the executor of her will. Could I launder the money so it felt clean? I wondered what Ella would do. I thought all my mother's assets would have crossed palms over a bottlo bench or been doled out dollar by dollar into a jukebox or a pokie machine. She must have still owned her house; letting it decline and gain value over the years. I wondered if some hipsters had purchased it 'as is,' pouring bicarb soda over the stench of vomit and unhappiness.

Pete turned around and yelled out to me as his beach fishing rod was yanked out of his hand by something splashing behind the shore break. Hard to hold on, he clenched his special fishing muscles, knuckles white, pointing west. Bon and Gus ran down to him in their rash vests.

'Dad, that must be Huey himself,' Bon said, worried, as the splash kicked up and the line arc linked fisherman to a long-lost hunter past.

'Fish, fish, I saw fish,' Gus called, running in behind Pete as he staggered backwards, not quite as fit as he used to be.

'We've got dinner, boys; fire up the barbecue, tell your mum.'

'I'm right here babe, watching.' I said, Sascha holding my calf.

Pete heaved and wound, biceps puffed up as if he'd put thumb to mouth and blown three big breaths. Finally, up out of the shore break, appeared a massive mulloway, bigger than Bon, not much smaller than me. Its massive brown eyes looked up at us, gasping for breath. As if in sync, I inhaled sharply. It must have been thirty years old or more.

'Oh Pete,' I said.

'Let the old man go?' Pete looked at me.

'Let him go, let him go,' Bon and Gus chorused, half out of fear that it could swallow them whole.

'We can have ham and cheese toasties for dinner.'

'Don't you tell the boys at Yuna!' Pete laughed as he reversed the hook out of the mulloway's bottom lip and turned him around. 'You've changed me, Jodie Daley!' Knee-deep, the mulloway, exhausted, submerged his body and wiggled towards the west.

I feel like there is no end to loneliness. Whether Pete was there or not, whether the children were sleeping or not. Whether the wind had kicked in or we were caught in a gap. Loneliness, she is my skin. I follow her up sandy tracks and across fields stapled by fences. She leads me to search deep inside my lover, brush in hand, sifting, sifting, to find bones that she has not yet touched.

There is now nowhere else to run as I have reached the shore. I am standing far away from where I have run. Toes in sand, I tilt forwards. If I run further it will have to be walking on water to Africa through sharks underfoot and pelagics below. On the edge of my own personal continent I know what it would mean to travel beyond. These days my heart is watched. I focus on the space inside my skin, now familiar. A twitching finger, an ache in my jaw, desire in my groin. I watch it all. From shallow to deep moves my breath. I used to sabotage breath from the outside. Reacting to the sun, the wind, the space outside that seemed so empty. Heart beating like a viral pop song. Now I bear witness to my own rhythms, scanning from the inside, an eternal search. I have found rhythms within rhythms within rhythms. I tie myself with vessel and intestine inward; holding on for dear life to my mast of bone.

ACKNOWLEDGMENTS

For my children and Steve who are the soul of the universe to me. For my mum for her loyalty, love and towering stacks of books who have made me who I am. For Nansy and Poppy Rae who calmed the chaos while I wrote. For Gpa Dex and Gma Wea and their encouragement, despite a preference for historical romances. For Bek who once sticky taped my writing all over her Scarborough home when I needed someone to do that. For Pammy, for always saturating me in love. For E, who without fail, every time I saw him since I left school, asked me when I was going to write a book. For Ronelle, for living the FIFO life of Reilly with me. For Kathryn Heyman for being there at the start and patiently bestowing on me some of her wisdom. For Fleur Porter who sat me down and set me boldly down this road. For Mish Stockwell and her lyricism and for putting me in touch with Jocelyn Hungerford, who was a masterful editor. For Andy at Publicious Book Publishing Services for his warmth and skills. For Samille Mitchell, who made me promise at midnight on a dancefloor to send my first draft to her, which I did. For Kelly Bennett, for being one of the most warm hearted and grammatically knowledgeable people I know (and coping with all my ellipses). For Nick Nick and Cat Cat for always loving me and telling me that I have a beautiful mind. For my brothers and their partners, who I hope will cope with the soft porn. For all the other incredible book aunties; their feedback and support: Kate Naughtin, Zoe Randall, Anthea Balgera, Liz Bottomley, Jill Sellar, Anne-Maree Hopkinson, Rachael Turner, Steph Essex, Helen Teakle, Karen Yardley, Simone Blom, Aunty Shagaroura, Kitty Boyes, Emma Petersen, and Camilla Sleeth who will hopefully read it when her twinnies turn 18.